P9-CAN-358

Soulshifter

BARBARA PIETRON

Soulshifter

Published by Scribe Publishing Company
Royal Oak, Michigan
www.scribe-publishing.com

Cover design by Miguel Camacho
Interior design by Inanna Arthen

ISBN 978-0-9916021-2-4

Publisher's Cataloging-in-Publication data

Pietron, Barbara.
    Soulshifter / by Barbara Pietron.
    pages cm.
    ISBN 978-0-9916021-2-4

[1. Death --Fiction. 2. Hell --Fiction. 3. Fantasy fiction.] I.Title.

PZ7. P6193 S68 2015
[Fic] --dc23   2015939733

Printed in the U.S.

To Cass, who tolerated my ever-present laptop and clicking keyboard every day during the month of November while I wrote this story.

CHAPTER 1

Revelations from the Dark Realm

Feedback shrieked from the electric guitar amp, annihilating the harmonious blend of drums, bass guitar and electric piano. Jack winced as he fumbled for the volume knob on his guitar, pretending he didn't see Tommy, the lead singer, shoot him a furious glare. Head down, Jack concentrated on the next few chord progressions, until Tommy launched into his signature vocal screaming. Then Jack stole a glance to his left and caught the eye of his best friend, Wes, who skillfully delivered the pulse of the track on his bass guitar. Wes lifted his eyebrows and Jack answered with a slight shrug and an apologetic frown.

It was one thing if Jack screwed up this opportunity for himself, but Wes had talked the band into giving Jack a chance this summer when they lost their lead guitarist to college. Jack didn't want to embarrass Wes, or give Tommy a reason to give his friend a hard time. The singer hadn't wanted Wes in the band either, but when the other members heard Wes play and realized he was a wizard on the bass guitar, Tommy had been out-voted. It had taken two years for Wes to earn the lead singer's grudging respect and Jack hated to mess that up.

They finished the set and Jack ducked out of his guitar strap, leaning the instrument against the cinderblock wall of Fletch's—the drummer's—basement. He ran both hands through his thick curls, for the first time thankful that his mom had insisted he get a haircut before school started. Shoulder-length for most of the summer, his dark brown mane was now tamed to a mass of loose curls that ended at the base of his jaw—not as rock and roll, but certainly cooler.

He turned and nearly collided with Tommy. "What's up with the feedback, Ironwood? We've got a gig in two days!"

"Sorry, man." Jack shook his head. He noticed John, the keyboardist, give him and Tommy a wide berth as he beat a hasty retreat. "Just having an off day. I'm low on sleep."

"Well, you better get it together by Monday. A lot of people come out to the park on Labor Day, and we don't need you making the rest of us look like amateurs." He spun on his heel and stomped up the steps before Jack could reply.

Fletch offered Jack a sports drink. "You've been playing good all summer. Just don't choke when you get on stage." He laughed, but his eyes were serious.

"Thanks." Jack took the plastic bottle and cracked the lid open. "I'll be fine. I promise." He took a long drink, letting the slightly salty, citrusy liquid soothe his dry tongue and throat before bending to put his guitar into its case.

An intermittent chink of metal on metal sounded from the base of the stairwell. "Ready?"

Jack glanced up to see Wes tossing a bundle of keys into the air and then catching them. "Yep." He noticed that Wes had decided to leave his guitar at Fletch's. They were going to rehearse again tomorrow, but Jack felt like he ought to go home and get in some extra practice. He followed his friend out to the minivan, which smelled like the burgers and fries they'd eaten on the way to rehearsal, and loaded his gear into the back.

After Jack plopped into the passenger seat and closed the door, Wes spoke up. "Dude." He drew out the solitary word and added a sigh, conveying both disappointment and sympathy.

"I know," Jack said quickly. "I'm not a hundred percent today. Yesterday was my end-of-summer spirit-walk."

Wes nodded. "That's what I figured when you said you were low on sleep. You missed an entire night, right?" He plucked a paper cup from the cup holder and put the straw into his mouth.

Jack wrinkled his nose. If there'd been any soda left, it must be pretty watered down by now. "Yeah, I was up Thursday morning until Friday. And I slept like crap last night."

Wes returned the cup and braked for a stop sign. He glanced at Jack. "Well, don't let Tommy get to you too much—you'll always have one strike against you because you belong to the sect. Even after two years, I still catch him giving me looks."

Jack nodded but didn't respond, deciding if he wanted to expand the conversation about his spirit-walk. He downed the last swallow of his sports drink.

"People fear what they don't understand," Wes spouted in an odd, high-pitched voice.

Jack turned to stare at the other boy—not because of the weird voice, but rather, the words. Profound thoughts were not what Wes was known for.

Wes burst out laughing at the look on Jack's face. "What? My mom always told me and my brother that."

Jack chuckled. "Okay. You had me wondering." He knew the comment referred to the sect. Like any religion or spiritual group, the Racamedi Transcendental Sect had its share of doubters and haters. But his friend's words also hit home with Jack's particular problem today. He took a deep breath. "So here's something I don't understand. In my spirit-walk, I ended up in the dark realm."

"And?" Wes sounded unconcerned. "My brother Jensen's a shifter too. He's been to the dark realm." He stopped for a red light and turned to face Jack.

"But Jensen's a cop. It makes sense that he might end up on the dark side of the underworld." Jack cracked his window and made a mental note to throw away the fast food wrappers when they got to his house.

"True. But you weren't actually there… you were there in spirit. So what's the big deal?"

"The big deal is that it means something. But I can't imagine how it relates to the purpose of the spirit-walk."

Wes studied Jack for a moment with a raised eyebrow, then noticed the light change and moved his foot to the gas pedal. "What was the purpose? Don't you just concentrate on what you want to get out of the walk?"

"Sorta. The spirit-walk before school starts is really just about guidance—trying to make sure you're on the right path and all that. But I didn't exactly spend a lot of time contemplating school beforehand."

Wes took a quick glance at Jack and then snickered.

"Dude, it's a girl, isn't it?"

Jack let his head fall back on the headrest. Everything with Wes somehow led back to girls, even when the subject couldn't be further from the fairer sex. But this time Wes had hit the nail right on the head. "Yeah," Jack admitted reluctantly. "Shera."

The other boy smirked knowingly. "Right. The hot girl at the regional meetings. Isn't she the daughter of one of the elders?"

"Yeah. I ran into her at the sect offices Monday. She was with her dad." Jack frowned, remembering his initial impulse to bolt when he saw them at the end of the hallway. But Shera spied Jack and rushed forward to give him a brief hug while her father looked on with confused disapproval. Shera reminded her dad that she and Jack had gone to school together until his family moved to Ketchton three years back. The confusion had left the older man's lined face, but the disapproval lingered. Jack felt his cheeks grow warm as he pictured the hole in his faded Metallica t-shirt, the pocket half ripped off his cargo shorts and his worn-out Van's sneakers through the eyes of Shera's father. Of course that had also been before his haircut.

Suddenly Wes laughed. "Dude, your daydreams must've been pretty dirty if they landed you in the dark side of hell!"

Jack smacked his friend on the shoulder with the back of his hand. "Ha ha. I'm not like you."

"Not just me! I bet every teenage male at those meetings has Shera in their spank bank."

"Shut up." Jack's voice was quiet but firm. "It's not like that for me." Unfortunately, Wes was probably right. Shera was stunningly beautiful. And it wasn't only her

9

father's position that elevated her in the sect; she was extremely gifted at reading auras. "I really like her. I spent most of the day before my spirit-walk trying to figure out what I could do to earn a high enough standing in the sect to be able to date her."

"Wow, you're really serious about this," Wes observed as the van bounced over the rutted dirt road that led to Jack's house. "So what did you see in the underworld? Did you talk to anyone? Did Shera come up?"

"No. I drank the tea, lay down and closed my eyes. When I opened them I was near a river in some sort of canyon. I wasn't met by a spiritual guide and didn't know what I was supposed to do, but eventually I found a path that led up the side of one of the canyon walls so I followed it. When I finally made it to the top, I was in the dark realm. The only thing I saw besides rocks and ash was a creature. It was hard to make it out in the gloom, but it had a dog-like head, a humped back and walked on two feet."

Wes rolled into the driveway, shifted the van into park and turned to Jack with round eyes. "Like an Enuuki?"

Jack shrugged. "A hump-backed Enuuki, maybe."

"Gnarly. A hell's messenger." Wes bobbed his head appreciatively.

"Sure, if you're not looking for some meaning in the entire incident."

"What did your adviser say?"

Jack sighed. "Brody said it would make sense eventually. He didn't seem too worried about it."

"Then you shouldn't worry about it either, dude. Come on, it's the last weekend of the summer and we've got a gig on Monday. It's gonna be epic."

"Yeah, okay. I'll practice the set again tonight." Jack climbed out of the passenger seat, stuffed the bag of fast food garbage under his arm, then slid open the van's side door to retrieve his guitar and amp. He headed toward the house, contemplating his friend's words. Wes was right. In order to play a good show on Monday, he needed to get his mind off Shera and his spirit-walk.

Pausing on the front porch, Jack chuckled wryly— actually, the odds of him becoming a rock star were probably better than the chance of him ending up with Shera.

Four days later Jack strode toward the back doors of the school amid the chatter and bustle of students getting ready to leave the building. Because the heavy traffic of kids was mostly headed for the same destination—the buses—the doors had been propped open and the hall monitor leaned against the wall nearby looking bored. A gust of chilly wind swirled around the exiting kids and rushed down the hallway, brushing Jack's bare arms. He stopped abruptly and a girl bumped into his back.

"Sorry," he mumbled to her 'what's your problem' frown. He'd just remembered wearing a jacket on his way in. Turning, he headed for the biology lab. Since his locker was on the other side of the building, this morning he'd gone straight from the bus to biology. This was only the second day of school and he was still figuring out how his class schedule fit in with visits to his locker.

11

Back-tracking up the hallway, Jack could see that the door to the biology lab was open and he accelerated his pace. Cool. He'd grab his jacket—assuming the teacher hadn't turned it in to lost and found—and still make it to the bus in plenty of time. The smells of ammonia and latex hit him, and he pivoted to step through the classroom doorway, then paused at the sound of angry voices. Retrieving the jacket wasn't worth walking in on a teacher and student confrontation. As he debated his next move, Jack realized the argument had nothing to do with school. It was a couple in the classroom and, by the sounds of it, they were breaking up.

About to retreat, Jack froze.

Did the girl just say what he thought she said?

He'd taken his adviser's and his best friend's advice and stopped worrying about his spirit-walk. With his head in the game, rehearsal on Sunday had gone well. At the Labor Day picnic, nervous, Jack lead-fingered the beginning of their first song, but the enthusiasm of the crowd spilled onto the stage and he soaked it in. By the end of the tune, he'd relaxed and lost himself in the music. They completed the rest of the set without a hitch and Tommy didn't make any disparaging remarks, leaving Jack stoked about his performance.

Later, as other bands took the stage, a girl asked him to dance and even though she disappeared into the crowd before Jack could get her name, he'd started school yesterday feeling pretty positive about things in general.

Now, standing in the doorway of the biology lab, his spirit-walk flooded back in distinct clarity. Jack leaned forward just enough to glimpse the arguing couple, then backed away and sprinted down the hall to catch his bus. His thoughts were spinning a mile a minute, formulating a plan.

He knew the meaning of what he'd seen in the spirit-walk.

He knew what he had to do.

His first step would be to get more information from the girl in the biology lab. Fortunately, she was easily recognizable.

And he knew exactly where to find her.

CHAPTER 2

The Approach

Jack spied Natalie as the horde of students broke apart. He pulled a notebook from his locker and flipped through it, watching from the corner of his eye as she approached. This was his last chance to talk to her today.

She was alone this time, no excuses. The realization pumped extra adrenaline to his already buzzing nerves. When she stopped next to him and began spinning the dial on her combination lock, Jack's throat closed up. He swallowed. Forced air into his lungs. "Hey, Natalie."

"Hi." The surrounding babble and slamming lockers nearly drowned out her automatic response. She didn't bother to glance in his direction.

The smell of overripe banana wafting from the open locker on Jack's right gave him every reason to keep his face turned toward Natalie. He closed his notebook and slid it onto a shelf. "Hey… uh… I'm sorry about your friend."

"Thanks." Though her flat, bitter tone didn't invite further dialogue, Jack knew time was short. If he was right about what he'd seen on his spirit-walk, a life depended on this conversation.

The din died down as the hallway cleared. The

15

locker on his right banged shut and Jack breathed a small sigh of relief—for the smell, and for the privacy. He tried again, getting straight to the point. "Uh... look, I believe you... what you saw, I mean. The thing that took your friend wasn't human."

That actually earned him a quick glance. "Yeah, right."

"Seriously, I—"

She cut him off with a sudden look directly into his eyes. "No one believes me." The raw despair in her voice dropped like a weight on his chest. She turned away and continued cramming books into her backpack.

"I—" Jack scrambled for something he could say to make her listen.

Natalie hefted her backpack onto one shoulder and pressed her locker closed. She paused, one hand resting on the locker, eyes downcast. "Look, I don't mean to be rude, but I don't want to talk about it," she said in a low monotone, then turned and headed for the exit.

Jack gave his locker door a shove and took off after her, fumbling for the right thing to say. His long legs quickly closed the distance between them. "Natalie, wait. Please. I've seen it too."

Her lips pressed into a straight line while her eyes remained fixed on the doors in front of her. Jack lowered his voice as they passed a cluster of students. "It's hairy, right? Pointy nose like a fox. Walks upright. Has a tail."

Natalie slowed her pace a bit and studied him without turning her head. A brief glimpse of the terror she kept carefully hidden escaped from her nonchalant façade. "Where did you hear that... that description?"

"From you." Jack cleared his throat. This is where he could really blow it. "I overheard you yesterday. Accidently," he added quickly. "I wasn't eavesdropping, I swear, it's just your description was so familiar... I'd seen that creature before."

Natalie didn't respond. Jack pushed the door and held it open. She strode past him without comment.

He followed her across the parking lot. "I can prove it to you."

She stopped abruptly and spun to face him. "How?"

Jack planted his feet and jerked his upper body backward to keep from knocking her down. "I... I can show you. Actually, if you have time I can show you now." He read the conflicting emotions on her face. She didn't know him. In the two days since school started they'd probably exchanged less than a dozen words: hey, excuse me, sorry... basic pleasantries for strangers with neighboring lockers.

Before she could reply, Jack offered a safety net. "Do you know where the Little River Gallery is?"

Natalie shook her head.

"How about Shiner's Dairy?"

"Yeah."

"The gallery is two doors down. Meet me there? In, say, twenty minutes?"

The sunlight revealed dark circles under her eyes. She stared across the parking lot and then focused on Jack. "I don't even know your name."

Jack put on his best friendly smile. "Jack. Jack Ironwood."

"Natalie Segetich."

Jack squirmed internally at her scrutiny. Would

17

his appearance sway her in either direction? His jeans were well-worn, but he'd intentionally chosen a pair that wasn't too ripped up. And he had on one of the new t-shirts he got before school started. His hair was unruly, but aside from using hair products or buzzing it off—both of which he refused to do—there wasn't much he could do about it. At least it was clean.

Finally she spoke. "What was the name of the gallery?"

"Little River."

"Fine. Twenty minutes." She walked away.

Jack blew out a relieved breath. He hurried back to the school to retrieve the books he needed for homework. His walk to the gallery would take about fifteen minutes. Natalie could easily get there in five if she drove directly there. Good chance she'd be waiting on him and, judging by her current mood, the last thing she needed was someone asking her why she was hanging around outside an art gallery.

A valid concern for Natalie Segetich.

Everyone knew her. To start, she was class secretary; her name had been plastered all over the school at election time last spring. Jack might have even voted for her, he didn't remember. Also, Natalie had been the star of last year's track team, singled out at school assemblies numerous times. And if exposure wasn't enough to make her well-known, looks didn't hurt. She was a petite brunette, just shy of being short, with large dark blue eyes that contrasted with her pale skin. Jack got the impression her popularity carried over from junior high and maybe elementary school as well.

At the other end of the spectrum, it was no surprise that Natalie didn't know Jack. Why would she?

He was merely one of the faceless masses. His family moved to the area when Jack was thirteen and had only one year left of junior high. He hadn't started high school with many preexisting friendships. His lack of notoriety never concerned Jack, though; he knew his success lay within the sect.

Bright sunshine and a warm breeze that still felt like summer accompanied Jack across the school grounds. Only the yellow-tipped maple leaves gave away the coming change of season. Though the town of Ketchton had lost many of its elms to disease back in the seventies, plenty of oaks, maples and birch trees still populated the area. By the time Jack cleared the track and football field to reach the urban neighborhood, shade was welcome.

He arrived at Little River Gallery winded and took a few minutes to catch his breath outside, scanning the street for Natalie's car. The burgundy SUV wasn't parked on the street so Jack went inside, knowing there was also parking behind the building.

He ignored the twinge of disappointment when a quick survey of the exhibits came up empty. Maybe she made a stop on the way. A woman emerged from the back of the room. "May I... oh, Jack, hello." Her smile rounded out her face to match her ample form.

"Hi, Mrs. Miggan." Jack had been a fairly regular visitor to the gallery when he started studying with his adviser, Brody Carter. Much of the art displayed here was the work of sect members. "I'm meeting someone," he added as explanation for remaining near the door.

"Ahhh." Mrs. Miggan nodded. "You know where to find me if you need anything."

Jack wandered around the front of the store,

attempting to examine the displays instead of brooding over whether or not Natalie would actually show. The distraction failed, however, since he'd begun formulating a back-up plan when she finally came through the door.

His relieved smile received a tired, blank look in return. "This way." Jack motioned with his hand for Natalie to follow and weaved his way to the left wall. He stopped in front of a clear acrylic box which displayed a painting on birch-bark. Natalie stepped next to him and gasped at the scene depicted by the art work. A dog-like beast on two legs carried a struggling victim slung over its shoulder. Its maw stretched out in a grin, revealing sharp yellow teeth. Red eyes seemed to reflect the hot glow on the horizon. The clawed feet traversed rocky ground, the terrain black as coal.

Jack watched the color drain from Natalie's already pale face as she scanned the painting. Her blue eyes darted erratically back and forth, then rolled up into her head as she collapsed. Jack lunged and caught her, lowering her gently to the ground. He swiveled his head right and left, seeing no one. He opened his mouth to call for Mrs. Miggan, then closed it, realizing he knew what to do. He slipped his backpack off his shoulder and positioned it under Natalie's feet to restore blood flow to her head. Her eyelids fluttered almost immediately and Jack let out a relieved breath.

When she opened her eyes, she looked first at Jack, and then at her surroundings. She groaned and put her hand over her face. "God. I fainted?"

"Yeah, sorry."

She shook her head and pushed up onto her elbows. "It's not your fault."

Jack offered her a hand and she took it. "Well, kinda. I should've warned you about the painting."

"Maybe." The corners of Natalie's mouth lifted for the first time, and though the smile was small and weak, it transformed her face. "I think it has more to do with lack of sleep and food."

"Mmm. Let me buy you an ice cream then—it's the least I can do."

She protested at first, but after a second wave of dizziness, Natalie admitted she'd better eat something and they walked down to Shiner's Dairy. As he paid the clerk, Jack considered the two days of lunch money well-worth the opportunity to sit down and talk to her. He waited until she'd had a few bites of her coconut and KitKat-filled yellow cake batter concoction before asking questions. "The painting… is that what you saw the night your friend disappeared?"

Natalie shuddered. "Yeah. You could pretty much put Emma's face on the girl in the picture." She gazed at her ice cream for a moment and then at Jack. "Was it fake? Did some creep see that picture and dress up like that thing?" The question lacked conviction. She knew the answer.

"I'd love to say yes, but no. It's real."

"You've seen it?"

The tone of her voice held an element of hope Jack hated to crush. "Yes. Not exactly in the flesh, but yes."

She ran her hand through her hair, pulling the thick bangs away from her face. "Why are you telling me this?"

"Well… partly because I didn't want you to think you were crazy." Jack watched Natalie's cheeks turn pink as she realized he'd heard the argument with her

21

boyfriend. He dropped his gaze, remixing the crushed Oreo cookies into his chocolate ice cream. "I'm sorry. Really. I don't make it a habit to eavesdrop on people. I'd left my jacket in the biology lab, but when I heard your... um... heated conversation I figured I'd just get it this morning. Before I walked away I heard you describe the Enuuki."

The door creaked and a mom with two kids in tow entered the shop. Jack followed their progress to the counter, avoiding eye contact with Natalie. He wasn't going to mention that he'd heard them break up because her boyfriend didn't believe her.

"Enuuki?" Natalie's eyebrows inched up. "The thing has a name?"

"It means 'hell's messenger.'"

She stopped eating.

"Usually, the Enuuki take souls to hell, but occasionally they take the living."

"And you believe this?"

Jack waited to answer. The way Natalie watched the door warned him of new arrivals. Moments later, three loud tittering girls entered, all talking at once. Natalie rolled her eyes and murmured, "Freshmen." When they made it to the counter, Jack spoke. "Yeah, I do believe it. I also believe you witnessed it."

Natalie pushed her ice cream around the bowl. Then she looked at Jack. "You think that's what happened to Emma."

Jack returned Natalie's stare. "You tell me. Is it?"

She closed her eyes for a moment. "Everyone keeps telling me it was a nightmare. I started to believe them." Her gaze went distant, then focused back on Jack. "When I saw the painting, it's like it all became real again."

Jack plunked his spoon into his empty bowl. "Your ice cream's melting."

Natalie looked down as if she'd forgotten the ice cream were there. "Why... how do you know about this... this thing?" She took a bite of ice cream and watched him struggle to put together an answer.

He took a deep breath and let it out slowly. "You've heard of the Racamedi Sect?"

"Of course, everyone in Ketchton has."

"I belong to the sect. It's a group of people who can commune with transcendental forces. It's mostly made up of families because the abilities are passed through bloodlines."

Natalie frowned at him.

"Never mind. All you really need to know is that I believe in a lot of things most people don't." Like the majority of students, Jack had heard about Emma's disappearance from her family's Labor Day weekend camping trip. But he hadn't given it much thought until Natalie's description the day before had instantly conjured an image of an Enuuki. He realized an Enuuki with a girl on its back would easily look humpbacked. That's when he remembered the painting at the gallery. "Last night I looked up articles about what happened to your friend. I wanted to know if what I suspected was possible. It turns out the campground you were at is near an old Native American burial ground."

Natalie's eyes widened at his statement, and small pink spots formed on her cheeks, although she continued to eat without comment.

Jack scanned the small shop. He knew how crazy this would sound to most people, but to Natalie—who was struggling with her own sanity—it might make sense. Leaning across the table, he spoke in a low voice. "Here's the deal: the line between the living world and the spirit world blurs on sacred ground; it's a likely spot for the Enuuki to pass through."

Natalie scraped the bottom of her bowl. She licked the spoon, contemplating Jack's words.

He forged ahead. "Was she—God, I hate to ask this—was Emma taken alive?"

Jack watched her face scrunch up and his heart ached. Natalie closed her eyes and swallowed hard. Finally she simply nodded.

He blew out his breath and the hair on his forehead fluttered. "Now I'm really gonna sound nuts."

Natalie snorted a humorless laugh. "Everything about this conversation is nuts. Just tell me."

"There might be a way to save Emma."

Her chin jerked up at his statement. "Save? It's been days. She's—" Her voice broke, but she stubbornly continued. "She must be dead."

"Not necessarily."

"Jack. First you say she was dragged to hell and now you're saying she's still alive?" She watched his every move like a child watching a magician.

"Look," he said, "I can't say I know everything about this, but I'm pretty sure a living soul must succumb to hell. You know, accept it. How long a person lasts depends on the strength of their spirit. I figure Emma's young—with a lot to live for."

Jack detected a faint glimmer of hope in Natalie's eyes and suddenly some of his determination to make her believe him dissolved into anxiety. The sweet smell, which was inviting when they entered the shop, now seemed cloying. He'd been so excited when he had the idea the day before. Was there a mission nobler than rescuing a damsel in distress? If he succeeded, he could easily become the Shifter Premier, like Brody, his adviser. That potential alone would make him a worthy suitor for Shera.

Now, looking into Natalie's hopeful face, Jack considered what would be lost if he failed.

She shook her head slightly—perhaps in disbelief, or maybe in an attempt to clear her thoughts. "But... how...?" She seemed unable to formulate the question she wanted to ask.

Jack took a deep breath as he glanced at the other customers. Then he leaned across the table and spoke softly. "I'm a soulshifter. I can visit the spirit world."

Natalie blinked. "I am crazy," she muttered.

"You're not." Jack shook his head. "It's an ancestral ability many sect members possess."

"How? How can you do that?" The challenge intensified her gaze, but she held her face carefully impassive.

"There are certain rituals we use, but mainly, it's a spiritual ability I was born with." When she didn't say anything, he continued. "Just give me a chance. Work with me on this. If you're not convinced in a couple of days that I am who I say I am, we can drop it and I'll leave you alone."

Natalie stared at the tabletop for a long moment, her face slack. "Why, though." It didn't come out as a question and Jack wasn't entirely sure she knew she'd spoken out loud. Then her eyes flicked up and met his. "Why would you do this? You don't even know Emma."

Jack stared at his fingers as he folded a napkin over and over into an impossibly small bundle. He

25

felt a twinge of shame. "I have to admit—it's a selfish reason. I want to become an elder in my sect, a high-level shifter. In order to do that I have to prove myself. We call it an Attestation." Although the position was actually a means to get what he ultimately wanted, he figured Natalie was looking for a reason, not Jack's intimate hopes and dreams.

"Oh." Natalie leaned her head on her open hand, obscuring her expression. The chatter in the background seemed suppressed by the silence that stretched out between them. With no clue to what she might be thinking, Jack half expected her to tell him to back off and never speak to her again.

"Had you told me this stuff a month ago," she said slowly, "about sects of… soulshifters that… that visit other worlds… about rescuing people from hell, I would've fallen on the floor laughing. But now, after what I saw…" Finally she looked up, chin resting on her fist. "I don't know what I believe. I don't know what to say."

"Say you'll help me."

Talking to Natalie was his first step, and though she was cautiously skeptical, she'd agreed to help. Next Jack needed to see his adviser. It was that thought that saved him when Natalie offered him a ride home from Shiner's Dairy.

Jack didn't have a car and he'd obviously missed the bus, yet he immediately refused when Natalie asked if he needed a ride. A hot wash of panic had spread through his chest at the thought of Natalie Segetich driving up to his house. As he scrambled for an excuse, the need to meet with his teacher provided a way to solve two problems at once.

Instead of taking him home, Jack asked Natalie to drop him off at the sect offices.

An awkward silence formed inside Natalie's SUV once Jack had delivered directions. After their conversation in Shiner's, Jack floundered for a pedestrian subject, but anything he thought of seemed trivial. Finally, Natalie broke the silence. "So everyone in the sect has a... power?"

"Mmm, I'm not sure power is the right word. We have various spiritual abilities."

"Such as?"

"Well, there's dowsing, which is being able to locate objects. There are aura readers who can obtain information about a person, things, or even a place, from the energy field around them. I have a friend who can learn about people or things by touching them. That's called psychometry."

Natalie was quiet for a moment. "That's kind of creepy. Does it happen to him all the time?"

"No." Jack chuckled. "That would suck. Unless the person is like, obsessed with something, he has to 'tune-in', for lack of a better word."

"Is there... does anyone..."

Jack studied Natalie from the corner of his eye, noticing the bloom of color on her cheeks. "What?"

"Never mind." The flush deepened, spreading to her neck.

Jack laughed. "Go ahead. I'd love to hear what the rumors are."

Her throat worked as she swallowed. "Okay, I

27

heard the sect was necromancers."

"Yep. Heard that one before. The truth is necromancy is a spiritual ability. But it's considered a black art. No one in the Racamedi Sect practices it. I guess us shifters come the closest to necromancers since we visit the spirit world. But we're generally contacting ancestors, not conjuring demons." He motioned to the left side of the street. "Turn left there, by the hardware store."

Further conversation was cut off by Jack's instructions through a series of turns, and minutes later, they rolled up in front of the sect office building. "Thanks for the ride." Jack slipped from the seat. "See you in school tomorrow."

Natalie simply nodded in reply, her eyes thoughtful.

Jack knew he'd given her a lot to digest. He hoped she wouldn't back out.

When he arrived at Brody's office, the door was open, so he knocked on the frame. "Got a few minutes?"

The older man behind the desk looked up. "Jack. Hello." He glanced at the wall clock. "Well, I've got a half hour and then I'm out of here." Jack's adviser managed to keep a straight face, but the crinkles at the corners of his eyes betrayed his easy-going demeanor.

"I know, Brody. I'm sorry for just dropping in." Jack delivered the apology with a smile.

Brody wore his salt and pepper hair close-shaven and flat on top. Relatively fit for his age, the button-up shirt hanging loose over his blue jeans hid any belly he might be accumulating underneath. He leaned back and motioned to the chairs on the other side of his desk. "Have a seat. Tell me what's on your mind."

Jack perched on the edge of a chair and explained his idea, receiving no more than slightly raised eyebrows (at the mention of the Enuuki) and narrowed eyes (at Jack's idea to retrieve Emma). When he was done, he watched as his adviser chose his reply.

Brody laced his fingers together over his stomach. "First, Jack, let me say this is a brave offer and a commendable idea."

Jack let out an imperceptible sigh of disappointment, waiting for the 'but.'

Instead, his teacher took a different approach. "You know we spirit-walk for knowledge and to seek advice from our ancestors. Our goal is always to keep balance between worlds. So your idea is relevant; the living don't belong in the world of shadows, especially not in the dark realm."

Brody paused for a moment gazing upward as he gathered his thoughts. "These types of disappearances have traditionally been rare. But for the past five years or so we've noticed a marked increase in such incidents. The council believes a large portion of missing persons cases today are actually Enuuki."

Jack realized he was bouncing a knee and pressed his foot flat on the floor.

"Thing is, this isn't my area," Brody continued. "What I know from council meetings is that our people have undertaken spirit-walks to the other side to retrieve living victims. Unfortunately though, I've never heard of a successful rescue."

Jack expelled a breath and sank back into the chair. "So it can't be done?"

"I don't know." Brody studied his apprentice for a long moment. "I'm not sure I'd say it's impossible—it just hasn't happened yet. Each attempt gains more knowledge."

"But where does that leave me?"

"I think, before you give up your worthy idea, you should speak to those who have the most knowledge, the ones who have been there." Brody sat forward in his chair and flipped open his laptop. "I'll give you some names and numbers so you can make inquiries. Then come back and we'll talk again. This time you can educate me."

Jack waited as his adviser jotted down the information, wishing he'd come here before talking to Natalie. He hated to think he'd gotten her hopes up just to let her down. Brody slid the paper across the desk and Jack stood, folding the sheet so he could shove it into his back pocket. "Thanks." He turned to leave.

"Jack." Brody's voice held a note of concern. Jack twisted around, raising his eyebrows. "One thing I do know: the danger in this idea begins immediately. Minions of the underworld are everywhere—searching for and trying to influence human weakness—and the dark lord will learn of your plans sooner than you think. And once he knows, Zalnic will try his best to dissuade you."

Jack stared gravely into his teacher's eyes. He nodded. "I'll be careful."

With the autumn days growing shorter, one side of the street was already cast in shadow. Brody's warning had the fine hairs on the back of his neck bristling, so Jack crossed to the sunny side, using the warm rays as a welcome tonic. Since his dad's auto shop wasn't too far of a walk, he'd texted earlier to ask for a ride home.

The sign on the door was already flipped to

"closed," so Jack circled around the back. Apparently he wasn't the only one taking advantage of the lingering weather; the back door of the shop was propped open. Jack stepped inside and let his eyes adjust to the darker interior—his dad had shut off the overhead lights in anticipation of quitting time. The smell of exhaust, grease and oil was almost as familiar as his mom's fish soup.

Jack stepped inside the door. "Dad? I'm here."

His dad appeared in the office doorway, backlit for a moment until he flipped the light switch. "I'm ready."

A pang of guilt squeezed Jack's heart as his father advanced across the garage floor. Barely perceptible, most people would never notice the odd way his dad moved his right leg. But Jack couldn't get used to it—no matter how many times he'd been told not to feel guilty.

"Mom's working and we're on our own," Jack's dad said as they stepped outside. He pushed the steel door shut and locked it with a key. "Since you're here, let's just grab dinner after we pick up Jase. I don't feel like cooking, anyway."

"Sounds good to me," Jack replied. That gave him about ten minutes to fill his dad in on his rescue idea and the conversation with Brody—there'd be no serious discussions during dinner with his six-year-old brother.

At the honk of a car horn Jack flipped his history book shut, rose from the couch and picked up his guitar case. He had intended to get some homework done between dinner and band practice, but found himself staring at the words on the page while his mind wandered elsewhere. "Be back around nine-thirty," he

31

called to his dad who was in the kitchen helping Jase with his homework.

Wes turned down the stereo when Jack rolled open the side door of the minivan. He wore a smug smile.

Jack raised an eyebrow. "Hey, how's it goin'?"

"Apparently not as good as it's goin' for you."

Pushing the door shut, Jack swung open the passenger door and shot his friend a puzzled frown. "What's that supposed to mean?"

"Here I was giving myself props for talking to that blonde in my lit class today and then I see you with Segetich on my way to the bus."

"So? Natalie's locker's next to mine."

"Nice try." Wes met Jack's gaze for a moment before he craned his neck over his shoulder to back from the driveway. "I saw you leaving together. Give up on Shera already?"

"Of course not. And we didn't leave together, I… I followed her out." As the words came out of his mouth, Jack realized it would mean the same thing to Wes, who viewed life mostly in black and white with very little shades of gray. Because of sect meetings, the boys were already acquaintances when Jack moved to Ketchton, then they ended up as lab partners in eighth grade and had been good friends ever since.

To Jack's amusement, his friend was something of a chameleon. He loved to talk smack about everything—girls, school, elders, whatever—but in direct contact Wes was polite and respectful, a model for all teens. He had a wild streak in him and was smart enough to know when to let it show.

Although Jack planned to tell Wes about his idea, he wasn't sure how much he wanted to say about

32

Natalie. Or how much Natalie wanted him to say. She might want to keep their partnership on the down-low to avoid questions. Since others thought what she saw was just a bad dream, there would certainly be ridicule if anyone knew what she was up to now.

As Wes concentrated on driving around the worst of the ruts in the dirt road, Jack attempted to circumvent the subject of Natalie. "So this blonde. What's her name?"

Wes grinned. "Kelly."

"You gonna ask her out?"

"Maybe. We'll see what happens in class tomorrow." Wes stopped at the black top road. "She was pretty friendly today." His eyes lit up as he recalled the exchange. "It didn't seem like she was just being polite or trying to blow me off."

"Wow. That's two points in your favor."

"You know it." Leaning forward to check for traffic, Wes blew his straight blond bangs out of his eyes before pulling out. "You're not off the hook dude. I still want to know what a triple-threat like Segetich was doing slumming with you."

Wes brought up another reason Natalie might want this kept quiet—Jack wasn't anywhere close to her league. Still, he feigned insult for his friend's benefit. "Thanks man, you're the best."

"Got your back bro." Wes chuckled. He glanced at Jack. "So?"

"I came up with an idea for my Attestation."

"Dude, I don't think banging a girl qualifies."

"Ha ha." Jack rolled his eyes and shook his head. "Do you want to know or not?"

Wes waved his hand for Jack to continue.

"You know a girl disappeared just before school started, right? Well, she was Natalie's friend, and I overheard Natalie describe what took her."

"What—not who?"

"She was taken by an Enuuki."

Wes's mouth dropped open. "Seriously."

"Natalie saw it. And her description made me realize that's what I saw in my spirit-walk. It wasn't a hump-backed Enuuki. It had a girl over its shoulder—and I'm going to rescue her."

"Nice." Wes gave him a brief look of admiration. "And get some tail while you're at it."

Jack laughed. "Of course that's my plan," he said sarcastically. "No. I need Natalie's help. And she wants her friend rescued. That's all."

"So this is about Shera."

"If I succeed, I'd have a chance with her."

"Dumb." Wes pulled into Fletch's driveway and shifted into park. He shook his head. "You're risking your life for a girl, man."

"That's not the only reason, just an added benefit."

Wes gave him a dubious look then opened his door and hopped out.

As both boys leaned into the side door to grab their guitars Jack said in a low voice, "Don't mention Natalie to anyone else, all right?"

"Sure. We'll make her code name 'Triple-threat.'" Wes smirked.

"What does that mean, anyway?"

"Long legs, tight butt and nice boobs."

Jack sighed and headed for the house. "I had to ask," he muttered.

34

CHAPTER 3

Research

The next day Jack didn't run into Natalie at her locker until after lunch. He started to ask her something until she shook her head and glanced behind him before turning away. An explanation for her behavior didn't take long.

"Nat!" Susie Chelton broadcasted her presence. "You haven't been to track practice. Don't tell me you're not going to be on the team this year!"

Jack had no idea what kind of politics were involved, but he knew fake when he heard it. Susie was not the girl you wanted to know your business. Or even your name. Problem was, he'd really wanted to get Natalie's phone number so they could talk to each other later—from home. No busybodies or inquiring minds.

"But you were so good last year!" Susie gushed. "If you don't run, I guess I'll have to do the hurdles."

Jack scribbled his cell number on a piece of loose leaf, bent down as if picking something up, and handed it to Natalie.

"I think you dropped this."

Natalie took the paper without looking at him and shoved it into a book. "You gotta do what you gotta do," she said to Susie.

He fared no better after school. Two other girls

were with Natalie and Jack stalled at his locker as long as he could without missing the bus. He just had to hope she'd looked at the paper and saved it. Otherwise he wouldn't see her until Monday—he had no idea where she lived. Since he ended up running for the bus he didn't get a seat near Wes, but as the bus emptied, Wes moved to the seat across from Jack.

"Hey," Jack said. "Any luck with the blonde girl? Was it Katie?"

"Kelly." Wes grinned and held up his phone. "Got her number. We might go out tomorrow."

"That's cool." Jack smiled. He braced himself as the bus driver downshifted. A high-pitched squeal accompanied a whoosh of airbrakes as the bus rolled to a stop.

Wes waited for a few kids to pass in the aisleway before he answered. "Yeah, except now I'm keyed up. Wanna do something tonight?"

"Can't. I'm doing research."

"Homework on a Friday?"

"No. Interviews. I need to learn everything I can about..." Jack looked around. Only a handful of kids were left, but still, he pointed down.

Wes pressed his lips together and nodded knowingly. "Elders?"

"Some," Jack replied, "but not all." His phone buzzed and he pulled it from his pocket to see he'd received a text from an unknown number. The message, however, revealed the sender immediately.

"Got your number, thanks. I'm busy tonight but I'll try to call later."

Jack saved Natalie's number. Hopefully if she called tonight, he'd have some information to share with her.

His friend stood as the bus coasted to the side of the road. "Later, man."

When he arrived at home, Jack retrieved the list of phone numbers Brody had given him and then sat and jotted down a script. Though he didn't read or repeat the words verbatim, having it there for back-up was enough to calm his nerves. Five phone calls earned him two meetings that evening and possibly one tomorrow with an elder from Jack's former division of the sect. He left a message at one number and received an adamant refusal from another.

After dinner, Jack stepped out into the cool night, grateful for the use of his father's truck. Once the sun had disappeared below the horizon, the crisp autumn air was quick to dispel any traces of warmth. It would have been a chilly walk to the Jenkins' residence.

Jack's dad had been noncommittal as he listened to his son's idea. He'd asked a few questions to which Jack knew he'd either answered poorly or simply didn't know the answers. So his dad finally just said to let him know what else he found out. After sixteen years, Jack knew his father well enough to know he wouldn't worry about something that might not happen.

His mother's reaction had been different. But then, his mom was the daughter of a shifter. It was from her bloodline that Jack inherited his ability. Excited about the prospect of her son becoming a prestigious member of the sect, she'd joined Jack in speculating whether his idea was a viable possibility.

Ultimately, the questions produced in both conversations had helped to prepare Jack for his interviews.

The first man's name was Arlen Jenkins. Although the name was unfamiliar, Jack recognized him from sect meetings as soon as he opened the door. Arlen's thick, gray hair was closely cropped, adding a youthful element to his tan, lined face. He wore a casual plaid shirt tucked into khaki pants with slippers on his feet. A sweet, spicy aroma enveloped Jack as he was ushered into the living room.

"Make yourself comfortable." Arlen lowered himself into a timeworn easy chair. Another recliner populated the same wall along with a small table between the chairs. Jack chose to sit on the couch across the small room.

"So you want to go after the girl who disappeared a few days ago?"

"Yes. I hope I can rescue her." Jack leaned forward, elbows on knees.

"What makes you think she was taken below? Or taken alive?"

Jack explained what Natalie saw the night Emma disappeared and how he'd shown her the painting in the gallery to confirm that his suspicions were accurate. The older man nodded in agreement, his eyes distant. When he didn't say anything, Jack asked, "So, you attempted this too, sir? A rescue?" He suddenly felt awkward, as if asking a man to relate a failed mission was somehow an accusation.

Arlen made a dismissive gesture with his hand. "You can drop the 'sir.' Arlen is fine." He looked slightly amused but his expression turned business-like as he spoke. "I asked you to see me first because I laid the ground work in the quest to save living souls." He reached forward and shifted an ottoman so he could rest his feet on it. "You said you're an apprentice shifter. How old were you the first time you spirit-walked?"

"Ten."

"So I can assume you know the purpose of a visit

to the shadow world—to gain insight and maintain a link with our spiritual energy or possibly seek advice from our ancestors. But we avoid the dark realm of Zalnic. Why?"

The question wasn't a test. Anyone taught to spirit-walk knew the answer. Obviously Arlen was leading to something, so Jack replied, "Shifters travel to the darkest realm in search of black magic. We don't practice black magic."

"Exactly. So entering Zalnic's kingdom was, in itself, a learning experience for me."

A woman entered the room carrying two plates. "You must be Jack," she said. "You like apple pie?" She offered him a plate.

"Yes, I do." Jack smiled and accepted the plate. "Thank you."

"This is my wife, May." Arlen took the other plate, caught his wife's hand and squeezed it before letting her walk away. She paused before leaving the room. "Coffee, Jack?"

"No, thank you." Jack noticed Arlen already chewing a bite of his pie. The plate was warm in his hand and the apple filling oozed from the flaky crust. Jack took a small bite, unsure how hot it would be.

"May's pies are the best I've ever had," the older man commented.

Jack nodded and swallowed. "It's good."

Arlen downed another bite before he continued where he'd left off. "The first thing I had to learn was not to die." He laughed. "Because I did die. More than once, actually."

Jack raised his eyebrows.

"The dark lord has sentries everywhere. They kill

on sight. Lucky for me, I simply returned to my body."

Arlen's wife disagreed. "Nothing simple about it." She crossed the room with a steaming mug and set it on the table next to Arlen's chair. "It took him days to recover."

"Well, one day maybe. Let me tell my story, woman," Arlen teased. He caught his wife's eye and winked.

"Just don't pretty it up, dear. The boy needs to know the danger he'll face."

Arlen's gaze followed his wife out of the room then settled back on Jack. "She's right. None of this was fun. But it was necessary." He sipped his coffee. "Eventually I made it onto the grounds of Zalnic's citadel and found the boy I was looking for. He was in a deep pit. My problem was that I had no substance there—no physical ability to affect anything."

"Like a ghost," Jack said.

"Right. Except when I entered the pit I found I could grasp and control things from the living world."

"What do you mean?" Jack slid his empty plate onto the coffee table in front of him.

"The boy. His jacket."

"But you still couldn't get him out?"

"By the time I reached him, he was lost. Mentally. He'd forgotten who he was and I couldn't bring him back."

"How long?"

"He'd been missing at least a month."

The elapsed time since Emma's disappearance worried Jack. She'd been gone five days already. "Did you ever try again?"

Arlen's face went slack. "Yes." He paused a moment, staring into his coffee. "A girl this time. She'd only been

40

gone ten days when I got to her. I helped her regain her memory of life in this world. Got her out of the pit." He put the coffee down and closed his eyes. "But I couldn't get her back here."

"Why?"

"I was spirit, she was flesh." Arlen suddenly looked very old. He swiped his hand down his face. "She was recaptured. All I did was succeed in making her relive the horror for a second time."

Jack blew out a breath and his chin sank to his chest. He wished he'd learned more before approaching Natalie.

Arlen read Jack's posture. "Don't lose hope. There's more, Jack."

Jack lifted his head and met the older man's eyes. "More?"

"We didn't give up on saving souls. I just learned the first lesson: a living soul cannot be rescued during a spirit-walk."

"But that's what we—"

Arlen held up a hand to cut Jack off. "That's not *all* we do, Jack. We're soulshifters. We have the ability to *descend*."

Jack looked at the man blankly for a moment, then his mouth fell open.

"That's right," Arlen said, staring directly into Jack's eyes. "If you want to retrieve a living soul, you must enter the underworld in the flesh."

Jack climbed into the pick-up truck and started the engine. He sat for a few minutes listening to the

41

uneven sputter of the motor and digesting what he'd just learned. He probably shouldn't have been so surprised. Thinking about it now, he almost felt like he should have known all along.

He'd been thirteen when he first crossed into the underworld in the flesh. His family was barely moved into their house in Ketchton and Jack had just met Brody. But his teacher back in Petoskey passed along the message that Jack was ready for his own tools.

When a shifter dies, he or she is always buried with the mystic instruments they've collected over their lifetime. As they travel on their journey to the afterlife, they shed the material items they no longer need. Young shifters descend to the shadow world to collect these items or—as they're taught—present their being in the realm where the items of power can find their new owners, because the tools must fit the practitioner.

Even though shifters can cross worlds on most any given day as long as certain conditions are met, the annual rite to collect tools is performed at the summer solstice. This longest day of the year lends a maximum amount of time for light to hold evil at bay, and the membrane between the known world and the world beyond is at its thinnest. Shifters bodily descend to the outer reaches of the underworld—the shadowland—by crossing the veil on sacred ground.

Since Jack had physically entered the other world every summer to obtain the tools of his trade, he knew he had to be bodily present to bring material items back into this world. Why wouldn't it be the same with people? He couldn't berate himself too much though; Arlen said he felt the same way once he realized his error. Because of his advanced age, Arlen had opted to pass along his knowledge and leave the physical travel to younger shifters. When Jack asked if he knew what happened to anyone who'd tried a physical rescue, Arlen declined telling another man's story. He did, however, survey Jack's list of contacts and encourage a trip to Harbor Springs.

Jack consulted the directions given to him over the phone. His next meeting was in an unfamiliar area just outside Ketchton, so he took advantage of each stop at a traffic light to make sure he was still on track. The neighborhood transformed from quaint old homes to small ranches and bungalows built in the forties or fifties. The yards appeared either unadorned or overgrown; even simple landscaping was scarce.

Jack wasn't one to judge. His own front yard wasn't much of a lawn by any stretch of the imagination.

He found the correct street but struggled to pick out house numbers in the dark. The sparse street lamps were located at intersections only and the mailboxes mounted on the houses instead of the curb certainly didn't help either. Moreover, low-lying clouds impeded the moon's assistance. His dad had mentioned the truck was running rough and Jack noticed idling slowly made it worse. Finally, he parked the truck and walked.

His new haircut left his neck exposed to the chilly air so Jack pulled his hood over his head. By the time he found the house, he'd jammed his hands way down into the pockets of his sweatshirt jacket, marveling that earlier it had still felt like summer. He hit the doorbell with his elbow. Studying his reflection in the glass of the outer door, Jack realized he probably looked like a thug and quickly swiped the hood off his head.

Nothing happened. Though a blind was pulled

over the front window, Jack could see the telltale flicker of blue light coming from a television inside. He contemplated the doorbell again, unable to recall if he'd heard it ring when he pressed it. He knocked.

This time he heard movement within the house. The blind fluttered and then the door opened head-width to reveal a woman's face. "Can I help you?" The words were more challenge than invitation.

"I'm Jack Ironwood. I'm here to see Kyle Burman. I called ahead," he added.

The door closed and Jack heard muffled voices. He waited, unsure if he'd been dismissed. Then the door swung open and the woman stood aside to allow Jack entry. He tentatively stepped inside.

"I'm Kyle," the woman said. "My dad said I should talk to you."

Jack tried to hide his surprise. He'd spoken to a man on the phone. The woman appeared to be in her thirties and had a small head out of proportion to her plump body. Tiny eyes, colorless lips and dark hair pulled into a severe ponytail only added to the illusion. She peered at him suspiciously.

"Hi, Kyle." Feeling awkward, Jack cleared his throat. "If you've descended to the underworld, I could use your help."

"I'll never go back." She turned away and moved down the hallway.

Jack followed. "No. I wouldn't expect that. I just want some information, that's all."

Wooden chair legs scraped the linoleum as Kyle pulled a chair from the kitchen table. She nodded toward the other seats. Jack chose the seat directly opposite and considered where to start. He tried to recall the phone conversation he'd had earlier which must've been with Kyle's father. Had the man led Jack to believe he was the one who crossed worlds? Or had Jack simply made an assumption?

"So… uh… you went on a rescue mission?"

Kyle only nodded. She sat with her hands cradled inside the center pocket of her faded Michigan State hoodie.

He decided a gradual approach to the real questions might be the only way to gain any information. "You must've been pretty young."

"Twenty-four."

"Was it your Attestation?" Maybe she had the same idea he did.

"No."

Jack frowned. "You volunteered?"

She shrugged. "I had to go."

"Why?"

"She was my little sister."

"Oh." Jack closed his eyes for a moment. "I'm sorry." He hadn't anticipated anything like this.

"Not my actual sister—you know the Big Brother program? I was her Big Sister. She was a sweet kid, though. I loved her like she was my sister."

Jack could see the tears welling in the bottom of Kyle's eyes. "Look, you don't have to talk about it. I should go." He moved to push his chair back but a loud thud on the table top made him stop and jerk his head up. Kyle's arm lay on the Formica surface and as Jack scrambled to equate the heavy sound with a human limb, he did a double take at her hand.

Mechanical. Kyle wore an artificial limb.

"No," she said. "Stay. My dad's right. The only thing

45

I can do now to make my sacrifice mean anything is to tell my story so others can learn from my mistakes. Our mistakes."

"You went with someone?"

"My mom," she murmured and turned her head away.

The small kitchen filled with an atmosphere of foreboding. Jack suddenly didn't want to hear Kyle's story. He could feel the grief, regret and guilt emanating from the woman. The recounting of events would only reinforce and sharpen her obvious suffering. Then she began to speak and Jack knew he had to listen. Whatever he chose to do with the information Kyle shared, the least he could do was give her his full attention.

"We thought we'd have a better chance with two of us. My mom would be the distraction while I retrieved Tessa. It seemed like it was going to work. My mom got herself in to see Zalnic. I found my sister in a pit. It took a little while to talk her back to who she was, but I knew her well. Once she was back to herself, I was looking for a way to get her out of there when I was discovered."

Kyle had withdrawn her arm from the table and returned it to her hoodie pocket. "As the guard dragged me into Zalnic's palace, I fought. He lashed out with a blade. It cut me here." She used the side of her hand to slice over her arm just below the elbow. "My mother was with Zalnic. When she saw me, my arm limp and bleeding, she begged the dark lord to let us go. I'm sure she hoped to cut our losses and return for my little sister more prepared."

Kyle drew in a shuddering breath before continuing. "He laughed. Zalnic. Laughed with... glee." She

46

forced the last word out, still in disbelief. "It was terrible. I get cold inside just thinking about it." She swallowed. "Then he let us go."

"Let you go?"

Kyle nodded. "We couldn't believe it either, but later, we understood." She ran her fingers over her ear, smoothing loose hair back toward the ponytail. "We made it back. My mom died within ten days. My arm never healed. Eventually they amputated it and replaced it with a fake." She waved the arm as she said it. "Zalnic won. That's why he let us go."

Jack wanted to ask why Kyle's mom died, but couldn't think of how to ask. Kyle spared him. "Even though she knew better, my mom had tea with Zalnic. Tea." There were tears in her eyes now. "Do not have tea in hell." She laughed then, a pathetic sound.

He didn't know what to say. So he just nodded.

"Apparently he's pretty persuasive. I'd tell you not to go at all if I thought it would make a difference." She swiped at her eyes. "But you'll go anyway." Her voice was bitter. "Just don't underestimate him."

"I won't," Jack said gravely.

Kyle met his eyes for a minute, seemingly evaluating his sincerity, then gave a curt nod and rose from the table. "That's all." She rose and left the room.

Jack saw himself out. Before he even stepped into the brisk night he felt numb. The blasting heat in the truck couldn't chase away the lack of feeling, though it eventually transformed into doubt. His idea had lost much of its brilliance. The prospect of danger didn't surprise him. He'd be entering the underworld after all, land of the dead. What he hadn't expected was a set of rules.

Rules that had deadly consequences when broken.

Jack couldn't help wondering if he was in over his head.

Jack was asleep on the couch in front of the television when Natalie called. He swiped a hand across his face and reached for his phone on the coffee table.

"H'lo?" he mumbled.

"Jack? I'm sorry. I woke you up."

"No." Jack blinked and peered at the clock. 12:20. "I was up watching TV."

"Oh, good. I know it's late but I didn't want you to think I blew you off. This is really important to me. More important than most anything else. Thing is, if I told anyone about it, I'd end up in a shrink's office. I know my dad was already thinking about it."

"It's okay, I'm glad you called. I have things I need to talk to you about."

"All right, but first I just want to say thanks for your discretion today. Susie Chelton has the biggest mouth in the school. And even though she pretends to like me, she can't stand that I beat her record last year."

"Yeah, I wasn't sure what kind of questions I might raise. You've got a reputation to uphold."

Natalie didn't say anything for a moment. When she did, her voice was tentative. "Just so we're clear. The issue isn't you personally—it's the whole, you know, underworld thing. I don't need people thinking I'm crazier than they already do." She paused. "If all things were normal, I would have no reservations about being... with you... friends, you know."

48

Jack practically heard her blush through the phone. Feeling the heat in his cheeks as well, he was grateful the conversation wasn't taking place face to face. "Uh, yeah, same here."

Duh, same here? She was Natalie Segetich! She could only improve his reputation.

As if he had one.

"What did you want to talk about? Did you learn more about saving Emma?"

"Yeah, actually, I did." Jack wasn't going to tell her he was trying to determine whether or not he still wanted to do this, he figured he'd just ask questions about Emma until he had a sense of the kind of person she was. But they started to talk and next thing he knew, he blurted out everything.

"The woman lost her arm? Her mom died because she drank something?"

"Yeah."

There was a pause. "Sounds pretty dangerous." Natalie's voice was low and even.

"I already knew it would be dangerous."

"You can't risk your life, Jack. For someone you didn't even know?"

He chose to ignore her first statement. "You can help me with that. Tell me about Emma. I need you to help me determine if there's a chance she's… she might be…"

"Still alive."

"Yeah."

Jack heard Natalie draw in a deep breath. "Emma was—is—a good person. I mean she wasn't angelic or anything, but well-liked. I think she was admired—you know, if others couldn't be her, they wanted to be with her."

Natalie sniffed. Jack squeezed his eyes shut and gritted his teeth. God, he was making her cry.

"Emma liked people—all kinds of people. She was the least discriminatory person I've ever known. The more different a person seemed to be, the more she wanted to get to know them. I suppose that's why so many kids liked her. No one was invisible to Emma."

"Wow, and I thought she was popular because she hung out with you."

She chuckled. "Hardly."

Jack detected another intake of breath and waited, thinking Natalie had something else she was going to say. He vaguely remembered Emma from the previous year of school. Long, curly brown hair. Attractive. Jack's impression of her was bubbly—she seemed to always be smiling. Just as he was about to say something, Natalie spoke.

"You were on her agenda."

"I was what?"

"Emma wanted to get to know you."

"I can't believe she even noticed me. I was never in any classes with her."

"We were locker neighbors last year too, remember? Anyway, she said she thought you'd be interesting. Looks like she was right."

"I'm interesting?"

"Uh… yeah. Soulshifter?"

He'd never thought about it that way—that others would be interested. He kept his membership in the sect on the down-low, aware that outsiders often considered them freaks. "Huh. Well, she sounds like a cool person to know."

"She was the best."

"Was she impressionable? I mean, could people talk her into things?"

"Emma would do most anything for anyone as long as it was for a good reason. But she marched to her own drum, you know? There were things she wouldn't do. No matter what."

"Brave?"

"Too brave. I think she was a borderline adrenaline junkie. I'd vote her most likely to go skydiving." Natalie lowered her voice. "Actually, that's what got her into trouble."

"What do you mean?"

Silence stretched out for a long moment. "She knew the burial grounds were there."

"She thought she might see a ghost or something?"

"No." Natalie's laugh held little humor. "Jack, you can't tell anyone this. Whether she makes it back or not."

"Okay."

"Promise."

"I promise."

"She thought it would be... uh... exciting to make out there."

Was Natalie saying what he thought she was saying? "The two of you... ah..." Did she mean they...? "You met up with your boyfriends?"

"No, it was just us."

Jack had no control over the imagery her comment conjured. A warm flush heated his cheeks.

"Wait." Natalie seemed to read his silence. "You don't think... Emma and I weren't... I didn't mean that the way it sounded. I was camping with Emma's family at the campground there. We decided to check

51

out the burial grounds because Emma wanted to bring Brian Winks there. We're not—" She breathed out in exasperation.

"No. I know. I wasn't," he lied. Jack cleared his throat. "Well, Emma doesn't sound like she'd give up easily."

"I can't imagine her giving up on life, and I don't want to—" Natalie's voice broke. She took a deep breath. "I don't want to give up on her. But you can't risk your life, Jack."

"That's why I'm talking to others first. If I learn the rules—and follow them—I won't be risking my life." He sounded confident, but he said it as much to convince himself as Natalie. "Which brings me to my next question: I need to talk to a sect elder in Harbor Springs. Would you want to go with me? Tomorrow?"

CHAPTER 4

Learning the Rules

Inviting Natalie to join him for the trip to Harbor Springs was admittedly Jack's way of getting a ride. He didn't have a car. Nor would he be able to borrow one. As a nurse, his mom worked weekends and his dad's old pickup couldn't afford a three hundred mile trip.

He knew it was an underhanded maneuver to preserve his ego, but somehow he couldn't just ask for a ride. When he called Natalie the next morning and explained the situation, she did exactly what Jack hoped—she offered to drive. "Where do you live?" she asked.

A swell of panic rose in the back of his throat. Shoot. He was an idiot. How could he have overlooked that detail? He didn't want her to see his house. "Uh… my mom's heading out soon, she can just drop me at your house. It'll be easier." Jack knew his mom was long gone and he had no idea of his dad's plans—or if he was even home.

"All right. I live on Meteor Lake. 968 Pluto. You might have to wait a few minutes; I still gotta hop in the shower."

"No problem." He may end up walking, but as soon as Natalie said Meteor Lake, Jack was convinced he'd done the right thing. The subdivision of huge homes was still under construction when his family moved into town. Though technically not far from where he lived, the upscale neighborhood was in another world.

His brother Jase, who was watching television in the living room, informed Jack that their dad was outside. Jack slipped into some shoes and grabbed a zip-up hoodie on his way out to the barn-like garage behind the house. The night's chill had yet to be chased away by the sun and he burrowed his hands into the pockets of the sweatshirt. He found his dad leaning into the pick-up truck's engine compartment. "Did you figure out what's up with the truck?"

Jack's dad glanced sideways at him and shook his head. "It's missing, as I'm sure you noticed last night. I replaced the spark plugs, which seemed to help. I'll check the timing next. Hand me that big flathead screwdriver, would you?"

Jack plucked a screwdriver from the toolbox and handed it to his dad. "I have a meeting today with a sect elder in Harbor Springs."

His dad straightened up. "You should've mentioned that sooner. I might've been able to drive Mom to work."

"Oh." The comment surprised Jack. He hadn't realized his parents put his venture at such a high priority level. "I didn't know that was an option. But I have a ride. A friend from school—she was best friends with the girl who disappeared. I was just hoping for a ride to her house."

His dad eyeballed the project in front of him. "Uh… it'll be a while."

"Yeah, looks like it." He gave his dad a small smile.

"I can always walk or bike. It's just over on Meteor Lake."

His dad raised an eyebrow but didn't comment.

Jack checked the time on his phone as he headed back inside. If he ended up walking, he'd have to leave soon. First though, he'd try Wes.

"Hey, can you use the van?" he asked as soon as his friend answered. "I need a ride."

"Where?"

"To Natalie's. She's just over in the Meteor Lake sub." Before his friend could start in with some dumb innuendos, Jack explained. "She's driving me out to Harbor Springs to see an elder there. I couldn't have her pick me up, you know?"

After a brief pause Wes said, "Yeah, I hear ya. Hold on."

Jack heard Wes yelling in the background. Then muffled voices. "When?"

"Soon."

Another few seconds of indistinct murmurs. "That'll work. I'll be there in fifteen, twenty minutes."

"Thanks."

Cool. He had enough time to grab a quick breakfast.

Jack plopped down on the couch next to Jase to eat his peanut butter toast and was still there when Wes rolled up the dirt drive. He bounced up and opened the door, giving Wes the "one minute" gesture. "Stupid Clone Wars," he mumbled under his breath as he bounded up the stairs. All of his notebooks were allocated to specific classes so he grabbed the one he used least: Biology. Then he snatched his sunglasses off the dresser on his way out the door.

Wes had his head back and his eyes closed when

55

Jack slid into the passenger seat. "Oh man," his friend groaned, opening his eyes and reaching for the travel coffee mug in the cup holder. He took a long drink. "You're lucky I gotta work today, or I'd still be in bed."

"Late night?"

"Yeah." Wes backed from the drive and started down the dirt road. "I hung out with Fletch for a while but then I went home and decided to get online for LOTRO. Man, I was on a roll. I leveled up twice and then ended up ganked by a band of five yahoos. Five against one! Who does that?"

Jack didn't game too often, but he knew what Wes was talking about. "That sucks. Did you tell them off?"

"Sure." Wes chuckled sarcastically. "As if it did any good." He turned on Red Apple Road.

"How long do you work?"

"Eleven to five. Six magical hours of layering meats and cheeses."

Jack laughed. "Actually, a sub sounds good right now."

Wes wrinkled his nose. "Speaking of subs, it's this one, right?"

Jack's stomach clenched at the sight of the brick pillars which marked the entrance to Meteor Lake Subdivision. He swallowed hard. "Yep. This is it."

"I can't believe you're going out with Segetich," Wes said as he slowed and flicked on his turn signal.

"Natalie. And I told you, we're not going out."

Wes shot Jack a sideways glance. "Seriously man, you realize this hero thing could get you some major action, right?"

"Is that all you ever think about?"

"Yeah." His friend looked genuinely surprised. "Don't you?"

56

Soulshifter

"No. Not always. Frequently, but not always," he added with a smile. "Besides, I want Shera."

"So. You might end up with her. Why not have some fun until then?"

Jack shook his head. Wes couldn't understand. He'd never had feelings like Jack had for Shera. His phone chimed, saving him from answering Wes's question.

It was a text from Natalie: *"Just FYI we're working on a school project together—going to the library."*

He texted back: *"Good plan thanks."* Good thing he'd grabbed a notebook. He wished he had more than that, but it would have to do.

"So have you talked to Kelly? Are you guys going out?"

"Yeah." Wes's mouth curved into a nervous grin. "We're going to the movies tonight." He was finally able to turn and cruised slowly into the neighborhood, gaping at the houses. "I get why you didn't want her to pick you up. Where to?"

"We're looking for Pluto."

"No directions? You didn't look it up?"

"Dude. No internet at my house, remember? I didn't know the sub was this big."

Wes opened the console and tossed something into Jack's lap. "Here. Type in the address."

Jack picked up the device and saw it was a GPS. It didn't take him long to figure out how to enter the address. He laughed. "It wants you to turn around."

The GPS brought them quickly to a looming red brick house. Four white pillars extended two stories, creating a large porch which ran the length of the house.

Wes whistled through his teeth. Four houses the size of Jack's could have fit inside Natalie's house. "It looks like a freakin' plantation house."

57

Jack sucked in a huge breath in an attempt to quell the nerves rising in his chest. "Just let me out here. Don't pull in the driveway."

Wes eased up to the curb.

"Thanks." Jack swung the door open. "Good luck on your date tonight."

"Luck? Who needs luck when you have all of this?" Wes swept his open hand from head to lap, indicating himself.

Jack laughed, shaking his head as he got out of the minivan. The comic relief was welcome right now. He ambled up the walk, giving his friend time to pull away. Given the length of the brick path, he could've used his regular pace and still wouldn't have reached the porch before Wes was out of sight.

The sun had inched high enough to give the surroundings vibrant definition. The lush, green lawn tempted passersby to take off their shoes and sink their feet into the soft carpet of grass. Fallen red leaves peppered the recently raked sea of green and colorful mums lined the shrubs in front of the house.

Jack had never felt so out of place. He wasn't even inside the house and already he felt underdressed.

The feeling was worse when Natalie's father opened the door. Though Mr. Segetich was about Jack's height, his expensive suit and stature elevated his presence in an intimidating way. He met Jack's eyes with a no-nonsense regard. "Robert Segetich," he introduced himself and extended a hand.

"Jack Ironwood. Nice to meet you, sir." Jack shook the man's hand, hoping his palms weren't sweaty.

Natalie's father motioned him into a room just inside the door. "Go ahead and sit down. I'll let Nat know you're here."

Jack set his notebook on the coffee table as he lowered himself to the leather couch. He leaned forward, forearms resting on his thighs, and concentrated on breathing normally. At least he wasn't taking her out on a date. This wasn't a big deal, he coached himself. School project. Going to the library.

Except that's not what they were doing at all.

Natalie's dad came back and sat down on the other end of the couch. He picked up Jack's notebook. "What's the project you're working on?"

Jack swallowed around a lump in his throat. Was this a test? Did Natalie already tell him something?

Mr. Segetich looked at him expectantly.

"We... haven't entirely decided."

"I thought we were doing the Renaissance." Natalie came around the corner and Jack breathed an inaudible sigh of relief.

"Yeah... uh... I guess we did talk about that."

When Natalie's father didn't reply, Jack glanced from the corner of his eye. A knot of dread formed in his guts when he saw the man flipping through his notebook. "Then why does this look like science to me?"

Jack's eyes flicked to Natalie briefly and then he met her father's suspicious stare. Acting surprised was his first reflex. "Science?"

Mr. Segetich held the open notebook out to him. Although Jack knew what he'd see, he looked anyway. "Aww, man. I grabbed the wrong notebook. My history one is the same color. I should write on the front or something." His strangled laugh sounded forced.

Natalie spoke up. "It's okay, Jack. I have my notes." She held up a binder.

"I'm sure they're better than my notes anyway." Jack stood and Natalie's father handed him his notebook.

He followed Natalie to the front door.

"When will you be home, Nat?"

She glanced at Jack. "Not for a while. We're hoping to knock most of this out today."

"Do you have your phone?"

"Yep. Bye, Dad." Natalie pecked her father's cheek and Jack opened the door for her.

Once they were safely inside Natalie's car and the front door to the house was closed, Jack blew out a large breath. "Whew."

"I know." Natalie backed down the driveway. "I hate lying. One lie always leads to more lies to back it up." She shifted into drive and accelerated down the street. "But we didn't really have a choice, did we?"

"No."

"Did you get directions?"

"Just take 31 up the coast. It's just past Petoskey, where I grew up."

They didn't say much as Natalie made her way through town to the highway. She turned on the radio and told Jack to flip through the stations. He had no idea what she would listen to so he settled on a station that played a wide variety of older rock music.

After a few minutes on the highway, Jack began to feel awkward. He had over two hours ahead of him in a car with a girl he barely knew. Maybe he should just nod off, taking himself out of the uncomfortable situation. That way Natalie could relax too and listen to whatever she wanted to.

Except he'd already sort of scammed the ride—the least he could do is keep her company. Plus, he should help her watch for road signs. He knew 31 took a few jogs onto other roads.

The radio station launched into a series of commercials. "I brought my iPod." Natalie rummaged through her purse and pulled out the mp3 player. She handed it to Jack, opened the storage console between them, and produced a cord. "Plug it in here." She pointed to a small outlet in the corner of her radio.

Jack plugged the cord into the radio and then into the iPod. "Playlist? Or shuffle everything?"

"There's a playlist called 'current.' Let's start with that."

Jack pressed play and continued to look through the music. He'd expected pop hits, so her alternative rock selection surprised him. He made a few comments about bands he recognized and soon they were talking about music.

"If you like metal, check out my playlist called 'jams.' I mostly play it when I'm ticked off." A shy smile accompanied Natalie's confession.

"I get that." Jack smiled in return. "That's what I like best about playing metal. It's a great way to blow off steam."

She shot a surprised glance his way. "Play? What do you play?"

"Guitar. My parents bought me a small acoustic guitar for Christmas when I was like eight, I think. I taught myself how to play."

"That's impressive. Were you banging out hardcore rock back then?" She kept her attention on the road, but Jack noticed the slight furrows at the corner of her eye and he chuckled.

"Not exactly. But by junior high I was playing classic rock. That's when I finally got my first electric guitar."

A sign indicating they were seven miles from Traverse City took Jack by surprise and his gaze flicked to the time readout on the radio. An hour had slipped by already. "Oh, watch up here," he warned Natalie. "We want to take Airport Road so we go around Traverse. If we stay on 31 we'll end up downtown."

They rejoined 31 at the bottom of the east arm of Grand Traverse Bay. The large body of water spread out before them, sparkling in the autumn sunshine. The highway edged the bay for a stretch and Jack noticed Natalie stealing glances in that direction. "Never been to Traverse City?"

"No. Apparently my dad doesn't have any business here."

"That's the only way you go on vacation?"

Natalie let out a humorless laugh. "Otherwise we couldn't write it off. Where's the fun in that?"

"Wow. If that's your dad's idea of a good time, remind me not to go to any parties at your house."

"If you do, bring your tax return." Natalie giggled.

The highway meandered inland, allowing only the occasional glimpse of water until eventually cherry farms dominated the landscape.

"So you said you want to be an elder in your sect," Natalie began. "Is that considered a job?"

"It can be. My adviser is full-time, so to speak. He's paid by the sect council."

"Is that what you want to happen?"

"Yeah, well, sorta."

"Sorta?"

"It's more like that's what I've always expected to happen ever since I was deemed a candidate for an apprenticeship."

62

"Mmm. What about before that? What did you want to be when you grew up?"

"You mean besides a rock star?" Jack laughed. "An archeologist—or actually, a paleontologist."

"Let me guess." Natalie grinned, the corners of her eyes crinkling. "You loved dinosaurs."

"You got it. Actually, I still do." Jack shifted in his seat so he was leaning against the door. "What about you?"

"What do I want to do? Or what did I want to be when I was little?"

"Both."

Natalie pulled the corners of her mouth into mock-seriousness. "First, of course, I wanted to be a princess." She giggled. "Then I got more realistic and decided I wanted to be a movie star."

Jack chuckled. "Is there a pattern there?"

"Ya think?"

"So what now? First woman president?"

She groaned. "Oh, sure, maybe in my dad's dreams. But I don't have such lofty goals anymore. I'd really like to be a teacher."

"Really? What subject?"

"A little bit of everything. I'd like to teach elementary. Maybe kindergarten."

"Wow."

"Yeah, wow. My dad thinks I'm nuts. 'Teachers don't make any money, Nat,' he always tells me."

"It's true. Most teachers aren't rich."

"I know. But you know what? I'd prefer to be happy. What good is a big house or all the latest gadgets if I'm miserable?"

"True."

She was such a surprise. He had a feeling when Natalie wanted to be a princess, she was probably already treated like one. She couldn't have wanted for much. Yet here she was, determined to carve her own way in the world. Though spoiled materially, the taint hadn't seeped into her person. She might look the part of rich daddy's little girl, but she didn't act like it.

"If you become the head shifter will you be happy?"

"I think so." Jack thought about all the things Brody did. "I know I wouldn't like the politics, but I do like the traditions and the ceremonies. Actually, I'm interested in all kinds of beliefs and customs. Have you ever noticed the similarities in different religions or mythologies? It's fascinating." He suddenly felt sort of shy and embarrassed. What made him spew all that out?

But Natalie didn't seem to think twice about it. "Well I guess you've got your college major right there—anthropology. Kind of a spin-off of the archeology/paleontology thing."

"Yeah. I suppose it is."

"And a good choice to back up your shifter training too."

"Uh-huh." Jack hadn't given college much thought. "Obviously you've done a lot of thinking about your future."

Natalie sighed. "I have to." Her tone was bitter. "My dad certainly has. If I left it up to him I'd be a corporate lawyer and defend his company from lawsuits."

"Okay, that would suck."

"No doubt. But the way I see it, my future belongs to me. I should be able to determine my own fate." She shot Jack a quick glance. "No offense. I mean, you're lucky. You want the future that's been laid out for you."

Jack nodded, but couldn't help wondering. Did he really want to be a sect shifter for the rest of his life? He'd accepted it for so long; he'd never considered other possibilities.

Wait a second. What was he thinking? Of course that's what he wanted. It was the only way he'd have any chance of having Shera.

Gracefully tall and lean with doe eyes, delicate features and long, jet black hair, Shera had never gone unnoticed by any boy—including Jack. But he'd always accepted that their places in the sect were on different levels. They were oil and water, they couldn't mix. Then, at a party in seventh grade, when Shera was dared to kiss any boy there, she'd chosen Jack. Suddenly he was imagining the unimaginable. Sure he wasn't born on her level, but maybe he could rise to it.

Though he was a competent soulshifter, Jack had no familial ties to boost his standing within the sect. Only by proving his talent was unparalleled could he hope to gain the respect necessary to date Shera. That's why, as Jack read the accounts of Emma's disappearance and realized the girl may still be alive, he instantly saw the opportunity he'd been looking for.

"Hey, turn this up. I love this song." Natalie broke into his thoughts and Jack reached for the volume knob. Wow—The Killers? This girl was certainly a lesson in not judging a book by its cover.

As they neared Atwood, Jack suggested lunch at a diner he'd been to with his family a few times. So they stopped for sandwiches and refueled the car. About an hour later they arrived in Harbor Springs.

After pulling into the driveway of a neat little log

home, Natalie turned the car off and fiddled with the keys still hanging from the ignition. "Should I wait or go in with you?"

Jack gave her a bewildered look. "Come with me. You're not my chauffeur."

"Good."

His chuckle earned him a 'give me a break' glance and then the two of them met in front of the car to walk to the house together.

Jack recognized the tall, solidly built woman who answered the door and scrambled to remember her name. He should, since he'd heard many stories at her knee, though he'd been quite young at the time.

Instead he introduced himself, unsure if she would remember him. "Hi, I'm Jack Ir—"

"I know who you are, Jack." Her eyes creased when she smiled. "Though I'll always think of you as this big." She held her hand about four feet from the ground. "You've done a lot of growing up."

"Yeah, it's been quite a few years since…" Suddenly it dawned on him and Jack grinned. "Lore with Laurie." That was her name. Laurie.

She waved him inside, chuckling. "I'm surprised you remember that. Go ahead and sit. I'll tell Ron you're here."

The home was more spacious inside than the exterior gave away. From the doorway they could see the living room's two-story vaulted ceiling. As they advanced into the room, their attention was immediately drawn to the wall of windows which revealed a breathtaking view of Lake Michigan. The modest furniture had a comfortable, homey appeal. They sat on a couch facing a stone fireplace.

A large man entered the room and waved Jack down before he could stand up. Jack remembered the elder from sect meetings before they moved to Ketchton though he didn't imagine the man would remember him. "You must be Jack." He leaned over to shake Jack's hand. "And..." His gaze shifted to Natalie.

"Natalie," she squeaked.

"Ron Winert." He sank into a seat near the wall of windows. The top of his head was bald, but the remaining fringe around the sides was still mostly brown. He had the lined, tanned face of a man who worked outside. "I believe I know your father, Jack. He worked at the marina?"

"Yes. Huritt Ironwood."

"That's right. If you had a problem with your boat motor, he was the man."

"That's him, except he works on cars now." Jack immediately regretted the comment. But Ron Winert was a local and a sect member; surely he'd heard about the incident and wouldn't ask any questions. In fact, the way the man's black eyes evaluated them with a sharp intelligence led Jack to believe Ron didn't miss much. He reminded Jack of a bird. A hawk, to be precise.

"So you're contemplating a rescue in the underworld."

Jack nodded. "Have you done this, sir?"

"Actually, no. I became an elder when a seat was vacated by a man who descended for a rescue attempt. He wouldn't tell anyone what transpired during his time below. The experience ruined him, though. He quit the council and became a recluse. Eventually he died, wasted away by despair or possibly guilt, no one is sure. Anyway, I made it one of my responsibilities to collect any piece of information gained in these ventures—in hopes it might aid future forays into Zalnic's realm." An orange striped cat sidled along Ron's chair and jumped into his lap. "Marmalade. I found her in the woods when she was just a kitten." He stroked the cat as she arranged herself on his lap. "So tell me, how long has this girl been gone?"

"Almost a week," Jack replied.

"You should still have some time then. Is she a fighter?"

Jack nudged Natalie. "Tell him what you told me." He explained, "Natalie is Emma's best friend."

As Natalie spoke, Marmalade jumped from the elder's lap and crossed the room. She sprang up on the couch between Jack and Natalie. Ron elected not to comment when Natalie finished. Instead he asked a question. "Have you spoken to Dan Manning?"

The cat rubbed her face on Jack's leg so he reached out to scratch her head. "I called him, but he refused to talk to me. He insisted I was foolish." Marmalade drew the length of her body beneath Jack's hand. She was silky soft, and he detected the vibrations of a purr.

The large man emitted a soft grunt. "To my knowledge, only two lives have been saved from the dark realm. Dan's nephew is one."

"Who saved him?"

"Dan himself. He saw the Enuuki, woke his wife, and they both followed the specter. Dan wrestled the creature while his wife fled with the boy."

"They all made it back?"

"Yes, no doubt because the boy never made it to Zalnic. But his wife still paid a dire price—she now wears a glass eye."

Jack glanced at Natalie. She stared as if frozen. "Are you saying she traded an eye for her nephew?" she asked.

Ron's gaze shifted from one face to another. "You might look at it that way. During the escape, she was cornered by one of Zalnic's pets, a blind salamander. She was bargaining her way out of the jam when Dan caught up."

Marmalade made her way over to Natalie and Jack could hear the cat purring in earnest as Natalie stroked her. "How did he fend off the salamander?" he asked.

"The details may be in my notes—which I intend to give you. Even so, if you undertake this errand, I think it would be worth your while to get Dan to talk to you."

"Yeah, I could definitely use his advice," Jack agreed. "You said someone else was rescued successfully?"

Ron cocked his head sideways, lending more to his bird-like appearance. "It depends what you consider successful. The victim made it back, but his rescuer never did."

"Do you know the survivor? Is he or she still alive?"

"I assume so. He must be barely in his twenties. Fortunately for him—although unfortunately for you—he has little memory of the ordeal. Hang on." The elder rose and disappeared through a doorway near the foyer. He emerged a moment later with a laptop. He sat back in his chair and powered it up. "I'm going to send you my files. I'm sure you're already aware you'll need to descend and enter the spirit world in the flesh?" When Jack nodded, he continued. "This is managed on sacred ground at the crest of the moon. It's a dangerous

69

undertaking, to say the least. You must not eat or drink anything from the other realm. You don't want to assimilate anything from that world into your body. Even dust. Wear shoes, pants, long sleeves."

"Gloves?" Jack asked.

The elder nodded. "Definitely." He paused to type something then pinned them with a serious stare. "Take the time to prepare. From what you've said about the girl who was taken, she'll be okay for a little longer. Better you enter the dark realm prepared than give Zalnic your souls on top of the one he's stolen. Try to formulate a plan that keeps the two of you together. It'll be safer that way."

"Oh." Jack's eyebrows lifted in surprise. "No. Natalie's helping me, but only I plan to travel below." He noticed Natalie jerk her head in his direction, but he didn't look at her. She didn't think she was going with him, did she? He'd never said so.

Ron asked Jack for his email address and sent his files while they waited. Then he looked up information on the survivor. "Ah, here it is. Eric Palmer."

Jack extracted the pen from the rings of his notebook and opened to the back page. He copied down the information as Ron dictated it to him, his mind racing with the possibility of speaking to a survivor. Even more encouraging was the man's address; he lived in Charlevoix.

Which was on the way home.

Natalie didn't say a word until they were in the car. She turned to Jack before starting the engine. "What do you mean I'm not going?"

"Natalie, I never asked you to actually come to the underworld with me. I knew you couldn't. That's why I explained that I was a shifter. Only I can descend into the spirit world."

"Teach me then."

"It's not something you learn. I thought you understood—I was born with the ability to cross worlds."

Natalie pressed her lips together and stared hard at Jack. As she detected the truth to his words, her face softened and he saw tears pool in her eyes. "I want to help save her."

"You are."

She blinked a few times and faced forward. After wiping her eyes on her sleeves, she started the car. "Okay, tell me where we're going."

Jack read from the directions Ron had given them. The elder had also offered to call Eric and give him a heads-up before Jack and Natalie showed up on his doorstep. Jack felt like he'd scored a wealth of information already. Maybe his quest was viable after all.

Eric lived in an apartment complex just outside the city. "Jack and Natalie?" he asked when he opened the door.

"That's us," Jack said. "Obviously Ron got ahold of you."

"He did." Instead of inviting them in, Eric stepped out and drew the door closed behind him. "I'm sorry, but I gotta be to work in forty-five minutes. I always stop at the diner on the way. You're welcome to tag along. There's not much I can tell you, anyway."

They followed Eric's little red hatchback a few blocks into town and met him inside the diner. Eric ordered a large coffee and a sandwich to go then took a seat at the counter. Jack and Natalie both ordered a soda. Eric didn't wait to be asked a question. "I remember the thing that took me." He shuddered. "I still have nightmares about it—about its red eyes. And even though I don't remember that thing saying anything to me, in my dreams it calls me 'son of pool' or something like that. Weird. Anyway, since then I've made it my business to know the location of sacred grounds and stay away from them."

The waitress placed a large Styrofoam cup with a lid in front of Eric. Jack waited until she headed into the kitchen. "What about the rescue? Do you remember that?"

Eric's eyes roamed the cold case behind the counter. "Bits and pieces. I heard someone call my name in the dark. Then I was led across a desert of black sand. Since the last thing in my memory was that creature, I screamed and tried to get away. But then I saw it was a human. He yanked on my arm and said something about a chasm, I think, because next thing I knew he pushed me into an enormous pit of some kind. I came to in the cemetery where I'd disappeared. I'd been gone eight days." He shook his head. "The other guy was never seen again."

"And you don't remember anything from when you were taken until you were rescued?"

Eric shook his head. "Nothing. You want to know if I ate or drank anything, right? I don't know. And I wonder every day if I'm poisoned or infected in some way or if that thing will come and reclaim me. And there's the ultimate question—why me? Do I have some kind of inherent evilness?"

Natalie spoke up. "No."

Eric leaned forward to see around Jack. A smile played at the corners of his mouth. "You sound pretty sure about that. Have we met before?"

"No." She breathed a nervous laugh. "I just know my friend Emma doesn't have an evil bone in her body. You were just in the wrong place at the wrong time."

Eric studied her for a moment. "You may be right. My research hasn't brought me to any conclusive answer."

"Research?" Jack asked.

The waitress presented a paper bag to Eric. The top was rolled and stapled shut along with the check. Eric smiled and produced a twenty dollar bill. "Thanks, Donna." He waited for his change before addressing Jack's question. He tilted his head toward the door.

Outside, he explained. "Like most victims, I wanted to know what I did wrong or if I could've done anything—changed anything—so it never would've happened. I wanted to make sure it wouldn't happen again. Since there were no ready answers, I started my own database of information on disappearances. I quickly noticed a pattern of teens and tweens that go missing when either on, or last seen near, sacred places. Both things have helped me to live a fairly normal life. As I said, I stay away from hallowed ground and now that I'm in my twenties, I believe I'm too old to be abducted again. I just wish I could really nail down the similarities and maybe spare someone else the experience—you know, possibly save a life."

"Would you share your database with us?" Natalie's request surprised Jack. He wasn't sure the information would be useful for them now. Emma was already gone.

"Sure." Eric smiled. "Why not?"

There was something about Eric's smile that bothered Jack. He considered interjecting that they didn't really need his data.

"I can give you my email," Natalie offered.

"Or mine." Jack blurted it out, surprised he'd even spoken. Natalie shot him a confused look.

"Got a flash drive?" Eric looked at Jack then back at Natalie.

Natalie held up her keys to show a flash drive hanging from the bundle.

Eric led them up the street to the cell phone store where he worked. They followed him inside where he motioned them to a workstation in the back. He logged in, then reached under his shirt collar and retrieved a lanyard from around his neck. Fastened to the end was a flash drive. He looked up through his eyelashes with a sheepish grin. "Yeah. I admit I'm a bit obsessed. Don't judge." He laughed. Once he plugged his device into a port on the workstation, he held out his hand for Natalie's. He slid hers into another slot, waited a few seconds, then began clicking the mouse.

Jack noticed a pack of post-it notes, peeled a sheet from the stack, and wrote his cell phone number on the paper. He stuck it next to Eric's keyboard. "This is my cell in case you think of anything else. Would it be okay if I had your number?"

"Sure, take my card." Eric gestured to the plastic holder on the other side of his monitor. "Transferring files... and... done. Eject." A moment later he pulled Natalie's flash drive from the machine. "Enjoy." He passed it to her with a wide grin.

Jack took one of Eric's cards and nudged Natalie away from the counter before she thought to grab one for herself.

Between giving Natalie directions back to the highway, Jack tried to pinpoint what it was that bothered him about Eric. He was friendly, congenial and forthcoming. But when Natalie commented about how well Eric had recovered from his ordeal and how nice he was, Jack merely grunted.

"Is something wrong, Jack? You haven't said anything in the last twenty minutes aside from telling me where to turn."

"No. I—" How was he supposed to answer that? Finally he said, "I'm not sure how you think Eric's research might help us."

"I don't know." She sounded surprised. "I just figured it wouldn't hurt to ask. We might wish we had it later."

She was right and he knew it. He had to shrug the chip off his shoulder—especially when he had no idea why it was there. "Yeah. Okay. I guess we can't have too much information."

"Cheese and rice!" Natalie's exclamation caused Jack to jerk upright in his seat. "We've been gone four hours! What am I going to tell my dad?"

Jack burst out laughing.

"It's not funny, Jack."

"I know, I know." Jack got himself under control. "Sorry. I never heard anyone say 'cheese and rice' before." He swallowed another urge to laugh. "Tell him… uh… tell him we went out for lunch and ran into friends."

Natalie handed Jack her phone. "Okay, that sounds good. Send a text, would you?"

"Uh, sure." Jack accepted the phone reluctantly. "Should I use 'cheese and rice' to make sure it sounds like you?"

"Yeah," Natalie replied with sarcasm and shot Jack a bland look. "I'd like to hear how you work that in. Just don't abbreviate anything. He hates that."

"All right." Jack still wore a small smile that disappeared as soon as he started tapping the keyboard on Natalie's phone. A slow typist and a lousy speller, abbreviations were his lifeline when it came to texting. He scanned the message before hitting send to make sure he didn't mess anything up, then deposited the phone into a cup holder. "Hey, let me know if you want me to drive."

"Okay, thanks."

Jack hooked up Natalie's iPod and they rode without conversation for a while. He wondered how he might persuade Dan Manning to talk to him. Maybe he could relay the things Natalie told him about Emma and convince him that she could still be saved. Influencing another person's opinion was never Jack's strong suit—he knew better than to join the debate team or entertain a future in politics. He stole a glance at Natalie.

He would try. He owed her that.

Natalie pulled into a gas station.

"Gas already?"

"No, pit stop. Will you get me a bottle of water?" Natalie reached for her wallet. Jack stopped her before she could pull it from her bag. He gave her a pointed look and rolled his eyes dramatically.

She laughed. "Fine." They walked into the convenience store together. Jack flagged Natalie down before she made it to the restrooms. He held up a bag of Cheetos. She smiled and nodded.

As they returned to the car Jack asked, "Want me to drive for a while?"

76

She scrutinized him for a moment, considering the offer. "Are you a good driver?"

"Uh, yeah. I drove around my grandparents' farm way before I took Driver's Ed." He reached for her keys.

Natalie closed her fist. "Are you careful?"

Jack huffed, but the corners of his mouth curled upward. He looked out toward the gas pumps, considering, and then settled his gaze back on Natalie's face. "Definitely, considering I'm always driving someone else's car."

"Okay." She opened her fist over his palm.

As they climbed inside, Jack handed her the bag of Cheetos. "Am I allowed to eat and drive? I might get orange stuff on your steering wheel."

"I have napkins. Try to keep the cheese on the wheel to a minimum."

About a half hour from home, Natalie's phone buzzed. "Shoot. My dad wants me home. Now. Client dinner."

"Client dinner?"

"Yeah," she muttered. "I shouldn't have to go. I'm not his wife."

"Won't your mom be there?"

Natalie snorted in disgust. "My so-called mom left when I was seven."

"God. Sorry." Jack felt like an idiot.

"Don't be. You didn't know." Natalie's thumbs flew over her phone screen. "Can you speed a little?"

Jack gave her an amused glance.

"Not enough to get a ticket though. I told him we need to put some stuff away and then I'll head home. Ooo—what about you? How far are you from my house?"

Jack's heart skipped a beat. "Not far at all."

Natalie put her head back on the seat and sighed. "Sometimes I wish he'd get remarried. I'm tired of trying to be two people."

"Does he date?"

"No. He buries himself in his job."

Jack wasn't sure what to do. If she needed to talk, he was okay to listen, but he felt like their friendship was too new for him to pry into her past.

"I guess it's partly my fault. When my mom left, my dad was heartbroken. I felt so bad for him that I took over a lot of the things she used to do, you know, so he wouldn't miss her so much." She laughed. "I guess that was my way of burying myself in work."

The playlist ended. Natalie turned off her iPod and stuffed it into her purse. She didn't turn on the radio. After a few minutes of quiet, Jack figured he'd put a question out there. If she didn't want to talk, she'd say so. "Do you miss her a lot?"

A silence stretched out and Jack thought maybe he should have just kept his mouth shut, but Natalie must have been mulling over her reply. "I miss... having a mom. But honestly, I might feel that way even if she'd stayed. It's kinda hard to explain." She took a deep breath. "My dad used to travel and move around a lot. He met my mom in Dubai and I was born there. I don't think they intended to have kids—at least not at that time. Anyway, we lived a few other places and then my dad took the job here, to settle down once I'd started school."

Natalie had the cord for her iPod in her hand and she kept twisting it around her finger as she spoke. "She couldn't take it—settling down, I mean. She married my dad because she loved the excitement of his transient lifestyle. Putting down roots in a small town was never her dream. We both knew it—my dad and I. It hurt when she left, but I can't say we were surprised." Jack felt her gaze on him and searched for something to say. "Sorry, I'm sure that's more than you wanted to know."

"I want to know anything you want to tell me."

"You do?"

"Sure. Why wouldn't I want to know you better?" He felt her stare. "What?"

Her mouth twitched up at the corners. "Nothing."

As he turned onto Red Apple Road, Jack had an idea. He pulled into the lot in front of a farm stand that was closed for the evening.

"Switch?" Natalie asked.

"I'll walk from here. You get home."

"No. It's not right. Do you live close by?" She swiveled her head around taking in the distinct lack of signs of other civilization.

"Right up the road." Jack pointed. "I can call my dad, but it's no big deal just to walk."

Natalie's anxiety about getting home worked in his favor. "All right then. Talk to you later?"

Jack nodded. "Yeah. Go."

He waved as she pulled back onto the road.

His street was only about a half mile away; his house another quarter mile. Jack set off toward the sunset—western Michigan's claim to fame. On the shore of Lake Michigan, watching the sun go down over the water was like watching a sunset over the ocean. Miles and miles of uninterrupted horizon.

Only a few miles from the lake, Jack caught a

glimpse of the water as he crested a hill, the sun a red half-circle floating on the surface. It would be dark before he got home.

The name of the street that dead-ended at his house was Bittersweet. Funny, that's kind of how he felt about it. They lived in an old farmhouse. Not the big, rambling kind—a tiny one. It had two stories: a small kitchen, living room and bathroom on the first floor and two bedrooms on the second floor. Since Jack and his little brother Jase shared a room, their parents gave the boys the bigger bedroom.

The overgrown property hadn't been farmed for decades and the barn roof had caved in long ago. Behind the house was an old chicken coop they kept in reasonable repair and used as a shed. Alongside the coop was a newer barn-like garage. Jack was old enough when they moved to take off by himself and explore, so he felt the acre and a half of property made up for the house's lack of square footage. The brook that trickled across the northwest corner of their tract soon became his favorite hang-out.

His only reservation was having friends at his house. Since the bus ride to school revealed the subdivisions other kids lived in (though none were as affluent as Natalie's) Jack was reluctant to invite anyone over. He let others volunteer their homes for group projects or suggested public places to meet. Only those he knew well, like Wes, had been to Jack's house. His home was his haven and he preferred to keep it that way.

The sun had slipped below the horizon, sucking the residual light along with it. The intermittent buzz of traffic on Red Apple Road faded as he started down Bittersweet Lane. Most of the sparsely scattered residences were set back from the road. A few open plots of land provided occasional relief from the surrounding forest and thick underbrush.

The scuffle of footfalls on loose gravel broke the silence.

Jack turned, but darkness cloaked the road. Whoever—or whatever—made the noise, was too far behind for him to make out. He continued on his way, increasing his pace slightly, ears tuned to pick up the sound. The intermittent scratch on the hard packed dirt or rattle of rocks seemed to increase in frequency and grow closer. Jack concluded it was a dog. Most people out here owned at least one four-footed friend and it wasn't unusual to see them trotting down the road. Good thing the uneven road surface encouraged drivers to proceed slowly.

Peering again into the gloom behind him, Jack adjusted his sightline lower to the ground and picked out the shape of a large dog. He guessed it must be black or dark brown since it blended with the night.

"Here, boy." He searched his memory of neighborhood dogs, trying to fit size and color—and ideally—a name. He wouldn't mind a little company for the rest of his walk. The Lemenors had a black lab, didn't they? Another glance at the black form revealed the outline of a raised muzzle scenting the air. No, too big for a lab. Maybe the Havers—

Jack watched as the head lowered, and he met the animal's glowing red eyes.

His next thought ran through his brain in slow motion: there wasn't anything in the area to reflect that color.

Then he heard a low snarl.

81

He ran.

Ahead of him, the porch light on his house resembled a small flashlight.

The sound of the creature's pursuit changed in cadence. Jack risked a glance over his shoulder, and caught the loping gait of the animal behind him.

Dogs didn't run like that. A cat might, though.

A very big cat.

A surge of adrenaline spurred him along faster. Jack clawed at his jacket, fumbling for the phone in the pocket. He bobbled it once, caught it and clutched it to his chest. He didn't dare try to enter his passcode—it would slow him down. What he needed was some kind of temporary refuge, but Jack was thoroughly familiar with the property flashing by beside him. He knew there was nowhere to hide.

The cat was right behind him. He didn't look—the prickles on the back of his neck told him all he needed to know. He couldn't afford to slow down.

The details of the porch illuminated by the light next to the door were coming into focus. "Help!" he yelled, panting. "Mom, Dad, help…"

Nothing changed at the house. Jack realized he had no idea if his family was even home. If the door was locked, he'd never get his key into it before he was attacked.

"Help," he screamed again, though his breath came in ragged gasps.

Whether real or imagined, Jack felt the heat of the animal behind him. His eyes darted to the garage. The large opening simply looked dark. The door was black—sometimes it was hard to tell if the door was up or down even from the house windows. Jack decided it was a better bet than the house. He made a quick dash to the right, hoping to throw the cat off for even a second, reaching deep for the strength to make it to shelter.

Hope swelled for a moment as the shadowy form of his dad's pick-up became visible in the garage opening. He could jump into the truck. It wouldn't be locked. He could make a ca—

A terrific weight slammed him face down into the dirt. Knives of fire pieced his shoulders.

He weakly lifted his head toward home, hoping to see someone coming to the rescue.

The porch light winked out.

CHAPTER 5

Underworld Guardian

Jack cracked his eyes open. Six inches in front of his nose a cherub-round face peered anxiously over the mattress. Jack rolled in an attempt to rise up on his elbow and grimaced in pain. A chubby hand reached up to push him down.

"Mom says you're supposed ta lay down."

"Okay." Jack managed a little smile. "Go tell Mom I'm awake."

"Uh-uh. I'm on Jacky watch. It's important."

"I promise not to move until you get back."

Jase's face regarded his brother seriously. "Better not."

"I won't." But Jase was already out the door and bounding down the stairs.

He was back a minute later with Jack's mom trailing behind him. She sat on the edge of his bed like he was a little boy. A worry crease indented her forehead. "How do you feel?"

"I don't know. I wasn't allowed to move."

Her smile didn't entirely erase the furrows on her brow. "Your brother's been watching over you—he was worried."

Jack groaned as he sat up. "Sore."

"You're pretty bruised up. Luckily your father scared the cat off right after it knocked you down."

Jack flexed his shoulders. He could feel bandages. "So it was a cat?"

"Apparently." His mom put her hand on his forehead. "Dad said it looked like a big black panther." The creases reappeared on her forehead and she didn't meet his eyes—there was more she wasn't saying. She felt his cheek to divert the conversation. "You don't seem to have a temperature."

"Is Dad home?" He'd get answers from his dad.

"He's at the Millers' helping them fix their tractor. He should be back for lunch." She rose. "Hungry?"

"Starving."

"I'm making pancakes. I'll bring some up."

"No. That's all right. I'll be down in a few minutes." He couldn't afford any lost time if he wanted to rescue Emma. The sooner he convinced his mom he was okay, the better.

His mother considered him, chin resting on her hand. "Don't push it, Jack. Send Jase if you change your mind."

Jack sifted through the clothes that had migrated to the bottom of his bed and found a t-shirt. Over the head wasn't so bad, but the bandages on his shoulders and his bruised torso made it difficult to maneuver his arms into the sleeves. He grunted in frustration and pulled the shirt off.

Jase looked up from the Transformer he'd been fiddling with on the floor. "Want me to tell Mom?" He was already on his feet.

Jack reached for a button-up shirt from the bedpost. "No." He produced a smile for the worried six-year-old as he stuck his arm into a sleeve. "Just pull this shirt over my bandages for me." Jack turned

86

and squatted down, noticing his legs felt fairly normal despite his slightly banged up knees. Jase wrapped the shirt across Jack's shoulders, making it easy for his big brother to slip his other arm into the sleeve. Then Jack recovered his sweat pants from the floor in front of the closet.

On the way downstairs he discovered his ribcage and back really ached, making the ladder-back chairs in the kitchen tortuous. He opted to eat on the couch. After the pancakes he called Natalie.

"How was the client dinner?"

"How do you think? Boring."

Jack chuckled. "Mmm. Don't know which was worse, my night or yours."

"What can suck more than an evening with your father's business associates?"

"A panther attack?'

"Right. Seriously, what did you do last night?"

"I got attacked by a panther. Really. Well, knocked down anyway. Hard enough that I'm hurting today."

"Chee… uh… geez, are there even panthers around here?"

"There shouldn't be. Unless one escaped from a zoo. Otherwise, I think it'd have to be a black cougar. Except it seemed too big for that. I don't know. I'm waiting to talk to my dad about it. He saw it too. He scared it off."

"Jack! I knew I should've driven you home."

"Oh come on, what are the chances? I walk places all the time. Besides, I'm fine. I'm more worried about how to get Dan Manning to help me. I think I should just go to his house and convince him that Emma can be saved—that she deserves to be saved. If you don't mind, could we go over the things you told me about Emma?" He caught movement from the corner of his eye and noticed his mom gesturing at him. "Hang on a minute." Jack pressed his phone to his leg. "What?"

"You're not going anywhere today."

"What? Why? I'm fine."

Standing in the kitchen doorway, she regarded him with eyebrows arched high on her forehead. "Who do you think bandaged you up?"

"I'm just sore. Come on, Mom. This is important."

She considered him a moment longer. "I'll discuss it with your dad when he gets here." She turned on the last word, closing the conversation.

Jack put the phone back on his ear. "Son of a b—" He broke off, remembering who he was talking to. "Uh sorry, looks like I got a few hours to figure this out before I can go see Dan."

"Do you think he'd talk to me?"

Jack heard a knock at the front door and watched as his mom crossed the room to answer it. "No offense, but if he won't help a member of the sect, I can't see him doing anything for you." His mom stepped back and Brody entered the house. "Hey, I'll call you back okay? My adviser's here."

Jack set the phone down as Brody sank into an armchair. "Your dad called me this morning. How do you feel?"

"Like I was on the losing side of a cage fight." Jack flexed his shoulders and winced. "The claw marks are the worst. The rest are just bumps and bruises."

The older man's gaze assessed Jack. Apparently satisfied with his student's well-being, he changed the subject. "Bring me up to speed. How'd things go in Harbor Springs yesterday?"

Jack relayed their conversation with Ron as well as the encounter with Eric. He ended with his walk home.

"Sounds like you made a lot of progress yesterday. Zalnic couldn't have been too pleased." Brody spoke softly, glancing quickly toward the kitchen. "How well did you see the animal?"

"Not very good. It was dark and the cat was so black it kept disappearing in the shadows."

"Tell me what you remember about it." Brody's face tensed in focused attention.

"At first I thought it was a dog—maybe a black lab. Then I realized it was too big. I was thinking about Haverson's bull mastiff…" Jack searched his memory for details. "Then I saw it sniff the air. The nose was too blunt to be a dog's nose. Then it…" Jack trailed off. The clatter of dishes and running water came from the kitchen.

Brody waited expectantly.

"It looked at me." Jack's eyes bugged out as he remembered. "Its eyes—they were red." How could he have forgotten that?

"A reflection?"

"No. I thought of that also. But there's nothing out there. Nothing that would cast a red reflection." The details of the incident suddenly flooded his memory and Jack shuddered, recalling the terror of the chase.

His teacher closed his eyes for a moment. "I suspected as much."

"Suspected what?"

"Remember I warned you? Zalnic will try to scare you off."

"He sent a panther?"

"Not a panther Jack, a hellcat. That's why your dad called me."

89

Jack paled. Hellcat? A guardian of the underworld?

His eyes grew wide as the thought of Kyle's artificial limb struck him. "But... Kyle..." He stammered, lifting his arm to convey what he didn't dare utter aloud. His gaze shifted to his mom standing at the kitchen sink, her back to them. Fear streaked through his chest.

A light dawned in Brody's eyes as he comprehended Jack's unasked question. He shook his head. "Not the same up here," he murmured.

Jack let out the breath he didn't know he'd been holding. He wasn't poisoned. Still, the full impact of his dangerous undertaking left an impression. Did he really want to go through with this? For a girl he didn't know?

Shera. He had to keep his eye on the prize.

And what about Natalie?

To his astonishment, the idea of letting Natalie down was almost as big a deterrent from backing down. Now that he'd invested in the partnership, aborting the mission would cost him.

Cost him what?

Her friendship? Was she a friend? They'd really only known each other a few days.

What about respect? How could Natalie respect him if he started this only to back out when the going looked tough?

Jack scrubbed his hand over his face. His head hurt. He wasn't sure why it should matter so much what Natalie thought of him, but it did matter.

"You're not required to do this, Jack." Brody rose and Jack lifted his chin to meet his adviser's eyes. "Think about it carefully."

Although Natalie didn't know it, she ended Jack's deliberation.

He was propped up on his bed, texting with Wes while paging through a Rolling Stone magazine, when a call from Natalie showed on his screen.

"Hey, Natalie. What's up?" He hadn't called her back yet because he didn't know what to do. He needed his dad's advice. Unfortunately, lunch came and went with no sign of his father.

"I think I have good news. When we talked earlier and you said Dan's last name, Manning, it rang a bell. It took me a while to figure out why, but then I remembered the glass eye and it hit me: Callie Manning. She works at the book store out by the mall. I kind of know her."

"Dan's wife? You think she might tell you something?"

"I already talked to her."

"You what?"

"I drove out to the mall to see if she was working and she was there. She took her break to talk to me."

Jack was amazed. "Just like that?"

"Yeah, except I didn't know all the questions you would've asked."

"Do you think she'll talk to me?"

"Yeah, I asked her. And Jack, she's going to try to convince Dan to help you."

"I can't believe it. You're awesome." A large part of Jack's uncertainty about moving forward melted away.

"Thanks, I finally feel like I've done something to help get Emma back." The breathless excitement in her

91

voice made Natalie sound as if she'd just run back from the mall.

"Tell me what you found out."

Callie's fifteen minute break allowed only a brief version of the Manning's descent to the spirit world to rescue their nephew. So Callie invited Natalie and Jack to come by later that afternoon.

"Did she say what time?" Jack asked.

"Anytime after three. She gets off work at two."

"I hope my dad gets home soon. If he says I can go, my mom won't argue with him. I'll text you as soon as I know something."

Jack was pretty sure he heard his dad's truck roll up just before they said goodbye. Twisting sideways, he let out a moan. Ughh. He had to remember to move slowly. Swinging his legs off the bed, he carefully stood up, then paused at the top of the stairs until he heard his father's deep voice.

When Jack entered the kitchen, his dad sat at the table eating a late lunch and chatting to his wife. His gaze followed Jack into the room while keeping up his end of the conversation. Jack poured a glass of juice, turned from the refrigerator and met his father's eyes. A slight nod confirmed he understood that his son wanted to talk.

Jack wandered into the living room and contemplated the TV. There wasn't much point in turning it on. The chances of finding anything to watch on a Sunday afternoon—or ever—were slim. Cable hadn't made its way down Bittersweet Lane. Though satellite was an option, it wasn't priority for the Ironwood family. If not for games loaded on his laptop, Jack would go nuts.

He settled for the Sunday comics. He only stared

at the colorful pictures for a few minutes before he heard the wooden scrape of a kitchen chair. The slightly uneven tread of his father's footsteps elicited an instant stab of remorse. Last night wasn't the first time Jack had been rescued by his dad. At least this time only Jack was hurt. The first time had been the other way around.

Ron Winert was correct; Jack's dad used to specialize in boat motors. He was once the most sought-after mechanic at the Lake Michigan marina. In the summer, on days his mom worked, young Jack went to the marina with his father. His dad taught him about boats and motors and found small jobs to keep him occupied.

Because the marina rented pleasure boats, his dad occasionally had to assess a crippled boat out on the water. On the fateful day, Jack had begged to accompany him, anxious to get out of the shop and speed across the water. His dad relented and took Jack along.

Normally, a speed boat ferried Jack's dad to the stranded vessel, waited for the diagnosis, and then either ferried him back to the marina or towed the disabled boat to the docks. This time, a woman had become extremely sick from the rolling motion of the helpless boat so the smaller boat ran her in to shore while his father worked on the pleasure craft's motor.

Distracted by their own crisis, no one noticed the freighter bearing down on them. The larger ship, unaware that the pleasure boat was dead in the water until it was too late to alter its course, bellowed a warning blast. After a mad scramble for lifejackets, the remaining five boaters hit the water along with Jack and his father.

Everything became muddled after that. Jack

remembered a lot of screaming and shouting and then the buzz of a small motor. The speed boat had returned!

Except it hadn't.

The sound came from a WaveRunner.

Actually, there were two of them.

Jack's father grabbed his son by the lifejacket and towed him toward the nearest WaveRunner. The driver had already taken one of the boaters aboard and another was clambering up. "I can only take one more," he shouted.

"Take my son." His dad spoke without hesitation.

"No!" Jack wailed, even as he was being hauled from the water. "You can fit… see… no…" he babbled. The two rescued boaters sandwiched Jack between them.

"I'll come back," the driver promised.

Jack's father nodded, then met his son's eyes. Whatever he was going to say was obliterated by an enormous crack as the freighter smashed into the pleasure craft. The WaveRunner driver gunned his machine and zipped toward shore.

They found Jack's dad bobbing among debris from the wreck. He'd been tossed about in the giant swells the freighter created and slammed by a large piece of fiberglass. The severed ligament in his leg was never quite the same.

Jack knew if he'd stayed at the marina, his father would've been on board the WaveRunner instead of in the water.

His dad returned to work at the marina, but his injury made it tough to balance on a pitching boat. Three years later, when the opportunity to take over an existing auto shop arose, Jack's father took it, and the family moved to Ketchton.

Although Jack still loved the beach and the sparkle of sunshine on water, he never went much farther than ankle deep into Lake Michigan. He'd swim in small inland lakes, or ponds and rivers, but had no interest in boats. The mere thought made him break out in a cold sweat.

His dad would be angry if he knew his son still felt guilty about the incident so Jack took a breath and carefully neutralized his expression.

"Mom said Brody was here this morning." His dad sank into the other end of the couch.

Jack nodded. "You already knew though, didn't you? That it was a hellcat?"

"I did. Saw the red eyes from the porch."

"How did you chase it off?"

"Light. Hopped in the truck and turned on the headlights—the brights. The thing kind of just… vaporized."

Jack looked down at his hands. "Dad?" He raised his head and met his dad's gaze. "Am I crazy to do this?"

"Jack, you're only crazy if you're careless and unprepared. What were you able to learn yesterday?"

Jack brought his dad up to date. Right up to his recent conversation with Natalie.

"Have you considered there might be a reason why she was taken?"

"Aside from being a teenager? It's random, Dad. Wrong place, wrong time."

"Are you sure?"

"Pretty sure." Jack thought about Eric's data. The survivor said he hadn't reached any conclusion aside from age. "Why would it matter, anyway?"

"The best way to defeat an enemy is to know how he thinks. Be one step ahead of him."

95

"You really think he can be defeated?"

"If he didn't have a weakness, he wouldn't be trying to discourage you."

"Well, it would definitely help if I could talk to the Mannings today. Mom didn't want me to go anywhere. Did she talk to you about it?"

His dad's lips curved and his eyes crinkled at the corners. "Yeah. You realize you'll always be her son first and a shifter second? She loves you, Jack. And so do I. But we figure you're old enough to know how you feel. Just don't overdo it."

A small part of Jack wished his dad would forbid him to go forward with his mission. But a much bigger part of him was bolstered by the confidence that came from his parents' support.

"Is the girl—Natalie?—going to pick you up?"

"No, we're going to meet at the Java Hut."

"Take my truck then."

His dad's pickup roared to life and Jack eased onto the dirt road, wincing each time the vehicle lurched over a bump. By the time he reached Red Apple Road, his teeth were clenched tight and he'd never been so happy to see blacktop in his life. An autumn-scented breeze complemented the gray skies overhead and the vegetable stand on Red Apple Road displayed various varieties of squash along with crates of bright orange pumpkins.

He saw Natalie's car in the lot as he pulled into the Java Hut. He parked next to her, directly in front of the sign near the door announcing: WE'RE NOT AN

INTERNET CAFÉ – WE'RE A COFFEE HOUSE WITH WI-FI FOR OUR CUSTOMERS' CONVENIENCE. Natalie's driver seat was empty. Jack took a breath and steeled himself for the drop to the pavement, but before he opened his door, Natalie appeared next to the truck with two cups in her hand. He rolled down the window.

"I got you a plain latte. You don't seem like the fancy-drink type." The corners of her mouth curled. "I hope it's okay. I didn't want you to have to get out and walk in."

Jack returned her smile and accepted the cup she moved toward him. "Thanks. Here, hand me yours too, and hop in." Natalie had to use the assist handle to climb into the pick-up and Jack hid his amusement behind a sip of coffee, grateful to stay in one place.

"Figured we had some time to kill, might as well get a coffee," she said once she was situated. "Is yours okay? Mine's a vanilla latte. I'll trade you if you'd rather have something with flavor."

"No, plain is great. I consider coffee a flavor."

"Ha ha, you know what I mean." Then Natalie's smile faded. "How're you feeling?"

"Sore. Grateful you saved me a trip inside."

"Well, I've got some interesting information. I spent some time this morning looking at Eric's database. It looks like he must have a connection with the cops or something because he's got missing person reports. Anyway, he put it all into a spreadsheet so you can search the fields for similarities. He's right. None of the fields have the same answers."

Jack raised his eyebrows and sipped his coffee.

"He did make the connection with the ages though—all teenagers, including a few preteens. I imagine he either knew or someone told him about the sacred ground part of his ordeal and then he confirmed that data on the other reports—one of the columns appears to be his notes on the locations. Anyway, what he didn't notice, or just neglected to mention, is the religion column. The answers vary widely, but when I really looked at them, I realized they pretty much said the same thing: the kids had no religion."

"Wait. I'm not sure I follow."

Natalie lowered her cup to her lap and swallowed. "The reports are from all over so lots of different people fill them out, right?"

"Right."

"Well everyone has their own way of saying 'no': none, n/a, no denomination, unknown, atheist... sometimes the field is crossed out or left blank, but it all means the same thing—none of the kids had a religious affiliation."

"Did Emma?"

Natalie stared at him over the rim of her coffee cup. "No."

"How does that figure in, though?"

"I'm not sure. But we're talking about a god taking people to hell—it's got to be relevant, right?"

Jack mulled it over. "Yeah—especially since the kids have no affiliation. Like, does it make them more attractive? Gullible? Easier to steal?" He thought about what his dad said earlier about knowing your enemy and looked at Natalie with a sly grin. "You may have found the key to our success."

She beamed at him. "Really?"

"No one else has mentioned this." Jack checked the time. "Let's head over to the Mannings' and see what they say. Are you okay with leaving your car here?"

Natalie nodded, pointed her key fob at her car, and received a satisfactory beep confirming the doors were locked. The drive wasn't too painful, as the route included all paved roads, but Jack still used the last of his coffee to swallow some ibuprofen tablets before going into the Mannings' house. He wanted to move without wincing. "Don't mention the attack while we're here," he said as they approached the front porch.

Natalie gave him an odd look, but Jack knocked before she could say anything.

A petite woman opened the door. "Hi, Natalie. And you must be Jack. I'm Callie," she said, ushering them inside. Her large, round eyes gave her face a youthful innocence bolstered by the long brunette hair she flipped over her shoulder.

"Thanks for agreeing to talk to us." Jack met Callie's eyes briefly, then glanced to Natalie, wondering how you speak to someone with a glass eye without appearing to stare at their handicap.

"Of course. And Dan will be joining us." Her emphasis on the word 'will' made it clear she'd told Dan the same thing. "Man, chilly out there today. You guys want something hot to drink?"

Natalie exchanged a smile with Jack. "No thanks, we had coffee on the way over."

"Okay, well, sit." She extended a hand toward the end of the hall. "I'll go find Dan." She disappeared behind a door and Jack heard the clip-clop of footsteps on wooden stairs.

The kitchen was immediately to their right, and they passed through a dining area on the way to the living room. Jack wondered at the odd arrangement—kitchen in front, living room in back—until he stood in the back room. Large windows made up the back wall and wrapped partway around the sides of the room. French doors led to a deck which spanned the width of the house.

The Mannings' considerable piece of property rolled lazily downhill to a pond large enough to swim and fish in. At least Jack assumed the fishing part, since a small row boat was pulled up on shore. The picturesque view could have been a watercolor or oil painting.

"Wow." Natalie sounded awed. "This was unexpected." They chose a couch situated on a side wall where they could see outside.

"I see you're enjoying the view of Manning Pond." Callie grinned as she entered the room. "We built it—you know, dug it ourselves—not sure what the correct term is. Our property backs up to state land and we figured why not create a habitat? Dan loves to fish, so we stocked it with bass, blue gill and perch. The ducks and frogs found it on their own." She moved a pillow on the couch across the room, sank into the cushions and pulled her feet up next to her. "When he was little, Ty caught frogs all summer long. He always wanted to keep them, but we explained they already lived here."

Ty must be their son. Jack wondered at her past tense reference until she continued.

"Of course, now the main thing he tries to catch is girls." She laughed. "I admit I'm a little anxious about him being away at college."

"He's going to be fine, Cal." A tall man entered the room wearing a t-shirt and jeans. Jack noticed the muscle definition on his arms and chest. The only clues to his age were his grey hair and the deep furrows on his forehead. He sized up Jack. "So you're set on going after this girl, huh?"

"Yes. We believe she can still be saved." Jack nudged Natalie and she stepped in, telling the Mannings about Emma.

"I heard you already had a run-in with one of Zalnic's minions. Do you realize the quantity of twisted creatures Zalnic has patrolling his realm?" Dan asked.

Natalie turned to Jack, eyebrows high on her brow. "You what?"

Jack shot a look at Dan. "How did you know?"

"Brody Carter called." He swiped a hand over his short hair. "Asked me to help."

"Uh... hello?" Natalie jabbed Jack with her elbow.

Jack sighed. "The panther? It was a hellcat."

"Hellcat?"

"Underworld guardian." Jack answered without looking at Natalie. "Zalnic's trying to shut me down before I get started."

"That's why you didn't want me to mention the attack," she muttered, crossing her arms.

Jack gazed from Dan to Callie. "We're hoping you might tell us what you ran into and any advice you have on getting around them—or fighting them."

The Mannings hadn't spent much time in the underworld, but they filled Jack and Natalie in on what they knew. "Just remember," Callie said with a hint of a smile, "the blind salamander isn't blind anymore."

"How did you... did it...?" Natalie struggled with her question.

"It had my nephew. I was responsible for him. I bargained for his life," the older woman replied matter-of-factly.

101

"That's how you got him back?" Jack asked. He wondered what they might have to barter with.

"The only reason we got Chris back is because we went after him immediately," Dan interjected. "I saw the Enuuki take him. Chris never made it to Zalnic's citadel. Your friend is most certainly under Zalnic's influence by now, somehow you'll have to convince him to release her."

"Oh." Dan's statement shut Jack down. He was certain Zalnic would want much more than an eye.

Natalie must've heard the resignation in his voice because she spoke up. "Um, was your nephew baptized or did he practice any kind of religion?"

Callie shot a surprised glance at Dan. Jack groaned. "Are his parents sect members?" Both Dan and Callie must be shifters if they crossed worlds so it wouldn't matter which side of the family the nephew was from. "If so, this blows our theory."

"What theory?" Callie asked.

When Jack didn't respond, Natalie answered the question. "We spoke to a guy who made it back."

Callie nodded. "We've met Eric Palmer," she said to her husband who bobbed his chin once.

"Right," Natalie said. "He gave us his database of disappearances he thought were the same as his. The primary factors seem to be teens and preteens taken from sacred ground." She paused and glanced at Jack. He flipped his hand in a gesture to continue. "I noticed something else I thought all the kids had in common, lack of religion."

"Chris doesn't blow your theory," Callie said quietly. "He was twelve, taken from a Native American historic site, and he didn't have any religious affiliations.

102

Soulshifter

He's my sister's son." She turned to Jack. "We're not sect members... or anything else." She exchanged a glance with her husband. "Years ago, while my brother was away at college, he got involved with a cult and disappeared. My parents hired a private investigator to track him down. By the time the detective located my brother, he'd already made a"—Callie's voice broke, but she continued—"a suicide pact."

Jack heard Natalie's sharp intake of breath. His hand rose automatically to reach out to her, but he just touched his neck instead and dropped the arm to his lap. Their relationship was odd—more than acquaintances, but not quite friends—he wasn't sure of the parameters and didn't want to make things awkward. Then he realized Dan was addressing him.

"—sure you get it Jack, the way others misunderstand the sect?"

Jack nodded. The sect was widely misunderstood.

"I knew Callie's father wouldn't allow his daughter to date me if he knew I belonged to a sect." Dan shot a quick glance at Callie. "I planned to tell Callie when things with her bother were sorted out, but after his death... I just couldn't. When I decided to ask her to marry me, I knew I had to come clean—with her, anyway. I decided to quit the sect. That way, when I told her, I could also say I was no longer a part of it, in case the idea of the sect spooked her."

"It did spook me," Callie admitted. "But Dan assured me he was done with it. Our family wasn't religious to start with and my brother's death cast suspicion on all organized religion."

"So our theory is still viable," Natalie said.

"Yeah," Dan replied. "It's viable—you just have to figure out how that helps get your friend back."

CHAPTER 6

Traditions and Ancestry

The meeting with the Mannings seemed to raise more questions than it answered, which left Jack feeling anxious. He paced his room after dinner, replaying the conversation in his head.

He'd taken Ron Winert's advice very seriously. He intended to be well-prepared. But his dad had added another layer to that advice—having an edge. And he felt like they were on the cusp of discovering the one tidbit of information that would ensure success.

"Jack?" His mom's voice carried up the stairwell.

"What?"

"Stop moving around. You should lie down and rest."

Jack sighed. He couldn't lie down. It was too uncomfortable. "Okay." There was no sense in arguing. He tossed his two pillows to the side of his bed which butted up against the wall, then paused with one knee on the mattress. Crouching down, he pulled a plastic container from beneath his bed and plopped it next to the pillows.

When he was as comfortable as he was able to be, he opened the container.

The first time Jack saw a soulshifter's codex, he was ten. That book belonged to his former adviser, David, who showed it to his protégé the day after Jack's first spirit-walk. "Now that you know your ability, Jack, it's time to learn how to exercise it." His teacher lifted the cover from a well-worn box.

The book David drew from the box back then was not the same one Jack kept under his bed, but the content was identical. The codex Jack now carefully removed from the plastic storage container was the one he found during his second summer solstice descent to the shadowlands. The finite number of ancient tomes meant not every shifter owned his own copy.

Jack decided there must be a reason this codex presented itself to him. It may not be relevant in this instance, but it couldn't hurt to take a look.

The delicate parchment crinkled under his fingers. A faint musty smell of basements and damp earth wafted upward with each turn of a page. The handwritten text contained the beliefs and observations of generations of shifters for use and reference in the future. Not everything in the book was fact—some entries were later contradicted by others. But many observations were repeated over and over.

Jack wasn't quite sure what he was looking for. He tried his best to ignore his scratched shoulders and pushed his scattered thoughts from the forefront of his consciousness as if preparing for a spirit-walk. Then he dropped his gaze to the book and scanned the handwritten entries.

About twelve pages in, something caught Jack's attention—the word 'non-believer.' He went back to the beginning of the passage:

I wandered the shadowland until I heard a voice call to me. To my surprise, my great aunt came to me from the mist. I knew she was a non-believer and didn't expect to meet her here. I asked her, "Auntie, I'm happy to see you, but tell me, how did you end up here?"

"I never promised myself to another realm, so when I passed into this otherworld, my grandfather came to show me the way."

After that we spoke of the sickness in our village.

Jack skimmed to the bottom of the entry.

No other reference to non-believers.

Jack slid the codex from his lap and stretched out his legs. The wall behind him supported his head as he stared, unseeing, at the opposing wall. This guy's great aunt never promised herself to another realm. Jack assumed that meant she had no religion; ergo, the woman theoretically could have been one of Zalnic's living victims. She ended up in the shadowland because it was the realm where her deceased grandfather resided. So Zalnic had nothing to gain by taking her soul if she would have ended up in his realm anyway.

Suddenly Jack sat up straight, wincing as his back and shoulders protested. Duh! If non-believers are destined for the realm of their ancestors, and the ancestors aren't part of Zalnic's domain, then he would have something to gain!

Was that the underlord's game? Stealing souls? From other gods?

Off of his bed and pacing the small room, Jack was on a roll. If Zalnic was stealing souls from other gods, wouldn't the other gods balk? Yes. Unless... they didn't know. "Because the victims didn't die," he said out loud.

Jack walked to his dresser and rummaged through the debris he removed from his pockets. "Ah," he exclaimed and picked up his phone. He hoped the number on Eric's card was his personal number. He had to know if Eric had ever been baptized and what his ancestral background might be.

After a quick conversation, Jack bounded down the stairs, oblivious to his aching shoulders. "Dad, can I take the truck and go up to the Java Hut?"

His dad looked at the clock. "Again? Aren't they only open for another hour?"

"No. It's open at least until ten. I want to get on the internet."

"You have school tomorrow."

"I know, but I can't really lie down. I'm probably not going to get much sleep anyway."

"Okay, home no later than ten though. I want you in before I go to bed."

Jack retrieved his laptop and scooted out.

Eric said Zalnic referred to him as 'son of pool.' Jack needed to know exactly who Pool was.

As the rich aroma of freshly brewed coffee engulfed him, Jack mused that someone would seriously have to dislike coffee to come in here and not order something. He set his laptop on a table and let it boot up while he ordered a latte. He scanned the café for familiar faces. Other kids from school often came in to use the Wi-Fi or just hang out with friends. The scene tonight, though, was fairly dead.

A lone girl sat with her laptop at a table near the windows and three guys carried on some kind of testosterone-fueled conversation in the back corner. The barista frowned in their direction after sliding Jack's drink across the counter. Jack glanced at the three again as he headed for his table, pretty sure he'd seen them at school. Suddenly it clicked—one was Natalie's ex-boyfriend. His name was... Brent? No. Brett.

As if Jack had spoken the name out loud, the tow-headed jock looked up at him. Jack gave the other boy a quick nod of acknowledgement, then sat down at his computer with his back to the table of guys. Soon, he was engrossed in Google searches.

Since Zalnic was an ancient god, it made sense to Jack that a correlation must be made to other ancient beliefs. Eric said he was mostly Polish on his mom's side and his dad's parents were from Wales. His search for 'Polish mythology pool' and 'Slavic mythology pool' found myths associated with a pool of water. He tried spelling pool—poul, poule, puul, pule, pul. Nothing. He had the same luck when he replaced Polish and Slavic with Welsh. Then he tried Celtic.

Jack leaned back in his chair with a groan. He'd walked in the door optimistic about being on a roll, now he was dead in the water. Maybe he was wrong. Maybe 'son of pool' meant something completely different. Or Eric heard it wrong.

Finally, he abandoned the search engines and scanned lists of Norse and Welsh deities. At the Welsh god Pwyll, Jack paused. No. Pwyll couldn't be 'pool.' The name likely rhymed with dill. Of course, he had no idea how to pronounce Welsh and none seemed to be offered on the websites.

The clock had rounded past nine-thirty. He had to leave soon.

He typed Pwyll into dictionary.com. The answer appeared on his screen: Pwyll [pool] **noun** *Welsh Legend.* a prince who stole his wife, Rhiannon, from her suitor, Gwawl, and was the father of Pryderi.

Jack caught himself before he whooped out loud. This was it! Zalnic referred to Eric as the son of the

Welsh prince Pwyll. His soul was destined for Annwn—the Welsh underworld.

Zalnic was stealing souls from other gods.

He called Natalie as he began shutting his computer down. "You were right," he said as soon as she answered.

"About...?"

"The religion." Jack shrugged into his jacket as he explained what he'd found while at the coffee shop and how he thought they might use the information. He tossed his cup, put his notebook on top of the laptop and slid them both under his arm. Backing out of the door, he never saw the fist coming at him.

Jack's jaw exploded with pain. His laptop slid to the ground and he heard his phone scuttle across the pavement. He crumpled against the side of the building. His arms were yanked roughly to either side, pinning him to the wall. Another blow rammed into his nose and Jack heard a snap. A wave of nausea settled in his stomach.

A face swam in and out of his blurred vision. The door to the coffee shop flew open and he heard a shout.

He was released immediately and slumped to the ground. The voice asking if he was okay seemed far away and then faded out as he slipped into unconsciousness.

Jack came to in the same spot where he'd fallen, with no idea how long he'd been out, though apparently long enough for the barista to retrieve a towel full of ice and apply it to his face. He struggled to regain his faculties. The counter guy held his laptop, notebook and phone and was saying something to the barista. Jack caught the last word: assholes.

A car skidded to a stop in the street. "Jack!"

Natalie.

Natalie? How could she—

He'd been on the phone with her.

She bolted toward him and knelt down. Her words ran together in a stream. "Oh my God what happened are you okay?"

Jack reached for the towel of ice. He shifted it away from his mouth. "I'b all right." Damn, his face hurt when he talked. "Abbushed." He flicked his gaze from barista to counter guy. "Who?"

The barista nodded. "The three assholes who were in the shop earlier."

Jack knew exactly who she referred to. He wasn't sure if he would've told Natalie or not, although it didn't matter because the counter guy blurted it out: "Jamie Caswell, Brett Hanley, and Harold Kosmarczky."

Natalie glanced at the guy and then down at Jack, her eyes wide. "Why would they do that? Do you even know them?"

Jack shrugged, winced at the pain in his shoulders, and shook his head.

The wail of a siren cut the discussion short. A police cruiser pulled up behind Natalie's car. The cop killed his flashing lights before getting out of the car and Jack sighed in relief.

After getting everyone's statement, the officer offered to take Jack to the hospital.

He declined. "The ice is helpig. I'll be fide."

Natalie frowned at him. "I don't know…"

"I'b fide." He stood a little unsteadily. "Cad I use the restroob?"

The barista opened the door for him.

Jack splashed his face with cold water repeatedly.

Aside from the weird angle his nose was at, it actually didn't look so bad once he'd washed the blood off. But it hurt like hell and he knew it would look worse tomorrow. There was a good amount of ice still in the towel so Jack transferred it into a bundle of paper towel.

Natalie rose anxiously when he emerged from the bathroom.

Jack fumbled in his pocket for the truck keys.

"No. You can't drive, Jack."

"Sure I cad."

"You need to keep the ice on your face or it'll swell even more than it already has. And you can't drive one-handed with obstructed vision."

Before he could argue, she snatched his keys from his hand. "Either you let me drive you home or you go to emergency."

Jack imagined an astronomical hospital bill, then reluctantly agreed to let Natalie drive him home. Without removing the bundle of ice from his face, he lowered himself into the passenger seat and carefully moved his head backward until it made contact with the headrest. The persistent throbbing of his face jumbled his thoughts, making it hard to concentrate.

He'd expected a stream of questions from Natalie, but she was quiet. What she finally did say took Jack by surprise.

"I'm sorry, Jack."

"About what?" he mumbled and rolled his head toward her.

"Brett." She glanced at him. "If you didn't even know those guys, then this is because of me."

It did seem to be the obvious explanation, but Jack had a hard time buying it. The only person at school who knew Jack and Natalie were spending time together was Wes. Aside from that first day at Shiner's Dairy, they'd never actually spent any time together in public.

Unless Brett was the kind of guy that stalked his ex-girlfriend.

When Jack failed to comment, Natalie didn't say any more until they were on Red Apple Road. "Tell me where to turn."

At the sound of her voice, Jack turned slightly to study her face: lips pressed tight together, shiny eyes. "Just past the Silos od the left," he instructed. "Thed go all the way until it edds." As she turned onto Bittersweet Lane, Jack's brain tried to reject the reality that Natalie was driving up to his house. He'd worked to avoid this, and now it was happening in a devastatingly humiliating scenario.

"Dadalie, it's dot your fault." Jack winced silently as they bumped over the dirt road. He put his hand on her arm. "Please, dod't feel bad. I just can't talk dow. Toborrow, okay?"

She nodded without looking at him and her throat worked as if she'd swallowed what she wanted to say.

Natalie pulled up close to the house, turned off the car, and then jumped out to open the passenger door. Jack shrugged off her attempt to help him out. "Could you grab by stuff?"

With his computer and other things in one arm, Natalie held the front door open for him. He watched looks of surprise register on his mom's and dad's faces as they took in his appearance. With a small gasp, his mom uttered, "Jack?"

He held up his hand. "I'b okay." He gestured toward Natalie. "Dadalie."

His mom was next to him instantly, examining his face. "Your nose is broken."

Jack nodded.

Natalie provided a short explanation—that Jack was ambushed by three guys outside the coffee shop. She left it there, didn't mention any names or possible motives, allowing Jack to say as much or as little as he wanted. Jack shot her a look of gratitude.

"Well, I should get home. Mr. Ironwood, would you like a ride to your truck?" Natalie offered.

He exchanged a look with his wife. "Maybe I should go get it." To Natalie he said, "Let me get some shoes."

"Thank you so much for driving Jack home," his mom said to Natalie. "Jack, follow me to the kitchen so I can take care of that." As his mom headed to the kitchen, Jack turned to Natalie. "Thanks."

She met his gaze for a moment. "It's the least I could do." Her voice was nearly a whisper. "I'm…"

"It's dot your fault." Jack cut her off.

Then his dad was back, preventing further conversation.

Before Natalie followed his dad out the door, she gave him a last troubled look.

He wondered if she regretted ever speaking to him in the first place.

When he woke the next morning, Jack felt like he'd been hit by a train. His body ached, his face throbbed and his head pounded. He peered at his clock through swollen eye sockets.

114

His alarm was off.

Jack was okay with that.

Last night, after Natalie left, he had met his mom in the kitchen, as instructed. She'd motioned for him to sit at the table, placed a shot glass in front of him and filled it with whiskey.

"You're going to need it," she'd answered his questioning look.

The liquor burned like heck on the way down and he chased it with the water his mom pushed toward him. Then she'd poured another shot. She had her healing kit on the table in front of her. Jack suddenly realized what the whiskey was for: his mom was going to set his nose. He'd quickly downed the next shot.

"Now these. They won't prevent your black eyes, but the caffeine will reduce their size." She'd shaken a couple of migraine formula acetaminophen tablets from a bottle and Jack swallowed them obediently.

His mom spread a small towel on the counter top and then opened the freezer and withdrew a handful of ice. She centered the ice on the towel and folded the edges in. The bundle was then wetted slightly and slid into a zip top bag. She handed the ice pack to Jack.

His mother had always possessed a natural talent for healing. Her grandfather had once been a great sect shaman. As the shaman title was now more honorary than functional, Jack's mom decided to put her talent to good use and went to nursing school.

Jack vaguely remembered the relaxed feeling as the numbing effects of the alcohol seeped into his bloodstream.

"What do you think? One more?" His mom held up the bottle of whiskey.

Jack raised the cold bundle to his nose and applied it gingerly. His eyes widened and he moaned as he nodded.

After giving the last shot a few minutes to take effect, his mom stood behind him. "Just lean your head back against me."

She took a couple of loose ice cubes from a bowl on the table and pressed them to either side of Jack's nose. The cold turned into a sting, and then the area became numb. Considering he knew what was about to happen, Jack felt pretty mellow.

The only sensation when his mom felt the break had been the pressure of her fingers. Then a sharp jolt of pain had made him sit up straight.

"Done." His mom moved his hand holding the ice pack up to his nose.

After that, the pain had faded pretty quickly. When Jack pushed the chair back and stood up, a wave of dizziness rushed to his head. His mom grabbed his arm. "It's the whiskey. Maybe you should sit back down." She eased him back into the chair.

His recollection of the remainder of the evening was a blur. Though he remembered his dad helping him upstairs, how he got into bed was a mystery. His jeans were off and his bloody shirt was nowhere to be seen. Thank goodness he'd had on a button-up.

Jack heard activity downstairs and remembered it was Monday—his mom's day off. Somehow the homey smell of toast and cinnamon permeated his swollen nose, making his stomach growl. He'd wriggled into his sweat pants and was contemplating a shirt when he heard the stairs creak. His mom came through the doorway with a tray.

"Back in bed."

Though Jack's smile was limited by his fat lip, the warmth he felt inside was undiminished. His mom used to do this for him when he was small and had to stay home sick from school. For the last couple of years he'd never been so ill he couldn't stay home by himself. He usually just slept the day away. After setting the tray on the bottom of his bed, his mom helped him into a shirt. Then she stacked his two pillows and retrieved Jase's pillow to add to the pile. When he was settled, she transferred the tray to his lap.

Jack's stomach rumbled again. Cinnamon toast and eggs. She'd even made him bacon. "After you eat," she instructed, "take the pills, then rest. That's what you're here for."

Jack's pounding head felt better as soon as he had food in his stomach. He obediently swallowed the pills, set the tray aside and reclined against the pillows. His mind, though, wasn't in a restful state. Images of the attack flashed in his head and he tried to make some sense of the debacle. Since Jack knew nothing of the guys who beat him up—even their names weren't familiar—one of them being Natalie's ex couldn't really be ignored. His relationship with Natalie must have something to do with it.

Which did not mean it was her fault. Not by a long shot.

Jack was also anxious to get on with the rescue plan since the information they'd uncovered yesterday was a major breakthrough. The thought reminded him that he may no longer have a computer or a phone. He pushed up from the pillows and groaned. He'd almost forgotten about his sore torso.

Wondering what his chances were of sneaking downstairs undetected and how much flak he'd get if he got caught, Jack advanced carefully across the room, willing the old wood floor not to creak. Then a glance at his dresser stopped him in his tracks. Stacked on the corner lay his computer, notebook and phone. He slid the pile into his arms and crept back to bed. The phone case looked pretty bad. In addition to plentiful scratches, cracks spidered from the corner that must have hit the sidewalk first and a piece had splintered away. The screen, however, was amazingly uncracked. He'd find out if the phone was functional soon, but he guessed it was fine. The investment in the hard cover had paid off.

He felt a stab of dismay when he moved the notebook and saw the scores in the top of his computer. His mind's eye pictured the machine skidding across the sidewalk. There were no obvious signs of impact though, so if the laptop had simply slid, he'd consider himself fortunate. When Windows started as expected, he breathed a sigh of relief.

He spent the day dozing or plucking on his acoustic guitar while he thought about the next step in rescuing Emma. As soon as school was over, he texted Natalie. When he didn't receive an immediate reply, he decided to take a shower. The hot water proved extremely soothing—his face still looked like hell—but he moved a lot easier. Stepping from the bathroom with a towel wrapped around his waist, Jack paused when he heard voices.

Since the house had been built before indoor plumbing, the bathroom had been added off the kitchen. The voices came from the living room. Jack listened from the bathroom doorway.

Soulshifter

Natalie was here?

Crap.

To get to the stairs, Jack had to cross the kitchen—which meant he'd walk past the doorway to the living room. He stepped back into the small room and pulled on his sweatpants. He made the trip to the stairway a quick dash, gritting his teeth as his body protested. After a slow climb up the stairs, he found a worn-in pair of jeans and gingerly pulled a soft, old t-shirt over his head. He combed his fingers through his hair. God, with two black eyes and a swollen lower lip he hated to talk to anyone.

Still, they had to get moving on the rescue plan or forget it. Time was running out.

His mom came to the bottom of the stairs as he started down. "The girl who brought you home is here."

"Natalie. I heard. Thanks, Mom."

"How do you feel?"

"Not so bad. The shower loosened me up and I think moving around has been a good thing."

"Glad to hear it." His mom touched his face lightly for a moment, her forehead scrunched in concern. Then she allowed a small smile and stepped aside. "I'm going to pick up Jase. We'll see you in a few minutes."

"Okay." Jack nodded.

Natalie sat on the couch. Her eyes stretched wide as she took in his appearance but she smiled to cover her initial reaction. "Uh… I texted you back but I guess you were in the shower?"

Did his mom tell her that? Or had Natalie seen him? And what did it matter, anyway? Jack took his phone from his pocket to hide the blush he felt creeping up his neck. "Yeah." He scanned the text and then

119

glanced up to catch Natalie's furrowed brow before she quickly turned away from his battered face. "It doesn't feel near as bad as it looks."

She gave a reluctant nod, then held up a laptop with a meaningful grin. "Check it out."

Jack raised his eyebrows. "Uh… new?" Her text had only said she was coming by with something to show him.

"No." She giggled. The sound was surreal—but in a good way—like the sun suddenly bursting from the clouds on an overcast day. "It's Emma's."

"O… kay."

Natalie grinned at his apparent confusion. "We need to know Emma's heritage, right? Well, I was trying to think of the best way to approach her parents." She patted the couch next to her and Jack sat down. "Then I realized I didn't have to ask them; Emma did a report on it last year. So I went by her house after school and asked if I could get some things out of her room." Natalie's smile faded. "It was rough… going in there. I stood in the hallway for a few minutes trying to pull it together before I could step through the doorway." She swallowed and closed her eyes for a moment. "I told myself I'd just grab her computer and get out. Then I remembered I had to find some stuff that was mine. Everything was untouched," she whispered, "like she'd be coming home any second." She gazed at Jack as tiny pools formed on her bottom lashes. "Before I left I vowed that we'd get her back."

"We will," Jack assured her.

The laptop finished booting and asked for a password. Natalie poised her fingers over the keyboard and pursed her lips.

"Do you know it?"

"Hopefully. I know a few of the passwords she uses. I'm not sure how often she changes them."

Natalie's first two guesses failed. She glanced at Jack. "What if I only have one more chance?"

He shrugged. "We gotta try."

"Mmm," Natalie mused. "What was going on over the summer..." Then she sat up straight and tapped out a few keystrokes. She met Jack's eyes. He nodded. She hit the enter key and—

They were locked out.

"Ugh," she groaned. "There goes my brilliant idea."

Before Jack could say anything, footsteps pounded on the porch, the front door banged open and Jase bounced in. "Jacky!" the six-year-old exclaimed, then stood still for a moment and wrinkled up his forehead. "You don't look good."

"Jeez, thanks, buddy." Jack laughed. Then he opened his arms and his little brother flung himself into them.

Jase gave Natalie a shy glance and then examined Jack's face up close. "What happened to you?"

Jack didn't want to lie, nor did he want to explain, so he employed distraction—which generally worked remarkably well with Jase. "Jase, this is Natalie. Natalie, Jase."

"Hi Jase." Natalie offered a friendly smile.

Then Jack's mom came through the door, a small backpack covered in graphics of smiling cars hanging from her hand. "Jase, please come and get your backpack. I shouldn't have to carry it in for you."

Jase extracted himself from his brother's arms and trudged over to his mom with a huge exaggerated sigh.

He took the backpack and half-carried, half-dragged it toward the kitchen. The way it swung from the straps evidenced that the pack wasn't very heavy.

Jack's mom shook her head, bemused. "Not sure what this is all about," she muttered to Jack and Natalie. Then she followed her younger son into the kitchen. "How about a snack?"

Jase's enthusiastic reply made Jack chuckle and he caught Natalie with her hand over her mouth stifling a giggle. "He's cute."

"He's all right," Jack admitted. "Most of the time."

Natalie's gaze dropped to Emma's laptop and her face fell. "I guess this is a bust."

"I'm pretty sure it'll reset in like a half hour. Do you have any other guesses?"

Natalie rolled her eyes. "We could be here a long time doing that. Maybe I should just talk to her parents."

Jack wondered what kind of strained conversation that would be.

"What about your friend? The one who can learn about things by touching them? Could he figure out the password by touching Emma's computer?" Natalie's eyes were round and hopeful, with a glint of excitement.

Jack pressed his lips together, thinking. "Mmm, it's a great idea, but I have a feeling he'd only learn things about Emma, not the computer." As he watched the light fade from Natalie's eyes, he hurried to add, "But I'm no expert in his ability. Let me ask him." He picked up his phone and began typing a text. "I'm just going to tell him our problem. He's got some pretty crazy computer skills too." Jack wasn't sure he wanted Wes around Natalie, but he couldn't stand the thought of her trying to get information from people who were distraught over their missing daughter.

Natalie scooted so her back rested on the couch and clasped her hands in her lap.

"Wes is a gamer," Jack explained. "When he's not playing his bass guitar, he's usually in front of the—" He was cut off by his text tone and looked down at his phone. "Awesome. He's coming over."

Jack's mom entered the room and set a large dish of apple slices in front of Jack and Natalie. "Here's caramel dip, if you'd like." She set a plastic container next to the apples.

"Everybody wants caramel dip, Mom," a small voice called from the kitchen.

Jack and Natalie both laughed. "Take it from the expert," Jack's mom said with a grin.

What Jack thought might be an awkward period of time actually passed quickly as he and Natalie chatted about mundane things like which apples were the best and whether caramel apples were better with or without nuts. Their bowl was nearly empty when they heard the hollow clump of feet on the wooden porch followed by a knock on the door.

Jack popped up from the couch. "That's probably Wes."

"Whoa," Wes exclaimed when Jack swung the door open. He took a close look at Jack's face. "Gnarly."

"Yeah, it's awesome," Jack grumbled as he let his friend in. Then with a stern warning look he murmured: "Be cool."

"As a cucumber." Wes grinned in return. Jack made introductions as Wes set a laptop down next to Emma's and began to unwind a cord.

"So we're going with technology," Jack observed.

Wes nodded. He opened the laptop he'd brought

and powered it up. "What I pick up from objects is usually emotion based." He plugged one end of the cord into Emma's computer and the other into his. "Think about any names, numbers or words she might use for a password."

Jack perched on the arm of the couch next to Wes and watched as a program opened. His friend leaned forward and tapped a few keys. "Okay, shoot," Wes said to Natalie. "Numbers first." Once he'd entered everything Natalie could think of, he sat back on the couch and looked from Jack to Natalie. "Now we wait. So dude, tell me you kicked the other guy's butt."

Jack shook his head. "Never had a chance. I was ambushed." He told an abbreviated version of the story, not wanting to dwell on the subject—especially in front of Natalie.

"So your ex saw you and Jack together and didn't like it?"

Natalie nodded. "I guess. He… he never seemed like that kind of guy, though."

When his mom entered the room, Jack was grateful for the interruption. "You didn't notice your father pull in, did you?" She stepped to the window to look for herself. "Elder Whitehead is on the phone."

Jack swallowed hard. Shera's father. Calling his dad. "No," he managed. "Haven't seen him."

Wes's eyes were big as saucers and he held up his hand for Jack to high-five. "Way to go, dude."

A flush worked its way up Jack's neck. He didn't return his friend's gesture. "He's a sect elder. He could be calling about anything." But Jack's thoughts were exactly the opposite. His dad's ability—telepathy—was seldom requested. Mental communication required the other party to also possess telepathic ability, and the capability was extremely rare. He also doubted Elder Whitehead was calling from Petoskey because he needed his car fixed. Scrambling to change the subject, Jack pointed to the computer screen. "How's the progress?"

"Do you think he's calling about your position?" Natalie asked.

"Nah, I haven't done anything yet," Jack replied as his heart beat double-time. He couldn't remember Elder Whitehead ever calling their house.

"Position?" Wes snickered. "Wouldn't that be up to you and Shera?"

Jack stood and flicked his friend on the back of his head. "Shut up."

"Ow!" Wes stopped laughing but still wore a mischievous grin. "C'mon man, how could I pass that up?"

Natalie swiveled her head from Wes to Jack and then back to Wes. "What're you guys talking about?"

"Jack's position," Wes stressed the word. "As son-in-law."

"Wait." Natalie leaned forward so she could meet Jack's eyes. "You're engaged?"

"No. No," he repeated again, more firmly. His cheeks burned. "It's just…" He struggled for a way around the subject, coming up blank. "He might want to arrange it."

"Arrange an engagement? People still do that?" Natalie blurted out. "I mean… uh… I know they still do… some places." Spots of pink appeared on her cheeks. "I just didn't think… around here."

An uncomfortable silence filled the small room.

Wes craned his neck and gazed up at Jack with

raised eyebrows. Jack stood with his arms crossed over his chest and glared at his friend. Wes furrowed his brow with a slight shrug as if to say 'what did I do?' and Jack shook his head.

Then Wes's laptop chimed. "Bingo. We're in," he announced.

Everyone was quick to focus on the computers.

"Okay, let's see if I can find Emma's family history project." Natalie scooted to the edge of the couch and began searching the documents folder.

Wes disconnected the USB cable and wound it around his hand. Then he powered off his machine. "What was all that?" he murmured as Jack followed him out the door. "I thought you were just 'working together.'" He put air quotes on the phrase.

"We are."

"So what's the big deal?"

"I don't know. It was embarrassing."

Wes looked at him doubtfully. "Whatever, dude." He turned to go, then stopped and looked over his shoulder. "Do you think you'll make it to practice tonight?"

"Uhh…" Jack moved his shoulders. They didn't feel too bad. "Yeah, I think so." Missing a practice would only give Tommy another reason to be displeased with Jack. And even though the singer tended to stress him out at times, jamming with the band was Jack's best pressure outlet, and he currently had plenty of pent-up tension he'd like to get rid of.

"Cool. See you later."

"Hey, thanks. I appreciate you coming over to help."

"Right." Wes shrugged. "You can pay me back

later." He grinned, then trotted down the porch steps.

Natalie looked up as Jack returned. "I found her family tree."

He sat down on the couch and studied the document on the computer screen. "Schmidt? Can you get any more German than that?"

"I don't think so," Natalie agreed, her eyes crinkling. "But I'm not sure about these." She pointed to the opposite side of the diagram. "We'll have to Google them. There's probably more than one website that lists the ethnicity of surnames."

"Yep. And then we'll need to look up the associated lore or mythology."

"Do you really think this could work, Jack?"

Her somber expression told Jack she didn't want to get her hopes up just to have them crushed, so he chose his reply carefully. "I think I have a better chance than anyone who's gone before me."

CHAPTER 7

Relationships

As the bus lumbered toward him, Jack instinctively took a step back to avoid the pursuing dust cloud. The door opened with a screech and he clambered aboard. His face looked a lot better this morning. Most of the swelling was gone and thanks to his mom, the black patches under his eyes were minimal and his nose was straight. Still, many curious stares followed him as he made his way to an open seat near the back.

He spent the next few minutes feigning interest in something on his phone until Wes got on the bus. Motioning with his head for his friend to sit behind him, Jack turned his back on the gawkers.

"So what's gonna happen when you see Hanley today?" Wes asked.

"Hopefully, I won't. But if I do see him, I'm going to ignore him."

"Dude, don't you want to get him back?"

"It won't solve anything. I'd just like to know how he happened to see me with Natalie. We don't even talk to each other at school." He hated to, but he had to ask. "You haven't been shooting your mouth off, have you?"

"Me? Why would I want to talk about you when I'm far more interesting?"

Jack snorted. "That's what I thought. So, what? Is he stalking her or something?"

"Beats me."

Jack asked Natalie the same question after second hour.

"Stalking me?" She switched out books in her locker.

"Think about it. How else could he possibly have known we've been spending time together unless he was watching you?"

Natalie scowled. "He better not be." She jammed a book on the top shelf.

Just then Jack was shoved, hard, into the locker next to his. Natalie looked up in surprise and then behind her for the perpetrator. He thought he heard her mumble 'cheese and rice' and then she marched down the hall after Brett who sauntered away, snickering.

"What's your problem?" She jabbed her ex's shoulder.

Brett turned around. "Don't touch me, tramp."

"Tramp? How dare you?"

"Oh please, your sheets hadn't even cooled off before you hooked up with your buddy over there. I bet you were cheating before we even broke up."

"WHAT?" Natalie rose up on her toes to get right into Brett's face. "You WISH you were ever in my sheets! Jack and I are working on a project together—not that it's any of your business. Get over yourself!"

Brett opened his mouth to say something, but Natalie cut him off. "And by the way, grow some balls and fight your own battles. Three against one—way to look like a coward!" She spun on her heel, snatched up her backpack, and slammed her locker door.

Brett attempted to laugh it off, but Jack swore he read confusion in the guy's eyes before he turned and drifted into the current of students.

Jack quickly finished at his locker and melted into the traffic, careful not to meet anyone's gaze. He felt like an idiot. Anyone who wondered what happened to his face had just been given enough clues to figure it out. And when they did, he was going to look like a wimp who needed a girl to stand up for him. But that was nothing compared to his bigger worry. Jack wished Natalie hadn't mentioned a project. The ruse was flimsy at best. It might have worked on Natalie's father, but if anyone at school noticed or bothered to check—he didn't have any classes with Natalie. The lie would likely make Brett angrier and Jack didn't need anything extra to worry about right now.

Lack of eye contact didn't diminish the prying eyes he felt boring into his bowed head or the barely whispered conversations that stopped when he passed by. He hated it. He preferred to fly under the radar, not be the blip that drew everyone's attention.

When Natalie didn't show up after third hour, Jack took the opportunity to get out all the books he needed for the remainder of his classes. He was ticked off and didn't want to be. Maybe if he avoided her for the rest of the day he'd calm down before he talked to her. Since he had a few classes with Wes, he dropped the extra books off at his friend's locker.

Unfortunately, Jack did run into Brett later in the day—or maybe Brett had sought him out. The latter was likely, because he challenged Jack to fight him one on one.

"There's nothing to fight about," Jack said firmly, meeting the eyes of his aggressor directly while continuing to his next class.

Brett stepped into Jack's path, forcing him to stop.

"You're a scavenger. Feeding on rebound chicks."

Jack rolled his eyes. Really? That was the best this idiot could come up with? He stepped around the other boy without saying anything.

"After school," Brett shouted behind him. "Just you and me. It's on."

In history class, Jack dumped his books on the desk next to Wes and slumped into the chair. "Brett just challenged me to a fight after school. One on one," he sighed heavily.

"Are you going to fight him?"

"I don't know. I don't want to. His reason for the fight is stupid, although he's managed to make messing up his face sound really inviting."

"Can you take him?"

"You mean without both of my arms pinned?" Jack said wryly. He shrugged. "Probably. My dad is a hand-to-hand master. He taught me how to fight when I was a little kid."

Wes eyed his friend dubiously. "He's pretty big, man."

"Big's got nothing to do with it. I'm fast and skilled. And I'm certainly not afraid of him."

"Do it, then. Get him off your back."

Jack shook his head. "I'm not going to go looking for a fight. If he approaches me, I'll try to talk to him first, but if he throws a punch, I will defend myself."

At the end of the day Natalie was with a friend and Jack didn't say anything to her. He gathered his books like any other day and headed for the bus. Wes waited for him at the exit doors and they stepped outside simultaneously. Ten feet from the bus door, just as Jack thought he might be able to climb aboard and just go home, he heard Wes mumble: "He's here."

Jack didn't look. He took another step toward the bus, not acknowledging when he heard Brett shout.

"Here he comes, man," Wes muttered.

"Hey, Jack-ass." The guy was a regular cut-up. Was this really the caliber of guy Natalie was willing to put up with?

Jack turned reluctantly. He didn't want to do this, but he didn't want to get sucker punched either.

"We had a date, remember?" The larger boy stood with his hands balled into fists, frowning at Jack.

"Look man, I don't even know what you want to fight over." Jack twisted his head toward Brett, the rest of his body still facing the bus—as if he had every expectation he'd continue in that direction.

"Natalie."

"Dude, you broke up with her."

Brett cocked his head slightly, again wearing that odd confused look.

Jack drew in a sharp breath. Brett's eyes. He could swear they just flashed red. Only for a second—so short that Jack had to ask himself if he'd actually seen what he thought he saw. He passed his books to Wes. "Watch his eyes," he said quietly.

"You're a scavenger that takes advantage of girls," Brett said.

It was as if the guy was on autopilot. "Really, what girls?" Jack played on the confusion, hoping he might snap out of it.

A crowd was beginning to form around them.

"Natalie."

"And?"

Again, puzzlement passed over Brett's face. Jack

had stepped outside the predetermined script. The other boy tipped his head to the side and this time there was no mistake. His eyes flashed red. Jack glanced at Wes. His friend frowned and nodded.

Brett reached out his hand and attempted a jab at Jack, but Jack quickly pulled his head back. He easily danced out of the way of Brett's next swing, too.

Jack knew it didn't matter what he said to Brett. The guy was programmed with a mission: to beat up Jack. The only thing he could do to stop the fight was to end it as soon as possible. He bent his knees slightly and put his hands up while his eyes followed Brett's movements. When Jack saw the opportunity he was waiting for, he clocked Brett in the side of the head. The guy sagged like a sack of rice and then toppled over.

Jack took his books from Wes. "Come on, we can still make the bus."

As Jack suspected, he didn't have to tell Natalie what happened. News like that traveled fast. He was still on the bus when his phone buzzed.

"*Heard about the fight. Guess I encouraged him, sorry.*"

"*It wasn't you,*" Jack replied.

"*Right.*"

"*Seriously. I'll explain. Are you heading home? I could meet you there.*"

"*Sure. Just got here.*"

The entrance to Meteor Lake subdivision was a regular stop on the route so Jack got off the bus there and walked to Natalie's house. She swung the door open with a frown, took stock of his face, and then quickly scanned the rest of him. Her eyebrows rose, smoothing the crease in her forehead.

"I didn't get hit," Jack responded to the unasked question as he stepped inside. His voice seemed to echo in the vaulted ceiling of the foyer. "I can hold my own in a fair fight." He shook his head with an ironic laugh. "You heard about the fight but no one bothered with the details?"

Natalie wrinkled her nose and shrugged. "Uh... no." She motioned Jack inside so she could close the door. "How does Brett look?"

Jack followed her into the kitchen, which opened to a family room, or great room, at the back of the house. His eyes widened as he took in the sweeping staircase and exposed second story walkway. The living room he'd been in on his first visit was modest in comparison to this vast space. "Probably just a bruised cheek or black eye. I only hit him once, just to knock him out. I don't know if he's usually a jerk, but going after me wasn't his idea."

She crossed her arms over her chest, eyes narrowed. "What do you mean?"

"His eyes reflected red."

Natalie gasped. "You mean he's possessed?" She rounded the granite-topped island in the center of a room at least three times the size of the Ironwoods' kitchen. Cherry wood cabinets accented with brushed aluminum handles flanked stainless steel appliances.

"Possessed, compelled, whatever you want to call it, he wasn't acting on his own."

"Great," Natalie commented sarcastically and opened the refrigerator. "Something to drink?"

Jack peeked over her shoulder. "Dr. Pepper. Thanks."

She handed Jack a can and then retrieved a vitamin water. "What'll happen to him?"

Jack slid onto a stool at the island and lifted the tab on his soda can. The snap and crunch of aluminum seemed magnified in the large room. He lifted his shoulders briefly. "I'm not sure." As the exposed carbonation hissed and popped, the distinct spiciness of the soda rose to assault his nose. He took a long drink, still considering Natalie's question. "He'll probably be fine as long as he stays away from me. He seemed kind of brainwashed; coached to believe I was taking advantage of you while you were on the rebound. When I stated some facts, he couldn't reconcile the information in his head—he was confused."

Natalie spoke softly, her eyes on the bottle in her hand. "He was never a jerk while we were dating... well, until Emma disappeared. Even then, he tried to be understanding for a while, but he just couldn't accept that I saw what I saw." Her gaze flicked up to Jack then returned to her fingers as she picked at the label on her vitamin water. "Now I feel kind of bad that I went off on him this morning."

Jack took another drink of his soda to avoid looking at her. "Yeah. It was kind of a scene."

After a moment of silence, Jack detected her breathed "oh," barely more than a whisper. "Is that why I didn't see you the rest of the day?" She phrased it as a question but her even tone indicated she already knew the answer.

Jack's gaze slid up to her face. "I've been trying to keep this on the down-low to protect *you*. Anyone in

136

the vicinity now knows we're up to something—and if they know we don't have any classes together, it's going to raise questions."

Natalie groaned. She rounded the counter and sat one stool away from Jack. "Dang it. I'm sorry, I didn't even think. Gosh darn my temper. I try to control it—believe it or not I'm much better than when I was younger."

Jack didn't reply.

"You're right, Jack. If my dad ever got wind that the 'project' we're working on is actually related to Emma's disappearance, he'd go ballistic." Natalie peeled the corner of the label away from the plastic bottle and then pushed it back up with her thumb. "So, what do we say if people ask? I guess we should get our story straight."

"I don't know." Jack swiped his hand through his hair. "Maybe it doesn't even matter. Planning this gets more dangerous every day."

"Do... do you want to call it off?"

"No. Just the opposite. I want to get to it. If I'm gonna get hurt or—or anything—it might as well be while I'm trying to rescue Emma. Not here while leaving a coffee shop or fighting some idiot at school."

Natalie dropped her hands into her lap. "Okay. When?"

"I'm thinking Thursday night." He'd had his sights set on Friday night, so he wouldn't miss a day of school—and more importantly, band practice on Thursday—but now that he had a plan, waiting simply provided more time for Zalnic to try and stop him.

Natalie stared at Jack's hand as he bent the tab on his soda can back and forth. "All right. I guess I'll tell my dad I'm spending the night at a friend's house."

The tab snapped off and Jack set it on the counter. "Why?"

She tilted her head to the side, frowning. "Because, I'll probably be gone all night?"

"No. You won't. You'll be here."

"I'm going with you, Jack." Natalie sat perfectly still.

He shook his head without looking at her. "We talked about this. You're not a shifter."

Natalie slid off her stool and threw her hands up. "So? Callie wasn't a shifter either! That's not an excuse. Obviously there's a way. We just have to ask the Mannings."

Jack frowned at her, flustered. "It doesn't matter. I'm the one who signed up for this. I never said you were going with me, just helping me prepare…"

"But didn't you say that girl had to talk her sister into leaving with her? You don't even know Emma."

She was right, but Jack didn't want to admit it.

Natalie stood with her hands on her hips. "I don't care if it's dangerous. Don't you get it? Emma was more than just a friend to me." Tears welled in her eyes, threatening to spill over her lashes. "First my mom, now Emma." She blinked quickly trying to dispel the tears as they leaked from the corners of her eyes. "I'm tired of being left behind. I—" She swiped at her wet temples, frustrated.

"Okay." Jack broke in. He couldn't sit here and watch her cry. He reached out and captured a hand, wet with tears. "Okay," he repeated softly. "You're right. I need you." What was he saying? How would he keep her safe?

Natalie stepped forward and put her head on his

138

shoulder. After a few shuddering breaths she whispered, "Thank you."

Feeling awkward, Jack used his free hand to pat her shoulder. His inclination was to put both arms around her and hold her so he could absorb some of her pain, but he couldn't. They were barely more than acquaintances; the gesture would be inappropriate and possibly misunderstood. He dropped the arm back to his side. She extracted her hand from his and crossed the room to a box of tissue. She passed one to Jack with a little laugh when she caught him rubbing his wet hand on his jeans. "Sorry."

He shrugged. "Just salty water."

"No, I'm sorry about getting over-emotional."

"You've been through a lot."

Natalie held his gaze for a moment and the wide, blue depths of her eyes communicated gratitude Jack knew she couldn't speak out loud. She blinked, blotted her eyes again and took a deep breath. "Okay, where were we?" She returned to her stool. "Oh yeah, I wanted to tell you. I did some research last night. The other names from Emma's family tree? Finnish, mostly."

"So Finnish or German, but we have no way to figure out which one to use."

"Well, I went a little further and learned this: Finland, of course, part of the Nordic countries, so Norse mythology. Then I looked up German mythology and guess what? Norse mythology is a subset of Germanic mythology, so we don't have to choose."

Jack must have worn a confused expression because Natalie slid off her stool. "Hang on a sec." She darted from the room and he heard her feet pound up the stairs. She was back in seconds with a handful of papers she set on the island in front of Jack.

"Nice. I can't believe we actually caught a break," he said.

"I also put a couple of books on hold at the library. Wanna go with me to pick them up?"

Jack grimaced. "I guess, but it sounds like I'll be up late."

"Don't worry." Natalie consoled him with a smile. "You're only interested in the head honcho and god of the underworld." She gathered up the pages and nodded toward the door.

On the way to the public library, Jack couldn't help wondering if they'd run into any classmates there. "So we got kinda sidetracked, but I agree that we should be prepared for people's questions."

Natalie glanced over at him. "Okay. Got any ideas?"

He did. He just didn't know if Natalie would go for it. "Well," Jack cleared his throat, "wouldn't it make sense to just go along with what most people will be thinking?"

They stopped at a light and Natalie turned toward him. "That we're going out?"

He squirmed a little in his seat and looked out the window. "Yeah."

The light turned green and Natalie accelerated. "It's the obvious answer, but I'm surprised you suggested it. How's that going to go over with your future fiancée?"

"Uh…" That was not the comment Jack was ready to respond to. "I don't have a fiancée. And it's not really relevant. She lives in Petoskey."

"Does she even know her father is doing this?"

"I don't know." Jack felt the heat in his cheeks and covertly drew in a calming breath.

"You know, if my dad tried that—and I wouldn't put it past him—I'd be pissed." She stole a quick glance at Jack. "I'm sure it's different if you grow up expecting it though."

"Yeah." His answer was clipped.

"I know it's not my business and you can tell me to just shut up, but is this what you want? Do you even know this girl?"

Jack blew out his breath. "Of course. We were classmates from kindergarten through seventh grade. Until I moved here. I... I feel like I've always liked her."

"And you think she'd be okay with this?" She flicked her finger back and forth between them.

"She'd understand," Jack responded, grateful that Natalie hadn't forgotten where the conversation started.

Her face was unreadable as she pulled into the library lot and parked. Sliding the gear shift forward, Natalie turned to Jack. "How about you? Would it be terrible to have to pretend to be my boyfriend? Because I do think it would stop the questions."

Jack couldn't help it. He laughed. "Seriously? What would be terrible? You can only improve my reputation at school—seeing as how, well, I don't have one. I was more worried about you. You're the one everyone knows."

"Well, I think that's a bit of an overstatement. You may not know a ton of kids because you haven't lived in Ketchton most of your life, but you haven't gone unnoticed by the female population. Emma's not the only girl who'd like to get to know you better."

"Come on. You're just saying that. It's not necessary." Jack reached for his door handle.

"I absolutely am not." Natalie grinned and opened her door. "And I have no problem with the plan."

He hoped Natalie didn't think her claims would bolster his confidence, because she'd only managed to put butterflies in his stomach. He'd never aspired to be noticed. "I wish you hadn't told me that about girls at school. Now I'm going to feel self conscious all the time," he said as they met in front of the car.

"Except you don't need to worry about it."

"Easy for you to say."

"No. Easy for me to do." She slipped her hand into his. "You don't have to worry about the other girls in school when you have a girlfriend."

She was right. It seemed he had a girlfriend.

For now.

CHAPTER 8

Betrothal

Jack's brain worked to comprehend how the hero Pryderi could have such a techno-sounding theme song. Eventually the wrongness brought him to consciousness. He'd been dreaming as his phone rang. Grabbing it from the night stand, Jack answered without bothering to see who it was, so as not to wake up Jase. "Lo." He flopped onto his pillow with the phone on his ear.

He heard only a tentative whisper. "Jack?" He pulled the phone from his ear to read the display. "Natalie?"

"Oh God, Jack, I'm so scared."

Jack sat up, fully awake. "What? Why?"

"Red eyes." She sucked in a jerky breath.

"Where?" Jack's heart thumped in his chest. Blindly, he searched for his jeans with his free hand.

"At my window. What do I do?"

"Turn on every light in your room. Right now." Jack found his jeans, but didn't put them on. What was he going to do? Rush over there? He'd only expose himself to the hellcats or whatever else might be out there.

"Okay. They're on."

"Downstairs, too. And especially the outside lights."

"Is it one of those evil cats—hellcats?"

"Could be. I assume all your windows have screens? If that's what's out there, they can't enter unless there's an opening. And they're made of darkness; they can't exist in the light."

Natalie laughed, but her voice shook. "My dad is going to kill me for having all these lights on."

"Tell him you had a nightmare."

"This is a nightmare."

Jack chuckled softly. "True." His smiled faded though, as he realized what the visit meant: Zalnic knew about Natalie.

"Okay, all the lights are on."

"Good."

"I guess I'll let you go." She sounded reluctant and still terrified.

"Wait." Jack pulled on a shirt and crept from his room. The days were still warm enough that his dad hadn't kicked the furnace on yet, so the house was chilly. Snagging the afghan on the back of the couch, Jack settled into the cushions and pulled the cover up to his chin. "Let's just talk for a while."

"Okay." He heard the relief in her exhalation.

"Hey, look, this is getting more and more dangerous. It's not too late to decide to stay here."

"No way."

"Natalie. If we split up, I can't protect you."

"That's why we have Dan and Callie to coach us on what to do."

Jack wasn't going to argue with her too much. Not after their little tiff earlier today. Instead he tried to think of something else to take her mind off the hellcat or whatever was out there. "So… do you have a favorite movie?"

The question proved to be a great conversation starter—as well as a distraction. After a while though, Jack heard the sleepiness in Natalie's voice. Before he could suggest they say good-bye, she simply stopped responding. "Natalie?" he half-whispered. With the house quiet around him, Jack detected her even breathing. He snuggled deeper into the couch and propped his phone between his ear and the pillow. He'd been up late reading a mythology book, so in no time he was asleep also.

"So do you get to kiss her?" They were on the bus, and Wes was on the edge of his seat—literally—as he leaned up against Jack's seat-back.

"I don't know." He should have seen this coming. Jack knew his friend well enough that he should have predicted the reaction when he told Wes he and Natalie agreed to pretend to be in a relationship. "We didn't go into details. We're just trying to cut down on speculation about the time we spend together."

"Making-out would definitely be more convincing. And if you wanted to, she couldn't say no or be mad, right?"

"Okay, Wes, do I need to explain it again?" The loss of sleep last night eroded his patience. "It's not about me getting away with stuff—it's about doing what we need to do without added hassle. You're trying to introduce hassle!"

"Okay, okay, dude." Wes raised his hands and snickered. "Just looking out for your best interest."

Still, the damage was done. Wes's suggestion had

145

taken root, and when Jack saw Natalie at her locker, he suddenly felt awkward. How would he act if he actually were her boyfriend? Would he kiss her? Hug her?

She looked fantastic in jeans with tall boots and some kind of blouse-like top. Had she dressed up for him? When she saw Jack heading her way, she gave him a warm smile that made his pulse surge a little. Just pretend, he thought, and returned her smile.

"Thank God for unlimited minutes, huh?" she said.

"Yeah, no kidding." Jack hung up his jacket and pulled out the books he needed.

Natalie leaned on her closed locker, books resting on her arm.

"Should I walk you to class?"

"It's what any good boyfriend would do," she whispered, smiling.

He chuckled to hide his embarrassment while mentally chastising himself. He had to stop over-thinking the scenario—stupid Wes! As they walked down the hall together, Jack found her hand.

No big deal.

"Hey, last night my mom told me there'd be a sect ceremony tonight. Do you think you can come?" Jack asked.

"Ceremony?"

"To send me—us—off, you know, like blessings and probably trinkets for good luck."

"Well, we could certainly use both of those. I think it'll be okay. Just let me know when and where." She slowed. "This is my class."

In what Jack thought was a very boyfriend-like gesture, he bent down to whisper into her ear. "Write

146

down your schedule for me, okay?" The message was benign, but if anyone was paying attention, it would appear intimate.

When he drew back, Natalie's face was flushed. She rose on her toes, kissed him quickly on the cheek, then ducked into the classroom.

Jack took a deep breath as he hurried to his class, refusing to think about the warmth that still lingered on the side of his face.

The rest of the day went pretty much the same. Natalie wrote down her schedule and Jack met her or walked her to class whenever it was practical. Students noticed. Two of Jack's classmates commented—one was a high-five. There was a tense moment when they passed Brett in the hall, but he blatantly ignored them. A red and purple bruise stained his left cheekbone.

"Want me to drive you home?" Natalie asked at the end of the day.

Jack hadn't thought about that. "Nah, it's out of your way, and I'll see you later anyway."

There was an awkward moment where he wasn't sure if she expected him to kiss her good-bye, but he decided not to. As he walked to the bus it occurred to him that he would have liked to kiss her, just not under those circumstances. Although chances were slim that it would ever happen, for some reason it was important to Jack that if he did ever kiss Natalie, he wanted her to know he wasn't pretending—that he truly wanted to kiss her.

Wes lifted his hand to high-five Jack as he shuffled down the bus aisle. Jack rolled his eyes at his friend, ignoring the gesture. "There's definitely a buzz going on about you two, dude."

"I'm not surprised."

Wes leaned close and spoke in a low voice. "Even if it's fake, this is gonna be good for you."

Jack sighed and changed the subject. "Hey, will you talk to Tommy tomorrow since I won't be at band practice?"

Wes didn't quite wince, but the skin around his eyes tightened. "What do you want me to tell him?"

As the bus lurched into motion, pulling away from the school, Jack furrowed his brow. "Mmm. He probably heard about the fight with Brett, I think the whole school did. Tell him my parents grounded me."

"He's not gonna be happy."

"I know, but I can't afford to delay the plan any longer."

Wes shrugged. "Sure. You got it."

"Cool, thanks." Jack lowered his voice. "Did you hear about the sect ceremony tonight?" When Wes crinkled up his forehead, Jack explained.

"I bet Elder Whitehead will be there." Wes punched Jack's shoulder. "Maybe Shera too. Hey, did your dad ever talk to him?"

"I don't know. Believe it or not, I've had other things on my mind lately," Jack responded dryly. The question though, continued to pick at his brain after he got home from school. He gave his mom enough time to hang up her jacket and wash her hands before he sauntered into the kitchen. With his head in the re-frigerator, Jack asked, "Hey, did dad ever find out why Elder Whitehead called?"

"Apparently he asked a lot of questions about your venture."

"Hmm." Jack didn't trust his voice to not convey his disappointment.

"You realize you're cooling off the kitchen and we haven't turned the furnace on yet," his mom teased.

With an embarrassed laugh, Jack selected an apple from the fruit drawer and closed the refrigerator.

"Oh yeah, he also asked if we'd made any marriage contracts for you yet."

He jerked his head up to find his mom's smiling eyes over a slight smirk.

"Really." He walked to the sink, trying to play it cool. His heartbeat picked up pace as he ran cold water over the apple and reached for a towel. When he turned, his mom stood at the counter, chopping an onion. Jack contemplated the apple. How could he pass up the obvious opening to ask a few questions? He leaned back against the sink. "Mom?"

"Yes?"

"You and Dad had an arranged marriage, right?"

"Yep."

"Did you resent your parents for doing that?"

"Well, to start with, that's mostly how it was done then, so I didn't think too much about it." His mom paused a moment, knife poised over the cutting board. "Actually, I had two arranged betrothals." She resumed chopping as she spoke. "Because my grandfather was a shaman, our family had some status and an agreement was made for me when I was maybe three. The other family was immensely pleased as my healing abilities emerged—until the position of functional shaman was phased out. I guess they felt their son deserved better than a registered nurse.

"After that, my family agreed to betroth me with your father. Even back then the usefulness of telepathy had diminished, making him lower in status than me,

149

but my parents jumped at the chance. That was what I minded the most."

Jack must have worn a surprised expression because his mom's face crinkled in amusement. "No, not your father—I thought he was quite a catch—what bothered me was the way my parents seemed so relieved after the contract was made, like they were lucky to get rid of me. I actually felt sorry for your dad getting someone else's leftovers."

Eyes shining, she stared into the past. "Fortunately, your dad didn't see it that way."

Jack realized he had a white-knuckled grip on the apple. He chalked up her watery eyes to the onion—the sharp aroma filled the small room—but he could swear she was blushing.

Awkward.

"Turns out I was lucky," his mom reminisced. "I never had to grow to love your dad. I fell in love almost immediately."

That was about all Jack could take. "Uh... cool. I should probably get to my homework now." He moved toward the door.

She reached out and touched his arm as he passed. "Jack."

He stopped, eyes darting to the side to meet her gaze.

"Do you want your dad to make an agreement with Elder Whitehead?"

Jack sighed and examined the door frame as if the answer might be written there. "I... I've always had a thing for Shera, but I thought she was untouchable—out of my league." He knew his mother was offering to influence his father on Jack's behalf. "Then that girl,

150

Emma, disappeared and I saw a golden opportunity to prove myself, to elevate my standing so…" He flicked his eyes to hers and shook his head. "But what if she… How do I know…"

Understanding dawned in his mom's eyes and she squeezed his arm. "Your concern for Shera's feelings says a lot about your integrity, Jack. I hope she deserves you," she said softly and then kissed his cheek before returning to the cutting board.

Jack's heart thudded unevenly as he realized he stood on the threshold of seeing his wishes come true. The surge of adrenaline should have been fueled by excitement, elation.

So why did he feel so frightened?

Jack shrugged into a dress shirt and was three buttons from the top when he heard Natalie's car pull up. She'd texted him earlier to let him know she would attend the ceremony and to ask for directions. Instead, Jack offered to ride with her so she didn't have to walk into the ceremonial lodge alone. She agreed gratefully.

He grinned at a yell from Jase followed by pounding footsteps on the stairs. "That girl's here, Jacky!" The six-year-old appeared in the doorway, face flushed and eyes wide. Jack laughed. "Well, go back down and let her in." Jase spun and thumped back down the steps.

Jack studied his appearance in the mirror. Spying a glass of water on Jase's nightstand, he wet his fingers and ran them through his shaggy hair. Unfortunately that's all he could do. Though his lip was nearly healed, his black eyes had faded from purple to puke green. Pretty gruesome.

151

A steady babble from Jase floated up the stairs—he was no doubt telling Natalie all about his cars. Cars were Jase's passion. Jack shrugged at his reflection and decided he should go rescue her. The seriousness on her face as she examined the car in Jase's chubby hand bloomed into a grin when she glanced up and saw Jack.

"Hi." She wore some kind of long, filmy shirt over leggings with boots. The lamp behind her created a striking silhouette of her shape beneath the translucent blouse. Jack suspected she had on more make-up than she usually wore for school—a healthy glow warmed her pale skin. Topped with the smile, the effect was stunning.

"Wow," Jack said. "You look awesome."

A blush deepened the color on her cheeks. "Thanks, you look pretty good yourself."

"Yeah, this shirt really brings out the green around my eyes, doesn't it?"

She laughed, but before she could comment, Jase inserted himself between them and held a car up to Natalie. "I got this one from Santa last year."

She took the car and turned it, properly admiring the vehicle from all angles. "I like this one," she said reverently. "Very cool." Meeting Jack's eyes, she stretched her eyes wide while her lips formed a silent 'O', conveying how adorable she found his little brother.

Jack raised an amused eyebrow. "Hey bud, aren't you supposed to change? There are clothes on your bed."

"But I want her to see my cars."

"You can show her more another time. Besides, we've gotta get going. I'll see you there, okay?"

Suddenly reminded of the ceremony, Jase bolted for the stairs.

The corners of Natalie's mouth curved up as she watched him scramble up the steps, then concern transformed her expression as her focus switched to Jack. He turned away. Already self-conscious about his puke-green eyes, he didn't need her feeling sorry for him. He walked to the kitchen to retrieve his jacket.

"Jack, do your eyes hurt to touch?"

"Nah, it's all pretty much for show now. Don't worry about it."

"Here," she let her purse slide from her shoulder to an end table and began rummaging through the contents, "let's try this."

Jack wasn't sure what she was suggesting until she opened the container in her hand. One half of the compact held flesh-colored powder and the other, a small brush. "Make-up? No. Seriously. I'm fine."

"It's cover-up."

As if that made him feel better about it.

"Let me try it, Jack. You can easily wipe it off. It's just powder." She didn't wait for an answer. Stepping close, Natalie dipped the brush and swiped it under his eyes. "It's pretty light for your face color, but it might be okay for under your eyes."

The top of her head came to Jack's nose level. As she lightly swept her fingers across the edge of his eye sockets to blend the powder, he breathed in the fruity smell of her hair. The tingle under his skin from her warm fingertips made him swallow any further objection to the make-up. Natalie took a step back and nodded. "Not bad. Check it out."

Jack inspected the results in the bathroom mirror. He was impressed. The greenish-purple circles under his eyes now nearly blended with his skin and, unless

153

someone was very close, he didn't look like he had on make-up. Traces of warmth remained on his cheeks where Natalie had touched his face, but he blamed the fluttery feeling in his chest on the upcoming ceremony and rescue. He took a few deep breaths to steady his pulse. "Get it together, Jack," he muttered under his breath. "Haven't even left yet."

Back in the living room, he bobbed his head in answer to Natalie's raised eyebrows. "Cool. Thanks."

Natalie's stream of questions during the short ride to the lodge revealed that Jack wasn't the only one anxious about the evening. He realized he hadn't yet asked Dan how he was able to bring Callie with him to the underworld. Jack had agreed to take Natalie with him assuming whatever the Mannings did could be replicated. But even at sixteen, he knew things were seldom as simple as they seemed, and the thought made his heart drum a little bit faster.

Then they pulled into the parking lot and the surprising number of cars—especially so early—added fuel to Jack's nerves. The simple ceremony wasn't supposed to be a full-blown sect event, yet inside, twice the amount of people he'd expected had already claimed seats in the large meeting area as more trailed through the door.

Natalie surveyed the room, wide-eyed. "We don't have to make a speech or anything, do we?"

"Not that I know of, and I'd like to think someone would've given me a heads-up. I just can't believe how many people are here. I thought it would mainly be the elder council and a few others."

Brody approached as they made their way into the room and Jack introduced him to Natalie. The older man held her hand between his for a moment, eyes closed, then nodded as if satisfied. "There are seats reserved in the front row for you." He gestured behind him to seating arranged in an oval. The majority of the circuit consisted of several rows with one noticeable section of about a dozen seats in a singular row. The reserved signs hung on chairs directly adjacent to the separate seating.

Sect members milled about on the outskirts of the oval, so Jack took Natalie's hand as they wove through the people and down an aisle to the front. He flipped a reserved sign so it hung over the back of the chair and motioned for her to sit. Then he did the same for himself and sat down next to her. He gestured to the single row. "For the council, so no one sits behind them," he explained.

Natalie nodded, then raised her eyebrows and glanced at his knee which was jigging up and down. "Nervous?"

Jack bobbed his head. "Yeah, maybe more than I was aware of. Funny, the last time I was the focus of a ceremony, I was nine, and I loved it."

"Probably because that time you weren't about to risk your life." Her voice sounded odd.

Jack studied Natalie's face, taking in the small creases in her forehead and the tense set to her lips. "Hey, are you okay?"

She nodded without looking at him. "All these people." She scanned the room. "They all believe, don't they?"

Jack frowned. "Believe..."

"In the underworld." Her voice was so low, he almost didn't hear her. She didn't wait for an answer.

"It makes what we're doing so real all of a sudden." She swallowed. "It's overwhelming."

Jack opened his mouth but she must have guessed what was coming because she spoke before he could say anything. "It doesn't change anything. As long as you're going, I'm going with you."

He could hardly tell her not to worry when his own anxiety was off the charts, so instead he wrapped his hand around hers and squeezed gently. She held on tightly for a moment and then relaxed her fingers. As he released Natalie's hand, Jack raised his head and his gaze fell on Shera, sitting directly across the oval, her eyes on him. He felt a flush of shame, as if he'd been caught with his hand in the cookie jar, but Shera smiled and gave a low-handed wave. He managed a return smile, the butterflies in his stomach doubling. Did she know her father had talked to his father?

Movement drew his attention and he couldn't help chuckling as Jase emerged from the rows of seats near Shera and cut directly across the open area toward them. He ran up to Jack and nudged his way between his brother's knees. Stretching up to get closer to Jack's ear, he whispered loudly, "I want to sit by her."

Jack met Natalie's grin over his brother's head. "Jase, why don't you sit in this seat?" Natalie patted the chair next to her. "Then I'll have someone I know on both sides."

Jase bobbed his head up and down and darted past Natalie to perch on the edge of the chair. He waved frantically when he spied his mom and dad.

Jack followed his brother's line of sight and his heart dropped to his stomach when he noticed his parents chatting with Elder Whitehead. He stole a

156

glance at Shera, whose attention was on the group as well. He tried to decipher the look on her face—curiosity? Excitement? Dread?

A hand clamped down on his shoulder and Jack jumped.

"Dude."

"Wes," Jack said, looking over his shoulder. "Hey, you didn't have to come."

"Sure I did." Wes shifted his gaze to Natalie who had twisted in her seat to see who Jack was talking to.

"Hi Wes, how's it going?" She swung her head to the side, flipping her hair out of her eyes.

Mesmerized momentarily by Natalie's innocent gesture, Wes blinked and managed to utter, "Uh... all right." He sat down behind them, then reached over to tousle Jase's hair. Jase batted Wes's hand and turned around to sit on his knees to avoid another sneak attack. "You've drawn quite a crowd, Ironwood," Wes commented.

"I know. What's up with this?" Jack swept his arm out, indicating the rapidly filling seats. "I expected family and the elder council and maybe a few people who had nothing better to do."

Wes shrugged. "It's big, dude. It's not every day someone volunteers to pay a visit to the lord of souls."

"Jacky's a hero," Jase interjected.

"Not quite, buddy," Jack told him.

Jase poked Natalie on the shoulder. "Are you going to be a hero, too?"

She turned to face him. "Maybe. I hope so." Jase asked her something else, but Jack lost their conversation when Wes caught his eye. His friend pumped a thumb over his shoulder where Jack's parents stood with Elder Whitehead. Wes raised his eyebrows.

157

Jack shook his head and held his hands palm up.

A hush fell over the hall as the elders began seating themselves. Anyone still standing quickly found seats. Jack's parents finally made their way down the aisle and sat down next to Jase. Jack leaned forward to garner some clue about the conversation they'd just had, but when he finally made eye contact with his dad, all he received was a smile.

The ceremony began as they all did, with a blessing from the local Shifter Premier—his adviser, Brody Carter. As Jack watched him perform the familiar rituals, he tried to picture himself in the role. This was a future he'd painted mentally for years: Jack wearing the black robes of Shifter Premier, his wife, Shera, sitting where Brody's wife was now, watching her husband with pride.

Tonight though, Jack struggled to project his face into the scene. As Brody launched into a speech about his protégé, panic started to wend its way from Jack's brain to his chest. His heart stuttered and pounded so loud he wondered if Natalie heard it. His adviser recounted Jack's accomplishments and inferred his future success as a shifter. The fear continued to permeate Jack's being, gathering into a ball in the pit of his stomach.

Oh man, he was about to either die or seal his fate.

He pulled in a deep breath and let it out slowly.

After Brody finished his address and returned to his seat, each elder rose in turn to offer advice or a blessing. The brief speeches seemed to blur into one another until Elder Whitehead stood up. Suddenly Jack's focus was crystal clear.

"An effort of this magnitude has not been offered

in many years. Only the bravest of warriors descend to the dark realm to dance with Zalnic. Elder Carter sees Jack Ironwood as capable of this task; worthy of one day becoming Shifter Premier."

Elder Whitehead paused dramatically to ensure he was the center of attention. "I extend to Jack my utmost blessing, the blessing of betrothal. Success in this venture deserves a substantial reward, so I offer the greatest gift I have: my daughter, Shera."

Blood rushed in Jack's ears drowning out the rest of Elder Whitehead's words. He felt, rather than saw, Natalie's surprised stare. His cautious glance across the room found Shera wearing a smile plastered over mixed emotions.

The crowd erupted into applause. Jack's dad clapped his son on the shoulder and drew him up from his chair. Then he was in front of Elder Whitehead, who now held his daughter's hand. The elder reached for Jack's right hand and joined it with Shera's before releasing them both.

The scene might have happened in one of Jack's many dreams. Except in his dreams, he smiled triumphantly and Shera beamed at him. In reality, she looked apprehensive and Jack's utter bewilderment prevented him from smiling.

With the roar of the crowd adding to the confusion, he stumbled along with Shera as they were herded from the room. He craned his neck to catch sight of his parents. The audience had surged forward and shouts of congratulations and well-wishes filled the lodge. When the mass of bodies shifted for a brief instant, he glimpsed his mom clutching his dad's arm while Jase yanked on her jacket. Wes stood with his mouth agape. And Natalie... was gone.

CHAPTER 9

Change of Heart

Jack and Shera were shuffled from the meeting hall to the back of the building where they were deposited into a studio apartment usually used by visiting sect elders. As soon as the door closed behind them, Shera breathed a sigh of relief. "Thank God it's you, Jack."

"What?" He fought his instinct to leave the room immediately and demand an explanation. He could still hear numerous voices jabbering in the hallway.

Shera dropped her purse on the small kitchen table and turned to face him. "I've agonized over this my entire life, and I'm just glad it's you."

Jack's confusion obliterated the potential flattery. "What's happening?" The council didn't intend for them to marry tonight, did they? The brief flash of panic that seared through his chest abated as he reasoned that their parents wouldn't expect them to marry before finishing high school. "Why are we in here?"

Shera plopped down in an easy chair. "Why do you think?"

Jack's gaze traveled around the room. Shera sat in one of two chairs arranged with a small couch around a fireplace. Immediately to his right was a kitchen area and in the far corner, a bed. His eyes grew round. "No. Your dad wouldn't."

161

"You don't know my father very well then. He believes in the old ways." Shera used finger quotes on the last two words.

Jack pulled his phone from his back pocket and called his dad. "What's going on?" he barked as soon as his dad answered.

"Well," Jack's dad cleared his throat, "I believe you've been given the opportunity to stay the night with your future wife before you go on your quest."

"You're kidding me." Jack paced from the door to the kitchen and back.

"Afraid not. But you don't have to stay, Jack. It's an old-fashioned formality."

A small sigh of relief escaped before his next question. "Are you still here? I think I may need a ride. It looked like Natalie left."

"We're on our way out. You can come with us, but you might want to at least talk with Shera for a bit. I can come back when you're ready."

Jack swiped a hand over his face. "Yeah. Yeah, you're right." If he just walked out right now, he'd hurt her feelings. "Okay. Talk to you later." He stuffed his phone into his pocket and turned to Shera, who'd very obviously listened to the conversation.

"So you're just going to take off?" She kept her chin up and her voice even, but the dejection showed in her eyes.

"No. No, of course not." He took a few steps toward the couch and jammed his hands into his jeans pockets. "I'm sure that sounded bad. I was caught off guard. This was the last thing I expected tonight. I'm supposed to be going to the underworld tomorrow." He dropped his gaze to the floor and rubbed the toe of his shoe on the couch leg.

"You didn't know our parents were in negotiations?"

Jack shrugged. "All I knew is that they'd talked."

"Mmm. Well, my dad didn't tell me either, but I suspected something like this might happen when he insisted I come with him. Especially when he said I'd miss school tomorrow."

Jack crossed to the other chair and sat on the edge of it. "Aren't you mad at your dad for just dumping you in here?"

"I could be."

"But you're not?" Jack thought about Natalie's reaction to merely the idea of an arranged marriage. She'd be spitting mad if this had just happened to her.

Shera gathered her long, black hair and pulled it over her shoulder. She picked up a piece, twirling it around a finger. "You know, when I was thirteen I asked him if I would have any input into who I marry—I wasn't trying to be rebellious or anything, just reasonable. Know what he said?"

"What?"

"I wasn't wise enough. Only those with years of wisdom can decide such things."

"Really."

"Really." She dipped her chin while maintaining a steady gaze. "The thing is, I love the sect. I love reading auras. If I ran away or something, I'd have to leave it all behind. I figured I might as well stick around and see how things turned out." She lowered her eyes then and her voice became softer. "I'm okay with this. I've always liked you, Jack."

Jack wanted to tell her he'd always liked her too, but his heart was beating too fast and he had a lump in his throat. If he choked on the words they would sound

163

insincere. He moved to kneel in front of the fireplace where a fire had already been lit. He picked up the poker and prodded the smoldering logs.

Shera got up and rummaged around in the kitchen. "Do you know the girl you're going to rescue?"

"Not really." Jack was glad for the change in subject. "You know, I saw her in school but didn't even know her name until I asked Natalie about the disappearance." He heard the click-click-click of the burner igniter and then the whoosh of a flame.

"Natalie. That's the girl going with you, right?"

"Yep." Jack moved to a chair, easing his shoulders back and attempting to breathe normally. His racing pulse dropped a little closer to normal.

Shera turned to face him and he couldn't help but be struck with her beauty. Her long legs were clad in tight black jeans that ended just above a pair of black flats. Her knit shirt was Caribbean blue, loose, yet somehow clinging to her curves. "You're friends with her?"

"I am now, I guess." He added the last, aware she was watching him closely. "I overheard her describing the Enuuki that abducted her friend, so I approached her." He thought back over the last few days. "I've really only known her for about a week." Had it actually been less than a week?

Shera returned from the kitchen, this time choosing the end of the couch closest to Jack's chair. She kicked off her shoes and curled her legs up on the seat. "Do you have a girlfriend?"

"No." Had she not brought it up, he probably never would have thought to ask the same. "Do you?"

Her eyes crinkled at the corners and he realized

how his question sounded. He smiled. "I mean, do you have a boyfriend?"

"I suppose either one is a valid question these days." She laughed. "So, no on the girlfriend, I'm straight. And boyfriend? Kinda. I have been seeing someone. Nothing too heavy duty though. You won't mention it, will you? My dad doesn't know."

"No worries. Is he sect?"

She shook her head. "A guy at school. He has no idea who my dad is."

Jack had mixed emotions about her revelation. Put in the same position as this other guy, how would he feel? Just starting to get to know a girl and then suddenly she's engaged? "He's gonna be destroyed."

Shera snorted. "He won't. It was just for fun. We knew it wasn't going anywhere."

The cavalier way she spouted out an explanation surprised Jack. Was she covering hurt feelings because she thought she had no other choice? Or was she actually that flippant about the situation?

At the sharp shrill of the teapot, Shera popped up to tend it. "You like tea, don't you?"

"Sure," Jack replied, though the idea of drinking tea seemed odd.

"I have a special blend for you to try." Her tone hinted at a secret, but she returned to their thread of conversation, chattering about working on the yearbook and how she'd met this guy and they started hanging out after meetings. With her back to him, Jack only half-listened while he watched her lithe and graceful form reach for mugs. Blue highlights caught in her straight, black locks which nearly brushed the top of her jeans. In the few years since Jack's family moved to

165

Ketchton, Shera had stretched out and left her girlish roundness behind. She'd been beautiful then. Now she was stunning.

The ramifications of their situation began to sink in. His dream had come true. So why had he decided so quickly to leave?

Because this wasn't how it was supposed to happen.

Jack had never considered himself the hopeless romantic type, but the circumstances were too forced. Not to mention that tomorrow was the most important—most challenging—day of his life so far. He needed sleep. And a clear head.

He'd have a cup of tea with her and then explain he had to go. She'd understand—maybe even be grateful for a chance to get to know each other a little better.

Shera crossed the room slowly with two steaming mugs. She set one on the table next to his chair and then carefully returned to her spot on the couch. Her gaze settled on him over the rim of her cup, watching through the steam.

Jack brought his mug up to blow on the surface of the tea. The earthy aroma of pine and herbs conjured instant memories of David and mysticism. He raised his eyebrows at Shera and lowered the mug to his lap. "Is this seekers tea?" Seekers tea was the last part of the preparation for a spirit-walk, transitioning the shifter to a more open frame of mind.

Her furtive smile came across as a warning to Jack. "It's a little different. But it'll calm your nerves."

"I don't think an altered state is a good idea for me tonight." Jack put his mug back on the table.

"Or it could be exactly what you need." She

166

breathed in the vapors rising from the mug, then took a long drink.

After that, the already unprecedented evening shifted to bizarre.

Jack watched Shera carefully as she steadily continued to drink, not sure what to expect. He knew seekers tea took effect quickly, but Shera wasn't forthcoming with the contents of her "special blend." A pure dose of seekers tea allowed the mind to wander freely, leaving the subject in a state of limbo. Shera, however, became Chatty Cathy. She only stopped spewing words to giggle.

He supposed the situation might have been fun had he imbibed the tea as well; the brew certainly seemed to remove inhibitions. Unfortunately, he could have done without knowing the personal things Shera decided to share. Some of the information troubled Jack. She was a much different person than the girl he once knew—or thought he knew.

Uncomfortable leaving her alone in such a condition, he stayed, debating what to do. At some point it would be too late to expect his dad to come pick him up.

Finally, the stream of chatter sputtered out and drowsiness set in. Each time Shera blinked, her eyes stayed closed longer. She slumped over the arm of the couch. After she'd stayed still for a few minutes, Jack spoke her name out loud. She didn't respond, so he rose, retrieved the quilt from the bottom of the bed and covered her.

As he tucked the cover up near her chin, she opened her eyes. "Jack." A lazy smile dimpled her cheeks.

"I'm gonna go," he whispered. "You sleep."

She snaked her arms out of the quilt and around his neck, pulling him down so she could whisper into his ear. "Don't go," she murmured. "Lay down with me."

As he drew away, she stopped him with a hand behind his head and pressed her mouth on his. Her lips were warm, damp and insistent. Taken utterly by surprise, he kissed her back. The moment wasn't slow and tender, but raw and wild and... desperate. Jack felt like a lifeguard trying to save a drowning victim.

He pulled away and Shera groaned a weak protest. Her eyes slid closed.

Jack texted his dad, then quietly slipped from the apartment. If it was too late for his dad to drive out, so be it. He'd walk if he had to—hellcats or not.

He had to get out of there.

After spending the bus ride fending off Wes's questions about the previous night, Jack arrived at school to find Natalie just finishing at her locker. He hurried over. "Hey," he said.

She gave him the briefest look and grunted.

"Look, sorry about last night, I had—"

"No explanation necessary. I'm sure it's none of my business."

"It's just that—"

She cut him off again. "By the way, we just had a fake break-up of our fake relationship. No need to follow me around the school."

Jack was astonished—not so much at what she said, but how she said it. She sounded so bitter.

He put his hand on her arm. "Natalie."

She jerked away, slammed her locker and stalked off without looking back.

Crap.

As the day wore on, Jack wished he had gone home sick after the conversation with Natalie. The present situation, combined with last night's confusion, piled on top of his anxiety about his upcoming venture. The jumble of emotions rendered him incapable of retaining any information from his classes. Last night his dad had offered to call the school this morning, but Jack declined, thinking he'd be able to talk to Natalie throughout the day.

Jack was pretty sure his dad had been sleeping when he received the text last night, but he drove out to pick up his son without question. On the way home, his dad's only comment was that Jack's call had surprised him. He thought Jack would have left earlier in the night or stayed until morning. Jack felt compelled to provide some kind of explanation, so he simply said, "It took a little while for me to figure out she's not the person I thought she was." His tone implied the conversation was over. He had no intention of recounting the night. He'd probably never tell anyone the entire story.

Everything seemed to be unraveling.

When Natalie still refused to speak to him before leaving school, Jack thought, fine—he'd go alone. It's what he'd wanted from the start. Wes blabbed on about one of his classes while Jack tried to figure out how to make the two-person plan into a one-person plan.

He'd most likely die trying or fail. No Shifter Premier.

No Shera.

Incredibly, the last thought was almost a relief. Failure would mean he wouldn't have to hurt Shera's feelings. His future would be a clean slate.

A buzz from his phone drew him out of his reverie. He looked at the text from Natalie: *Where and when?*

After a long moment, he slipped the phone back into his pocket. Rather than fail, he could call the whole thing off. He would become a paleontologist, find a girl and fall in love—real love.

His lifelong dream had become surrounded by bars that Jack didn't want to get stuck behind.

His phone buzzed again.

He ignored it.

"Good luck, man."

Jack snapped back to reality. Wes stood with his hand out as a few kids piled off the bus and the driver glanced impatiently into his mirror.

"Thanks." Jack shook his friend's hand. He'd planned to remind Wes about talking to Tommy, but he didn't really give a crap about the moody lead singer right now. Besides, maybe he'd show up at band practice after all.

Long before he'd reached the end of Bittersweet Lane, Jack recognized Natalie's car parked in front of his house. As he drew near, she got out and leaned on the car, arms crossed on her chest, and watched him approach. "Something wrong with your phone?" she called when he was within ear shot.

"Oh. You're talking to me now?"

"Regardless of our personal feelings, we have a job to do."

Jack proceeded past her and unlocked the front door. "I think we should call it off." He stepped inside.

170

Natalie rushed onto the porch and placed a hand on the door before he could close it behind him. "No, Jack. We're doing this." She followed him into the house.

He set his books down and turned to face her. Her eyes were full of hurt and determination. Jack watched tears well up and threaten to escape down her cheeks.

His newfound resolve crumbled. His grand plan to back out had a major flaw: Emma. He may have many doubts about his future right now, but two things he knew for sure—he couldn't let an innocent girl perish and he couldn't crush Natalie's hopes.

With a heavy sigh, he dropped into a rocker. "My dad said Dan wants us to come by tonight. And it's a good thing, because we need to know how to get you to descend."

Natalie had found a tissue in her pocket and dabbed at the corner of her eyes. "When?"

"I don't know. I have to call him, but probably after dinner."

She nodded. "I have a few new things on Norse mythology in my car. Do you want me to go over it with you?"

"Yeah." While she ran to her car, Jack took a couple of deep breaths, hoping to ease the tightness in his chest. He wished last night had never happened. He wanted his relationship with Natalie to be like it was yesterday.

They managed to discuss mythology civilly until Jack's dad arrived with Jase. His little brother flitted about and talked incessantly, lightening the strained atmosphere. Finally, his dad herded the younger boy into the kitchen.

"Sorry about that," Jack mumbled. "Maybe we should go to your house."

"No, Jase is great. And I prefer it here."

Jack shot her a questioning glance.

"My house seems clinically impersonal compared to being here. This is a home." She said the last in a quiet voice and rearranged a few papers without looking at Jack.

"Does your dad expect you home for dinner?"

"No. I told him I wouldn't see him tonight. That I'd spend the night with a girlfriend."

"Stay for dinner then."

"No, it's all right. I have stuff at home I need to gather up. And change my clothes."

"Okay, do that now, and then come back. We'll eat dinner here and then head over to the Mannings'."

She was tempted, Jack could tell. "Will it be okay with your mom?"

"Actually, dad's cooking tonight. There's always plenty, but if it makes you feel better, I'll check with him."

Dinner was a good call on Jack's part. By the time they were on their way to the Mannings', Jack and Natalie were able to have a fairly normal conversation. Her emotions though, were still guarded. The previous night hovered like a threatening rain cloud.

"Come in," Dan said. "Sorry we couldn't make it last night, Jack."

Jack winced. "It's all right," he mumbled.

Dan motioned them toward the couch. "Did you end up with anything you can use?"

Natalie plopped down, her arms wrapped over her

chest. Jack endeavored to sit neither too close nor too far from her. He cleared his throat. "We pretty much already heard everything given as advice—don't eat or drink, don't stay too long… The rest were blessings." He didn't look at Natalie.

"Thought so. Well, I have something for you." Dan left the room and came back with a paper-wrapped bundle. He set it on the coffee table and carefully pulled away the layers, revealing two greenish-yellow stones and rawhide. Sliding his finger under a piece of the hide, he lifted it, revealing a roughly fashioned necklace. He touched the stone. "Brimstone." Handing the necklace to Jack, he picked up the other and passed it to Natalie.

"I found these on one of my summer solstice descents to the shadowlands." He watched as Jack inspected the primitive pendant. "You notice the inscription?"

"Yeah, but I can't read it."

Natalie held hers under a lamp. "I don't think it's English."

"You're right." Dan said. "My adviser took them to the oldest shifter alive at that time who was shocked to see such an ancient item return to this world. Fortunately he was able to manage a rough translation of the script. Something like: *The warrior pure of heart travels the land of souls unseen.* My adviser guessed this meant they're amulets which render the wearer invisible to the many deadly guardians of the underworld. They're untested, though." He shook his head with a frown. "Callie and I took off without any preparation. I didn't even remember I had them until after we'd returned.

"You know," he added thoughtfully. "That old

shifter said there was a reason these amulets returned to the living world. Our ancestors try to anticipate our needs and send the requisite tools. I figured I screwed up by not using them, but who knows? Maybe this was always their purpose."

Jack slipped the cord over his head and tucked the stone into his jacket. "Thanks." His chest felt enlarged, as if his heart had expanded. Dan hadn't even wanted to talk to him at first and now he'd just given them more help than all the elders put together last night. "This means a lot." He didn't quite choke up, but his voice sounded rough.

"I just hope they help." Dan rubbed his palms together. "So what's your plan? Did the religion thing pan out?"

Jack shifted his gaze out the window then back to Dan. "As much as I'd love your input, I feel like we shouldn't discuss it. Both of us have been stalked." He glanced to Natalie who fiddled with her amulet on her lap.

"No problem. I think that's a wise decision. I wish you the best of luck. Whatever the plan, I hope it works."

"Thanks, me too," Jack replied quietly. "We need to know how you got Callie to descend with you. Did you... hold hands? Or something like that?" God, that was going to be awkward now.

"Physically, I held her. We wrapped our arms around each other as if nothing could tear us apart."

Jack squeezed his eyes shut briefly.

Natalie sniffed and shifted in her seat.

Dan flicked his gaze from Jack to Natalie, his eyebrows drawing down to form a crease in his forehead. "What's going on between you two?"

174

Natalie didn't look up, leaving Jack to field the question. "What do you mean?"

"Come on guys, I felt the tension as soon as I opened the door. What happened?"

"It's nothing," Natalie piped up. "It's over now."

"Really? Jack? Is it over?" Dan looked from one to the other, waiting for an answer. Natalie's eyes remained in her lap and Jack didn't say anything. He didn't want to chance making her angry all over again.

"Okay, listen." Dan stood up and paced in front of them. "This is important. Unless you work this out, you won't even get started."

"What do you mean, we won't get started?" Jack asked. He noticed Dan finally had Natalie's attention.

"You're the shifter." Dan poked his finger at Jack. "She's not." He jerked his thumb sideways at Natalie. "The only way you'll get her to cross the veil is if you're as one. Body and mind. You've got to be together in this one hundred percent. If you have any differences, you'd better work them out."

"It's not even relevant," Natalie said quietly.

"Everything is relevant. You can't be at odds with each other." Dan locked eyes with each of them in turn. "Even though I held on to Callie for all I was worth, I didn't expect her to descend with me. But she did. And the only explanation I have is that her determination matched mine. We had one singular goal between us. We went unprepared and without a plan, but we were one when it came to purpose."

No one spoke or moved for a long moment.

"I may not have been behind this in the beginning, but you've made me a believer. I'm pulling for you guys." Dan's voice was soft now. "I think you have a decent chance to come back alive—with your friend. Promise me you'll talk. Clear the air."

Jack looked at Natalie. She met his eyes and nodded briefly.

"Okay then, I guess you guys should get going." Dan walked them to the door. As they stepped out on the porch, he added a last word of advice. "Remember, there's a reason Zalnic is the lord of souls. He's a master at playing on your emotions. He's ruthless and will take every advantage without mercy. You can't afford to be distracted. Make smart decisions with your head. This is one instance where following your heart will most certainly get you killed."

Jack gave an affirmative nod and they headed for Natalie's car.

"Good luck," Dan called.

"Thanks." Jack glanced over his shoulder and raised a hand in salute. They were certainly going to need it.

Although Natalie didn't say anything when they got into the car, Jack decided there'd be no better time to talk. "So… uh… why were you so upset today? I had no idea that would happen last night or I would've given you a heads-up."

She didn't say anything until she'd backed from the driveway and was driving away from the Mannings' house. "I know I overreacted." She sighed and continued in a low voice. "Yesterday was… it seemed too real. And then I realized…"

Jack contemplated her death grip on the steering wheel and then noticed the way her eyes shone in the street lights. "Realized what?" he prodded gently.

"It's what you wanted all along. That's why we're

doing this. So you can be worthy of her." She swallowed and pressed her lips together.

Jack wished he could deny it, but she was right. And he had to come clean. "You're right, that was part of it. But I did also want to be the Shifter Premier."

Natalie snuck a quick glance at him. "Did?"

"Maybe I had Shera built up too much in my mind. I mean, I knew her when we were kids, but she's different now." Turning to face the windshield, Jack let his head fall back on the headrest. "Everything's changed. I don't know what I want anymore. Not her. I'm sure of that. So maybe I'm wrong about the rest. I'll always be a shifter, but maybe I could be something more."

"Aren't you… engaged?"

"It can be undone."

"It can?"

"Yes. It happened to my mom. My dad was her parents' second choice."

They both fell silent. Twice, Jack heard Natalie take a breath as if she wanted to say something else. But they arrived at Jack's house without further conversation. When she pulled her keys from the ignition, he spoke up. "Wait."

She paused and turned her head just enough to see him from the corner of her eye.

"There's more. Tell me. We have to clear the air completely."

A tentative silence stretched out as Jack waited for Natalie to speak. "Did you…" She began and then shook her head. "Never mind. It doesn't matter."

"Just say it." The porch light illuminated the bottom of her face and Jack watched as Natalie pursed her lips and then squeezed them into a line. "For Emma," he urged.

She took a deep breath. "I waited. Last night. I waited outside. I saw your family come out without you." She kept her gaze carefully trained on the windshield. Her thumb worked back and forth over the jagged side of her car key. "They left without you."

"My dad picked me up later." But Jack realized how he got home wasn't what was bothering her. "When they led us from the meeting room, they put us in an apartment in the back where visiting elders stay." Natalie turned away, peering out the side window and Jack continued, telling her simply what she wanted to know—what she needed to know. "We talked. She told me a bunch of stuff I didn't like—things I really didn't want to know—and then she fell asleep and I called my dad."

Natalie turned to him, eyes wide. "That's it?" She scanned his face and then locked eyes with him.

"That's it. Are we okay?"

She nodded. "I'm sorry, Jack. It shouldn't have bothered me, I know. But it did. I blame it on yesterday at school." She managed a weak laugh.

"Yeah. I know what you mean," he replied gravely. Because he did.

He knew exactly what she meant.

They gathered their supplies at Jack's house and said goodbye to his parents. Jack's mom hugged him extra-long and then squeezed his hands. "I'll call school in the morning," she said. "Even if you're back by then." She hugged Natalie too.

"Watch each other's backs," Jack's dad said as they stepped off the porch.

"Did you make arrangements for someone to call school for you tomorrow?" Jack asked.

Natalie shook her head. "I took care of it today. I'm accompanying my dad on a weekend business trip." She grinned, but uncertainty held her eyes tight.

They stopped for gas just outside of town and Jack picked up a large cola to keep him fueled up. Natalie declined his offer for something from the gas station convenience store, opting to drive through a coffee shop just up the road for a large mocha. By the time they were on the road to Mesick, it was just after ten o'clock. Natalie turned on the radio and they rode for while, lost in their own thoughts.

Jack should have been thinking about facing down Zalnic, but he wasn't. He was thinking about Natalie. Yesterday. The thrill of seeing her face light up when he rounded the corner to meet her. The way her small hand felt in his, soft and strong at the same time. How she was just the right size to fit in the crook of his shoulder, as if she belonged there. She was right. It had been too real.

So what happened if they were successful? Would they assimilate back into their previous lives? The occasional 'hi' at their lockers?

God, he hoped not.

He pictured the doubtful evaluation Natalie's dad had given him when they were supposedly working on a project together. How would her dad look at him if he arrived to take her on a date? No, he didn't think it would fly. The Jack Ironwoods don't get the Natalie Segetiches.

Regardless of what the future may hold, he promised himself one thing. Natalie was coming back. Alive. Whatever it took.

A half hour later, as they neared their destination, Natalie turned off the radio. "Talk to me, Jack. I'm starting to freak out a little."

In the greenish glow of the dashboard lights, she looked white as a ghost. "Okay…" Jack floundered for a topic far from their current undertaking. School. "I saw flyers that they're casting for the spring musical. Are you interested? Even if you're not going to be a movie star anymore?"

She laughed. "Yeah, actually, I am interested. Last year I couldn't because of track—that's one of the reasons I quit. I'm not sure if I'd want a speaking part though. But I'd love to be part of the chorus."

"There's a chorus?"

"Duh," she teased. "It's a musical."

"If you say so."

"Jack! You've never gone to a school play?"

"Nope."

She breathed out with exaggerated exasperation. "Well, it's about time. If I'm in this play, I expect you to see it. And if I'm not—you're going with me to see it. What road am I looking for?"

Jack chuckled. "You're not looking yet." He pointed off to the right where the moon was still fairly low in the sky. "We have plenty of time. Let's go into Mesick and find a bathroom, maybe a snack too."

The normality of stopping for fast food subdued their anxiety. Although Jack offered to drive the rest of the way, Natalie declined, claiming her mind was better off occupied. Then they back-tracked to the west side of the Hodenpyl Dam Pond.

When Jack had researched the area, he learned that the 'pond' formed by a dam in the Manistee River served functionally like a lake that was popular with boaters, fishermen and campers. More importantly, hundreds of years ago Native Americans had built their burial mounds along the shore of the river.

"Are we going to the campground?" Natalie asked.

"No. It's too late. I considered making a reservation, but thought it'd look suspicious with only a car parked in a site. I figure we'll find somewhere to park close by."

Once past the campground, they turned and went back the way they came to look for a safe place to park Natalie's car. She didn't want to leave it on the side of the road. "If my dad gets a call, I'll be grounded for life."

They decided to seek out an unoccupied summer home. Post Labor Day, quite a few lake houses would be closed and ready for winter. They could park in front of one and traverse the shoreline back to the burial grounds.

After scrutinizing four possibilities, they settled on a small cottage. Dock segments were stacked neatly offshore and the covered boat parked near a shed appeared buttoned down for the season.

"The owners still might come up for the weekend," Natalie said.

"Maybe, but that should give us until tomorrow night before anyone would see your car." Assuming the owners had to work Friday, which Jack didn't bother to say out loud.

Natalie parked. They got out and retrieved their backpacks from the back seat. After making sure the doors were locked, Natalie bent down and shuffled alongside the car.

"What're you doing?"

"Looking for a place for the key. Ah, here. Come see."

Jack rounded to her side of the car. She reached her hand up under the sheet metal just behind the front tire. "Feel this?'

He followed her arm down to her hand and felt a small ledge. "Yeah."

"That's where I'm leaving the key."

She didn't have to explain. Jack got it. This way she couldn't lose it in the underworld, but more importantly, if only one of them made it back to the car, the key would be here. "Good thinking."

"A little trick I learned camping with Emma's family."

They set off along the shoreline, clambering over the small piles of rocks which divided each property's narrow strip of sand beach. Out in the open, the three-quarter moon provided enough light to see by. The occasional undeveloped lot required flashlights to slog through the marshy grass and weeds.

The smell of wood smoke alerted them to the campground ahead. A few minutes later, Jack caught a glimpse of colorful lights. He stopped and waited for Natalie to come up next to him. "We're here."

He heard Natalie's shaky breath and reached for her hand. Her arm stiffened, but then she gripped his fingers tightly. Although Jack didn't feel frightened, his adrenaline had definitely kicked in, making him hyper-aware—his senses razor sharp. "You lead," he said in a low voice.

Natalie picked her way from the beach into the sparsely populated campground. Despite the chilly temperature, a few groups still huddled by their campfires. Natalie stopped and nodded toward an RV where flameless embers glowed in the fire pit. A small light lit the doorway to the otherwise dark camper.

"I'm pretty sure this is the site we were in. There should be a trail up here," she whispered.

"How did you know about the burial mounds?"

Natalie pointed to a sign and directed her light at it. It read: Burial Mound Trail.

He caught her smirk and chuckled. "Right."

"Plus, in the daylight," Natalie kept her voice hushed, "the trees are thin enough that you can see the mounds."

She hesitated at the trailhead. Jack squeezed her hand before releasing it, then stepped on the path first. Once they were enveloped by the forest, he stopped, turned off the flashlight and closed his eyes. Natalie drew up close enough for him to feel her body heat on his back. After a few moments, his eyes had adjusted to the dark and he could make out the silhouette of the landscape. "I see them," he murmured. To his left, the ground swelled fifteen to twenty feet higher than where they stood. In the distance on the right was another, smaller hill.

Natalie pointed to the large mound on the left. "We were at the top of that one." Her voice wavered slightly.

Jack turned his light back on and helped Natalie as they left the trail, pushed through the thicket and climbed up the rise. The otherworldly presence of the mound permeated his feet, spreading a slight vibration throughout his body. Near the top, Natalie tugged on his arm. He looked back to see her moonlit pale face, eyes wide with terror. She shook her head.

"It's okay." Jack stepped close. He touched the front of her jacket where he knew the brimstone amulet rested on her chest. "We're protected, remember? Dan gave us back the element of surprise. Nothing is waiting for us." He looked into her eyes and repeated the mantra which fueled her resolve. "For Emma?"

She gazed back for a second, inhaled deeply, then finally nodded.

They reached the summit of the mound and Jack searched the gray sky, breathing in the earthy smell of forest. The moon hung suspended above the treetops, an occasional wispy cloud drifting across its yellow light.

Natalie shrugged out of her backpack and stepped up behind him to look over his shoulder, her fingers clutching his jacket sleeve. "Now what?" she whispered.

"We can descend when the moon reaches its apex—the highest point in the sky. Brody said it would be around one o'clock." Jack pulled his phone from his pocket. "It's just after midnight."

Natalie shivered and took a half step closer to Jack, peering into the surrounding darkness anxiously. "So what happens when it's time?"

Jack returned his gaze to the rising moon, careful to keep his tone light. "I'll be able to feel the membrane—the veil between worlds—and I'll push against it. Or, actually, we'll push against it together."

"Oh." Natalie didn't retreat from her position, but she stiffened and released her grip on his jacket.

Even though they'd cleared the air, the emotional confusion caused by the fake relationship was going to make getting close awkward. Jack let his backpack slip to the ground. "We might as well sit for a few."

They sat for a while listening to an occasional noise from the campground—a door slam, the murmur of voices, footsteps on blacktop—or the rustle of an animal nosing through the dry leaves on the forest floor. The moon inched its way up the sky. Natalie pulled on her gloves, then drew her knees up so she could wrap her arms around her legs.

"Cold?" Jack asked. When she nodded, he moved next to her, hoping she'd benefit from his body heat. As he studied her from the corner of his eye, he noticed she was staring at their backpacks. He assumed she'd come to the same conclusion that he already had: if they wore backpacks, there'd be only one way to embrace—face to face.

A few minutes later he checked the time and then contemplated the moon for a moment. "I think we should get ready. I don't want to miss it."

Natalie got up and rubbed her hands together before reaching for her pack. As she swung it up from the ground, Jack said, "Try putting it on in front."

"What?"

"I've seen a lot of Jase's friends wearing their backpacks on their chest. Try it that way."

Her eyebrows rose, but she stuck her arms through the straps and pulled the bag to her chest.

Jack hefted his pack onto his shoulders and came up behind her. He slid his arms around her waist. Part of him couldn't help but notice her soft warmth and the tropical scent of her hair, but he pushed the thoughts away, concentrating on the hum which reverberated from the mound. He felt for the barrier.

There. He sensed a hollowness to the left. "Lean with me," he breathed, and they pressed in that direction.

185

Jack pushed into the membrane with his shoulder but immediately shifted out of line with Natalie as if her shoulder had encountered a wall. "Damn," he muttered.

"What happened?" Natalie's voice sounded an octave higher than usual.

"This isn't going to work." Jack stepped away and dropped his arms to his side.

"It has to." She wriggled out of her backpack, shrugged it onto her back, then stepped up to Jack and hugged him close. "Try it again."

Unfortunately the result was the same.

"I'll just go," Jack said.

"The hell you will." Her adamant response startled Jack into a smile. "If Callie could do it, so can I." She crinkled up her forehead, thinking hard. "One in body..." she muttered. Then the wrinkles disappeared and her eyebrows shot up. "Wasn't it summer?" She yanked her gloves off and unzipped her coat.

"What?" Jack struggled to catch up with her line of thinking as Natalie reached forward and pulled on his jacket zipper. "What are y—"

"Their nephew visited them in the summer," she said. "They wouldn't have had all these layers of clothes. Unbutton your shirt. Is that tucked in?" She plucked at the collar of his t-shirt.

"Yeah." He was already working on his buttons.

Before he could finish, Natalie had slipped her hands under his shirt to pull his t-shirt from his jeans. "Hurry." Then her cold hands were making their way around his waist and onto his back. "My shirts aren't tucked. Get your hands on my skin."

Jack obeyed, pressing her tightly against his chest, fingers splayed on her bare back. He could feel her heart flutter on his right side as his own thumped on the left. The membrane flowed around them like gelatin, but as Jack began to slip through, Natalie lingered.

She hooked her arms under his by curling her fingers over his shoulders. "No!" she gasped.

But Jack had entered the gravitational pull of the other world and couldn't stop his momentum. Natalie's face contorted in anguish. God, was this hurting her? He started to release her.

"No, Jack," she pleaded. Then he felt her lips on his and her resistance waned. He pulled her closer. They kissed in a vortex—a crazy carnival ride that strove to tear them apart even as they strained to stay together. Jack doubled the effort by covering her mouth with his. Her lips parted and she gasped, drawing in his breath.

One.

They broke through.

CHAPTER 10

The Underworld

Jack fell hard on his back, driving his pack against him and trapping Natalie's arms. The impact broke the kiss.

"Ouch." Natalie wriggled on top of him, attempting to pull her arms free.

"Hang on." Jack freed his arms from her clothes and hugged her loosely, rolling both of them to their sides. Then he rose up on an elbow so she could extract both of her limbs.

"Are you okay?" Jack anxiously watched her bend and twist her arms.

"Yeah. My arms were just kind of squeezed between you and your backpack."

Jack stood and helped Natalie up. "We made it—thanks to you." He regretted the last three words as soon as he said them because immediately his hands remembered the softness of her skin and the warmth of her lips. An awkward silence hung between them for a moment.

Natalie shrugged a little and dropped her gaze, shifting her pack. "I thought you were—"

A screaming yowl split the air. Jack yanked Natalie to a crouch and they scrambled for a nearby boulder.

As he'd glimpsed in his spirit-walk, the landscape

in the darker realm was much different than the shadowlands where he met with ancestors in spirit or entered on the summer solstice. The rocky and barren panorama surrounding them reminded him of pictures he'd seen of a national park in Utah—except the warm brown, orange and reds of those photos were replaced here by cold and bleak shades of gray. And in place of the graceful rock formations of the world above, stone protrusions rose violently from the terrain while boulders resembling giant used charcoal briquettes dwarfed the patchy, withered brush. The pencil sketch effect was completed by a colorless sky and broken only by a single orange glow on the horizon.

"Cheese and rice!" Natalie hissed. "What was that?"

"Not sure. Hellcat maybe."

She closed her eyes and took a deep breath. "Why is it cold? I thought hell was supposed to be hot."

"There's no sun. It's kinda like being in a desert at night."

"What's that then?" Natalie pointed to the smoldering break in the color scheme.

"That's where we're headed—to Zalnic."

Natalie eyed the abundance of open space dubiously and Jack followed her gaze. "Good thing Dan gave us the brimstones." He stood and adjusted his backpack. "Ready?"

They tried to move quickly, yet quietly, though the rocky terrain made it impossible to avoid kicking up gravel and dust. The air had a slightly acrid smell that lingered bitterly in the back of their throats. Since the amulets they wore were untested, they crouched down or dodged for cover at every grunt, cry or disturbance from the undergrowth, leaving nothing to chance.

As Jack was contemplating what seemed to be a haze in the distance, Natalie abruptly stopped and grabbed his arm. "Do you hear that?"

He was about to say he didn't hear anything, then closed his mouth and turned in a circle. She wasn't referring to a scuffle or animalistic call. "It's like a... buzz?" he asked. Natalie nodded. The drone intensified and Jack instinctively pulled her down to a squat.

A huge shadow rushed overhead close enough to make their hair flutter in the blast of air.

"What was that? A hell-bird?" Natalie whispered.

Jack shrugged. "I didn't see it good enough, but it was at least the size of a hawk—maybe even eagle-sized."

They were about to rise when the drone sounded again overhead. Searching the sky, they hunkered down in the scrub. Suddenly Jack threw his arms protectively over Natalie's head and pushed her down to the ground. "It's a bat." He turned his head sideways and watched as the dark form dove.

"A bat the size of a hawk?" Natalie squeaked.

"Shhh. Don't move," Jack breathed. Seconds later he flinched at the scrape of claws grazing the back of his jacket.

"I guess the brimstone can't protect us from echo-location," he murmured, rising to his knees. "They know we're here. We need to distract them."

As Natalie reached out to gather some stones Jack grabbed her wrist. "Gloves," he reminded her. "We should've had them on already. Were your hands on the ground?"

"I don't think so." She pulled gloves from her pockets and Jack did the same as the droning sound began to build again. He scanned the bleak sky as the noise grew louder. "Start throwing."

Natalie sat back on her heels and hurled rocks into the gloom. Jack waited until her supply was almost depleted before he started pelting his rocks into the air. "Get your head down," he instructed when she was out of ammunition.

Jack barely saw the black form swoop past them. As the buzz faded he said, "Let's get to that next bunch of boulders."

After duck-walking to the cluster of huge stones, Natalie took advantage of an outcropping and shrugged out of her backpack to scoot under the ledge. Jack hunched down in front of her. He fired a few more stones in the direction they'd come from, to draw the bats away. "Let's just stay put for a few minutes."

They watched as shadows coalesced out of the gloom to form huge wings spanning nearly six feet across. The bats cruised low over the area they'd just vacated. Sensing nothing, they eventually moved on.

Dashing from one form of cover to the next, Jack and Natalie worked their way forward. As the opportunities for concealment became fewer and farther between, Jack also noticed the ground became compressed and less dusty. In the distance he could still see some rock formations, but less boulders and more scrub. Soon they were picking their way through brambles protruding from muddy earth.

"Ugh," Natalie groaned at the sucking sound as she pulled her foot from the muck. "We could lose our shoes in here."

"No doubt," Jack agreed. "Be careful—you do not want that to happen."

"And it stinks like rotten garbage."

She was right. The smell was noxious. Suddenly

Jack froze—except for the hand that darted out to grasp Natalie's arm. They stood immobile, listening to the crack and snap of brittle scrub. Moving only his eyes, Jack strained to detect movement. "There," he breathed, barely indicating with his head to their right.

The creature seemed more an absence of light than a physical entity. At least ten feet in length and as thick as Jack's thigh, it slithered through the brush, so black that it blotted out the dark sludge of the bog.

After crossing their path, the snake-like anomaly disappeared. They remained still for a long moment, turning only their heads to stare at each other. Jack imagined the look on his face was that of amazement and alarm, but Natalie's eyes were wide with horror. "Either our brimstone necklaces work, or it was blind." He spoke in a low voice, hoping either observation might alleviate some of her fear.

She blinked a few times, and then inhaled slowly through her nose, blowing the breath out her mouth. "Okay. I'm okay." He wasn't sure if she was trying to convince him or herself. When he let go of her arm, she grabbed his hand and held on.

They worked their way forward, hand in hand, seeing only one more spectral bog-snake before they reached the smoke.

The terrain beneath their feet changed yet again, becoming parched and crusty. The going was easier for their feet, but once they were enveloped by the dark mist, decreased visibility slowed their progress considerably. The expectation of something creeping from the shadows into their path had the hair on the back of Jack's neck on end. If not for the illumination glowing steadily in the distance, they would have surely been lost.

"What is it?" Natalie asked. "It smells burnt, like smoke."

He shook his head. "I don't know. No one I spoke to mentioned it. I feel like we shouldn't breathe it in, but what else can we do?"

Natalie pulled off her glove, reached into a jacket pocket, and withdrew a small pack of tissue. She pulled one from the package and handed it to Jack. "It may not make a difference, but it certainly can't hurt."

Jack nodded and took the tissue. He opened it and pressed it over his nose and mouth while Natalie did the same. Then they rejoined hands and continued the trek.

All of Jack's senses were assaulted by the smoke. It felt like fine sand clinging to his skin. Despite the tissue, the smell—which reminded Jack of singed hair—invaded his nose, evoking images of funeral pyres and mass graves. He swore he could taste ash on his tongue. Misty soot seemed to fill his ears, dampening sounds, making it impossible to discern if the echo of beastly calls was real or if his imagination was running wild from sensory overload.

That he missed falling into the crevasse, Jack attributed wholly to his spatial awareness and experience as a shifter. He'd been staring forward, working to overcome the natural trepidation of walking blindly when suddenly his instincts told him to stop. He jerked Natalie's hand and she drew up next to him, clutching his arm. "What is it, Jack?" she whispered, searching the surrounding fog.

"A hunch." Jack scanned the ground in front of him, some sixth sense informing him of a void ahead. He shuffled forward slowly, moving their joined hands behind his back, allowing him to proceed first. The cavity appeared quickly. One, possibly two more steps and they'd have tumbled to their deaths. His heart thudded unevenly in his chest. Invisibility was not a safety net here. He turned to Natalie and lowered the tissue from his face. "We should get out of here."

Natalie nodded.

He took a step back in the direction they'd come from and she tugged on his arm. "What are you doing?"

"Getting out of here." He let go of her hand to throw his arms into the air. "No one warned us about this crap—the bog, the smoke—any of it. Which means it's here for us, to prevent us from ever getting to… Zalnic." He was going to say Emma, but caught himself. He sighed, discouraged. "What's it gonna be next?"

Natalie searched his face then looked beyond him. He could see her measuring the distance to their goal. "We've come this far," she said quietly. She stared down at the large gap behind Jack. "Do you think there're more?"

"Why wouldn't there be? I'm sure the ground is full of them to make sure we plummet to our deaths."

Natalie looked directly into his eyes. "I think he's misjudged you, Jack. He expects you're a cocky head-strong teenager with something to prove. But you're not. You're generous and sensitive and considerate."

Jack snorted. "Those things aren't going to keep us alive."

She didn't look away, struggling for an adequate response. Then she said, "You stopped. How did you know there was a hole there?"

"I… I sensed it, I guess."

"Humph. Sensitive. Kept us alive." She smiled triumphantly.

He laughed dismissively, but it still relieved some of his pent up tension. "You must really want to stay if you're reaching that much."

"I'm sure I don't know what you mean," Natalie claimed with mock-offense, grinning. Then her face became serious. "Don't you think you'd sense another one? Because I think you would."

Jack closed his eyes and shook his head. "I would hope so," he finally said with a sigh.

"Then we keep going."

"Fine. Tissues up." Jack covered his nose and mouth, holding his free hand out to Natalie.

Fortunately, he was able to sense the huge fissures dotting the smoky landscape, although the presence of the deadly gaps forced them to zigzag their way toward their destination. It had been quite some time since they skirted around the last crevice. Jack was concentrating so hard on avoiding the next one, he didn't notice the transformation of the smoke until Natalie spoke up. "Am I used to it, or is the burnt smell gone?"

Jack lowered his tissue and breathed in. "No, I think you're right." He stopped and studied the horizon. Silhouettes stood out clearly against the crimson luminosity in the distance. Zalnic's lair. He suppressed an involuntary shiver.

"Is that his... palace?" Natalie stared over his shoulder.

"I think so. Except I was thinking more 'lair.'"

"Yeah." She uttered a strangled laugh. "It sounds more evil. Unfortunately it also sounds scarier."

The smoke thinned and dissipated as they moved forward, leaving them in the dark of a moonless night that was as much a blessing as it was unnerving.

Three times they nearly walked right into the path of a roving beastie. Yet they made better time since the dark allowed them cover to advance quicker. Jack was convinced he'd been right about the bog and the smoke since, from what he could tell, the landscape here closely resembled the area where they'd crossed over. He wasn't sure how it could be darker now than when they'd arrived, without the sun to rise and set. Perhaps this deeper darkness was just another obstacle.

As they drew nearer to their destination, movement became discernible in the weak light emanating from Zalnic's fortress. Sentries, whose forms were unidentifiable at this distance, patrolled a wall which encircled the compound. A structure within the walls protruded at least four stories into the air. If not for the lighted oblong openings, the bulky uneven shape could have been mistaken for another huge rock formation.

"There's no more cover," Natalie murmured as they peered from behind a large boulder. "And it'll get lighter the closer we get to the wall."

"We should be okay with these." Jack fingered the rawhide around his neck. "I've been watching the pattern of the guard. Just to play it safe, we can make a break for the wall while he's on the far side." He traced the path of the sentry for a few more minutes. "Now," he said, and they raced for the wall.

The guard marched upright, on two legs, with an odd loping gait. Though its back was to them as they approached the fortress, the shape of its head was clearly inhuman. Just as they reached the wall, the creature turned toward them and Jack confirmed what he'd suspected, the guard was an Enuuki. He pressed his back into the stone bulwark, pulling Natalie with him. She squeezed his hand painfully and he knew she recognized the creature.

The way the Enuuki seemed to stare at them, tongue lolling from the side of its distinctively canine mouth, sent a chill down Jack's spine. The creature's pointed ears stood straight up, twitching, while its eyes shone red over a long muzzle and maw of sharp teeth. The sentry froze, pulling in its tongue.

Jack's heart thudded in stunned dismay, realizing what those actions indicated—they'd been spotted.

"It's looking at us." Natalie's voice was barely audible.

"Mhm." He released her and inched his hand toward the side pocket of his backpack, fumbling for the opening before locating and extracting his hunting knife.

The hybrid coyote-like guard lowered its head and crept forward, nostrils flared.

Jack removed the sheath from his knife and passed the cover to Natalie without taking his eyes off the creature. She uttered a stifled moan.

The Enuuki bolted forward, teeth bared.

Jack crouched and Natalie let out a panicked squeal.

The creature skidded in its tracks, wary, and lifted its muzzle to sniff the air.

Perplexed at first, comprehension came over Jack like a ray of sunshine. "It doesn't see you," he breathed, and edged away from her.

With a snarl, the beast lunged.

Jack dove and somersaulted between the animal's legs, springing back to his feet and spinning to face the next attack.

He was fast, but the preternatural creature was faster. It pummeled him to the ground, jarring his knife from his grasp. Jack sank his fingers into the Enuuki's neck before it could rip his own throat out. The beast's rough fur pierced his gloves and bit into his skin like rusty metal wire.

"No," Natalie screamed.

The Enuuki looked over its shoulder while keeping Jack pinned. Its head swiveled back and forth searching for the source of the high pitched scream. Finding nothing, its red eyes returned to Jack. The creature's lips were drawn up into a gruesome grin, exposing large canines. A drool of saliva dropped on Jack's cheek.

Natalie came into view, running toward them.

"No," Jack croaked. His arms shook with the strain of holding the creature at bay, but he wouldn't let go now. To his greater alarm, he saw Natalie rip off her necklace and start throwing stones at the Enuuki. What was she thinking? The guard whipped its head around and Jack heaved with all his might, throwing the beast off balance. It yelped and quickly gained its feet.

Sizing up the two targets, the creature bounded after Natalie. She produced a hatchet, took aim and flung it before she turned and ran. The blade actually met its mark, slightly grazing the beast's shoulder. Unfortunately this only fueled its fury. With a low snarl, the Enuuki dropped to all fours and closed the distance.

Jack scrambled to his feet. He retrieved his knife and took off after Natalie. He saw her dump her backpack, causing the creature to dodge and nearly trip.

Taking advantage of the stumble, Jack took two more steps and chucked his knife. The blade sailed through the air and Jack felt a moment of elation as it embedded itself into the guard's back. The brief burst of triumph disappeared when the beast howled in agony.

Jack cringed in alarm. The noise would surely draw reinforcements. "Put your necklace back on," he yelled, passing the fallen beast and heading for Natalie.

"I dropped it," she panted. "With my backpack, I think."

Jack tore his necklace over his head and put it on Natalie.

The Enuuki writhed on the ground and yowled even louder. Jack yanked his knife from its back and slit its throat, careful to wipe the black blood on the beast's wiry coat. Already he could hear a ruckus rising from behind the wall. He collected Natalie's backpack and found her necklace a few feet away. He decided they'd have to sacrifice the hatchet in order to escape.

"Run." Jack pointed to the compound. He followed Natalie. "We've got to get inside. They'll search out here first."

Though the fortress wall was high, not much care had been taken to smooth the outside surface. Jack guessed the attempts to break into hell were few. He stopped where a protrusion formed a sort of ledge partway up. "Ever been rock climbing?"

Natalie shook her head. She looked stunned and clutched her stomach. "I think I'm going to be sick."

"You don't have time." Jack dropped his pack and squatted, bracing his back against the wall. "Climb up me." He forced her to focus on what they were doing so she'd stop thinking about what just happened. "Start here." He patted his thigh. "Then my shoulders. Hurry!"

Natalie blinked. Her expression hardened and she stepped on Jack's thigh. The sound of trampling feet spurred her on. Jack kept one eye on the corner of the wall. When she had both feet on his shoulders, Jack said, "Brace yourself," and he slowly stood up.

Natalie reached for the bulge in the wall and hoisted herself onto it.

"Tell me what's on the other side." Jack shouldered his backpack and began to climb the wall.

"Nothing here, but there's a building or something a little ways down."

"Climb up and head in that direction."

By the time Jack hoisted himself onto the ledge, Natalie straddled the wall. She leaned forward on her arms to scooch along on her butt. Jack scrambled up behind her and followed in a crouch.

Natalie paused when she reached the structure, waiting for Jack to catch up. A moment later he squatted next to her. Although the flat roof was in their favor, the jump entailed more than a simple drop. The considerable space between the building and the wall necessitated a leap outward. "I'll go first." He stood, bent his knees slightly, and launched himself into the air. He landed lightly on his feet just inches from the roof's edge.

Natalie had turned so she was sitting with both legs dangling on the inside of the wall.

"Throw me your pack."

She grimaced, but did as he said, gripping the top of the wall tightly with one hand as she eased the backpack from her shoulders.

Jack caught the pack and set it aside, then opened his arms. "Now you."

Natalie eyeballed the expanse he expected her to cross and then peered at the ground. "Maybe I should take my chances and jump straight down."

Jack shook his head. "No, you'll twist your ankle or break a leg. You don't have to stand up, just squat low on top of the wall so you can push off with your legs. You can do it, Natalie," he encouraged. "You're a runner. Your legs are strong."

She stared at him for a moment, until the spine-chilling scream of a hellcat broke her consternation. Then, flipping one leg back over the wall so she straddled it again, she worked her way from there up to her knees. Turning toward Jack, she pulled her feet under her one at a time.

Jack planted his feet and bent his knees, but as soon as Natalie flung herself outward he knew she wasn't going to make it. She plummeted toward the rough edge of the rooftop with a small squeal. Jack rushed forward and shot his arm out to snag her torso, jerking her to him. They both tumbled backward on the roof.

Natalie rolled off him and lay there for a minute panting, hand on her heart.

"That's not how I thought it would go," Jack said raggedly, "but at least you had a soft landing."

She turned to him and breathed out a shaky laugh. "Yeah, thanks for that."

They fell silent as they heard voices from outside the wall. A raspy, garbled voice barked out something Jack thought was another language until he made out the word 'escaped.' The angry snarl that came in reply, however, needed no interpretation. "All I know is that an alarm was sounded. Anyone or anything roaming the grounds that's not a sentry needs to be brought in for questioning."

Jack met Natalie's eyes. He rolled to his knees and

helped her up. "This makes getting in to see Zalnic easy. I'll let them catch me. But we have to find Emma first."

They dropped off the flat roof and skulked along the perimeter of the wall. Jack wondered if the compound was as it appeared to be—a giant rock formation. Most of the dwellings were hollows bored into stone, reminding Jack of the pictures in his history book of Anasazi cities. The place seemed largely deserted, though there was no telling if the alarm had caused the potential inhabitants to take cover or join the search.

Far from the front gate they came across a smaller version of the stone dwellings with a distinct ghost town quality. "We need to get out of sight," Jack said in a low voice.

Natalie scanned the row of dark openings. She swallowed. "I… I'll go. See if it's safe."

"No. I'm a better fighter." Jack took a step forward but Natalie yanked on his arm.

"But I'm invisible."

He didn't like it, but she was right. Jack crouched behind a patch of black, spiky bushes and watched as Natalie disappeared into the nearest dark hole. His pulse pounded as he waited for her return. A minute later he detected light and then breathed a sigh of relief when she appeared in the doorway. She motioned him inside.

They crept as far back as they could in the cave-like hovel. The dusty stagnant air reeked of decay and despair. Jack knew he couldn't stay there for long without feeling like he was suffocating.

"Ugh," Natalie muttered, covering her nose and mouth with a hand.

"I know. We won't stay long though, just enough time for the excitement to die down so we can look for Emma." Jack took off his backpack and sat against the wall.

Natalie joined him, staying close to his side. "Why did the amulet work for me but not for you?"

"Apparently, I'm not a 'warrior pure of heart.'" His tone was grim. "I initiated this rescue because I wanted to get something out of it."

"Still, it doesn't seem fair. I mean, you're risking your life."

"For my own gain." Jack snorted a bitter laugh. "Except now I'm trying to figure out how to get out of what I thought I wanted."

After a few moments of silence, Natalie spoke up. "So if you changed your mind, why are you still here?"

He was there because he'd told Natalie they'd get Emma back, but he wasn't going to admit it. If he died here, he didn't want her to carry that burden the rest of her life. So he answered generally. "Integrity, I guess. Respect, you know, from my parents, Brody, the sect."

"Honestly, I think you had both of those things before doing this," she said quietly.

"Well, it doesn't really matter if the amulet works for me. If they're bringing intruders in for questioning, I need to be seen."

"After we find Emma."

"Exactly."

As expected, they found Emma in a pit.

Since they hadn't seen any sign of the pits before

taking shelter, they continued along the fortress perimeter. Not far from their Anasazi hide-out, they heard chatter and an occasional shout combined with scrapes and bangs of activity. They crept forward until they reached a low stone wall. Taking advantage of the cover, they hunched down and followed the enclosure in search of the source of the noise.

Jack peered over the stone wall at a settlement of underworld sentries. Unlike the hollowed-out shelters they'd seen elsewhere, the guard's dwellings were built of irregularly shaped stones piled together. About five or six deformed humanoids were erecting a new structure in front of a long, squatty building resembling a stable.

He touched Natalie's shoulder and pointed to the long building. Her face appeared ghostly pale but she nodded without hesitation and crawled back the way they'd come. Once they were out of the sentry's sight, they clambered over the wall. A quick dash brought them behind the stunted structure. They stole along the sidewall until the group of guards came into view. For all the attention the creatures paid to what was going on around them, Jack imagined he and Natalie could have sauntered into the stable-like area unnoticed. As he was about to round the corner, he heard Natalie draw in a sharp breath followed by a muffled squeak. He spun, expecting to see her captured, but she stood alone, with large round eyes over her hand covering her mouth.

"What?" he whispered.

She closed her eyes and breathed deeply, dropping her hand from her face. Then she looked at Jack. "They're... bones. Human."

He peered around the edge of the building. How

could he have missed it? The structure wasn't being built of stone but of human bones—the skulls made it obvious. He swallowed over a lump in his throat and squeezed Natalie's hand. He raised his eyebrows and when she nodded they slipped around the corner.

In the building's gloomy interior, Natalie nearly stumbled into the first pit. She threw her arms out and pinwheeled them for a moment before Jack grabbed the back of her jacket and hauled her backward. "Thanks," she breathed. "I think we found the pits."

Jack crouched down, making sure his flashlight was well past the rim of the hole before he turned it on. The glow of his light reflected off of the stark white bones of a human skeleton. Peering over his shoulder, Natalie dug her fingers into his arm.

"It's old," Jack assured her.

The next pit was empty. They found Emma in the third. The floor of the cavity was furnished with a small three-legged table or stool and a thin mattress atop a layer of hay. Natalie called softly to her friend, but Emma didn't acknowledge the voice or the flashlight. She sat on a ledge carved into the wall, with her face turned toward the dirt. Her knees were drawn up with her arms wrapped around them. She wore a faint smile.

"That's disturbing." Natalie's voice wavered. "She must be delusional. What if I can't get her to come around—or even listen to me?"

Her question revealed a raw fear she'd kept at bay thus far. Jack wrapped his hands around her forearms and gripped them firmly. "All you can do is try." He locked eyes with her. "You didn't come all this way to give up, right?"

She responded with a quick nod. "Right."

He smiled and released her. Then he pulled a bundle of rope from his pack. "Ready?"

At her nod, Jack tied the rope around Natalie's waist. He looped it around the wooden frame of the building and twisted the end on his arm. "The walls look rough, like the wall we scaled to get in. See if you can find hand and foot holds, but if you slip, I've got you."

Natalie nodded but she didn't move. "Jack, I…"

"What? It'll be okay. You can get her back. I know you can."

She shook her head. "It's not that. I feel like I should…"

Jack had a hard time reading her expression in the murky half-light. He waited.

"The kiss… you know, when we crossed over…"

"Yeah. See, that was a great idea. You'll do fine with Emma."

Natalie sighed. "It wasn't an idea, Jack. I thought you were going to go through without me. I didn't know if I'd ever see you again. That's why I kissed you."

"Oh."

Even in the low light, she must have been able to make out the dumbfounded look on his face because she actually laughed a little. "I just wanted you to know," she said softly.

His brain worked to put together a response though he could hardly process what she was trying to convey. "Thanks, I… I'm glad you told me."

"Okay. Now I'm ready." She sat down on the lip of the hole, flipped over on her belly, and began wriggling down. Jack backed up and pulled the rope taut. Natalie met his eyes and then slipped over the edge. He pushed her recent revelation to the back of his mind—this wasn't the time to get distracted.

Jack slowly let the rope play out. He wished he could watch her progress, but to have the best leverage, he needed to stand back from the edge. If she slipped, he'd feel it. When the rope went slack, he'd know she reached the bottom.

He debated on leaving the rope behind. The area must be patrolled periodically. The rope would raise questions, possibly give Natalie away. Jack gazed out toward the tall citadel in the center of the compound. No doubt that's where he'd find Zalnic. He may need the rope to escape. Then he shook his head. He'd find alternatives. If he took the rope from the pit, Natalie would have no way out if he didn't make it back. He had to make sure she had every chance to leave this place alive. The thought of her trapped at the bottom of the dark cavity caused a lump in the back of his throat.

He should have said something before Natalie went over the edge—told her how much he cared—but he wasn't prepared. He'd just have to make sure he got the chance later.

The rope jerked and Jack gripped it tightly, leaning back. In his mind's eye he pictured Natalie dangling at the end and scrambling for purchase on the rock wall. Finally the strain on the rope eased. Jack counted to ten and then continued the feed until the line went slack.

After confirming that Natalie had, indeed, reached the bottom, Jack secured the rope to the frame of the building. Then he kneeled at the edge of the pit. Natalie had pulled a small electric lantern from her pack and turned it on. She saw Jack and gave him a thumbs-up. He pointed to the rope, giving it a jiggle. Then he pointed to her and Emma and walked his fingers up the rope. She nodded.

He was about to get up when he thought Natalie said something. He paused and waited for a repeat. This time he read her lips. "Be careful," she mouthed.

He gave her a thumbs-up, then a quick wave. He watched for a moment as she extracted a large binder from the bag.

Photo album. Jack hoped it worked.

He turned toward the center of the compound and once again sized up the citadel. Then he dodged around the side of the building and made for the low stone wall. He intended to be caught as far away from Natalie as possible.

Jack crouched on the side of a structure behind the citadel, eavesdropping on the guards' conversation inside. Oddly, the shed-like outbuilding appeared to be constructed of wood, though what kind of wood, Jack couldn't say. The boards seemed charred, as if pulled from a fire. He swiped a finger across the matte black surface, surprised when his glove didn't come away with a smudge of ash. Remembering the quarters built of human bones, he decided not to ponder the black wood further.

"... didn't find nothin' so we checked the prisoner."

Jack's heart skipped a beat. Oh God, no. Natalie. The rope would give her away!

"Everything was status quo, so we think it might be somebody coming in, not out." The voice cackled. "Go figure. Anyway, we've been ordered to search the grounds thoroughly."

209

Jack breathed a small sigh of relief—apparently the guards had checked on Emma before Jack and Natalie found her. But Natalie would no doubt be discovered during the next search. He'd better get caught and cut off the hunt before it went any further.

His keyed up muscles twitched as adrenaline surged through his veins. He took a couple of deep breaths, contemplating his next move. Then, trying to block out the ramifications of what he was about to do, Jack rounded the corner and stepped into the guard shack. His eyes went round with fear and then he darted back out at a full run.

He had to make this believable.

Though he'd had only the briefest glance inside the rough shelter where the guards sat, he had no problem appearing terrified. The sentries inside looked like men—hideously disfigured men—but not beasts. A rotund figure sat at a table jawing on a bone in a shape that Jack was happy not to have the time to identify. The pudgy hands gripping the obviously raw piece of carcass seemed to have as many stumps as full digits. Jack's impression of the guard draped on a chair tipped back against the wall was that the left side of his face appeared melted. His left eye socket was merely a sag of skin.

A yelp, followed by the sounds of a scramble, convinced Jack they'd taken the bait. He took off in the opposite direction of the prisoner pits.

Allowing himself to be captured would be one of the hardest things he'd ever had to do. There was no guarantee the orders hadn't changed to 'kill intruders on sight.' He also had to assume he'd come to some kind of bodily harm—a daunting thought with the bruises

210

from his last beating not yet faded.

Jack dashed behind a building and pressed himself against the wall, panting. Then he edged to the corner and peered back the way he came. As soon as he saw the one-eyed guard, he broke cover, grimacing at the glimpse he'd caught of the cudgel in his fist. He was contemplating whether he should slow, or trip, or look for a dead end, when Pudgy seemed to come out of nowhere. The guard threw something, and the next thing Jack knew his legs were tangled in a rope and his ankle screamed in agony as he crashed to the ground.

He decided to play possum, hoping to avoid a fight. Pudgy boasted to One-eye of his prowess with his handmade bola. "Yeah, yeah, it worked because I herded 'im to ya," One-eye argued. "Likes of you woulda never caught up to 'im." His cackle sounded more like a smoker's hack.

The toe of a shabby boot nudged Jack's hip experimentally. "He landed hard," Pudgy assured his partner. Then a cruel kick landed in the soft part of his torso. Jack gritted his teeth to stifle a grunt and willed his muscles to remain limp.

"Tie 'im up then."

Heavy breathing accompanied the guard's actions as he stripped Jack of his backpack and bent to pull his arms from under his body. He roughly dropped one wrist on top of the other behind Jack's back and began to twist a rope around them.

Jack's heart hammered in alarm while his brain triggered fight or flight instincts which he struggled to suppress. Then he was rolled to his side and slapped firmly on the cheek. "Wake up Laddie. It's your lucky day." One-eye's fetid breath alone was enough to get

Jack to move. He groaned and fluttered his eyelids before opening them fully.

"On yer feet, Sunshine." As the one-eyed guard prodded him with his club, Jack managed to roll to his knees and stand up. Pudgy stood in front of Jack, winding his bola around his fat fist. "Whatcha crazy boy? Don't get too many intruders down here."

Jack said nothing.

One-eye wacked him behind his knees. "Git movin.'"

The guards led him inside the citadel. Though it was what Jack intended, he found he had to force one foot in front of the other. His hesitation didn't go unnoticed—the backs of his legs would be black and blue. Immediately inside the doors was an area reminiscent of a church vestibule. The entry doors swung closed behind the small group with a clang that rang out like certain doom. Barely visible in the muted light, large double doors dominated the center of the inner wall with a single door to either side. Pudgy opened the door on the left and waited while One-eye prodded Jack through.

A fire blazed in a small hearth, spreading a welcome warmth throughout the room. As Jack entered, a man rose to his feet in front of a door at the opposite end of the chamber. Instead of hair, the top of the man's head was mottled in shades of black and red. He opened his mouth, but before he could say anything, he saw One-eye behind Jack.

"Inform the master. We've caught the intruder."

The next few minutes seemed to stretch into hours as Jack waited, terrified, for his audience with the lord of souls. They left him alone in the room, though he had no doubt all doors were locked or guarded—or both. Eventually the man with the mottled head returned. "He'll see you now." He showed no expression—not even malevolence—while reaching into his tunic to remove a jagged blade. Jack shrank back as the guard stepped behind him. Bony fingers gripped Jack's forearm and he tensed, heart hammering wildly. There was a jerk on the rope binding his hands and then his arms swung free. That he was allowed to approach Zalnic unbound was particularly unnerving.

As he passed into the next chamber, a low growl raised the hair on the back of Jack's neck. Protruding from the dark recesses, he made out a coyote-like muzzle dripping with saliva. A motion from the guard shushed the beast and then he extended his arm out into the cavernous room beyond and gazed dully back at Jack.

Jack shuffled forward. Chunky black columns rose to the ceiling. As he emerged between them, he saw an identical row lined the opposite side of the room. Centered between the rows of columns, at the far end of the large room, Zalnic's empty throne stood on a dais.

Every sect member grew up hearing stories of the underworld god who reposed in a seat built of human bones. But unlike the roughly assembled outbuildings built by the guards, this structure was comprised of intricate work and delicate pieces. Jack gaped at the skulls which served as ornamentation, selectively placed at the top corners of the seat back as well as at the end of the arms. As he drew closer, revulsion churned in his stomach and threatened to climb up the back of his throat at the realization that the bones and skulls were too small to be adult.

"Welcome, Shifter." The voice issued from the black recess behind the throne. Zalnic's fiery red eyes materialized and the shadows seemed to coalesce until they fashioned the rough shape of a man. The crescent shape which composed the top of his angular head rose into peaks on either side, forming horns. The lord of the dead relaxed on his throne and watched Jack approach. When Jack stopped a respectful distance from the dais, the ruler of the underworld spoke again. "Jack Ironwood, I presume?" His voice rasped with the quality of gravel on cement.

That Zalnic knew who he was didn't surprise Jack, but the sound of his name coming from the lips of the underworld god made his blood run cold. All the things he'd planned to say turned to ash on his tongue.

Zalnic raised his eyebrows, causing his horns to twitch, an uncomfortable reminder of the specter's nature. "So… Jack—if I may call you Jack?" He didn't wait for an answer. "You realize you're quite late for the summer solstice?" He rose from his throne, disturbing the darkness from which he was made. Shadows trailed behind him like the train of a bridal gown as he stepped off the dais. "And for that matter, quite far from the artifact caves as well. If you're simply lost, perhaps I can direct you out?"

As the lord of souls approached, Jack's nose was assaulted with the odor of burnt ruins. Nothing like the familiar smell of summer campfires or smoldering autumn leaves, but the lingering odor after a house fire or a car crash—the stench of tragedy and loss. Repulsion inhibited his need to breathe and his hand rose unconsciously to his throat.

Yes. Yes, he wanted out.

Then his fingers brushed the brimstone amulet under his jacket, jarring him into a moment of clarity. "I intend to leave, but I expect to take the girl back with me."

"You brought a girl with you?"

Panic squeezed his chest. "Of course not." Jack pushed for a haughty tone to cover the blatant lie. "You know very well I'm talking about the girl you stole from the living world."

"On the contrary, I have no idea what you're talking about. I assure you, I have not stolen anyone." Zalnic paced leisurely, stroking his chin.

"A witness saw your Enuuki take her."

"Really?" Zalnic stopped to face Jack. "Come on Jack, seriously? Any sort of pedophile or serial killer could wear a mask. I hear these disguises can be quite extraordinary these days."

"It would take more than a mask to look like an Enuuki."

The underlord shook his head, and the moving shadows distorted his features for a moment. "Mmm. The memories of witnesses can often be faulty. Children go missing frequently—I suggest you speak to your local law enforcement."

"No. The frequency of missing children is your cover. I'm taking the girl back to the living world and I expect you to release her soul." Jack was careful not to use Emma's name. He didn't want Zalnic to think he had personal ties to the prisoner—he wanted the transaction to remain businesslike.

Zalnic stopped moving and regarded Jack for a moment. "All right. For your satisfaction I will question my Enuuki. But I ask you this, if an Enuuki did take a living girl—without my permission, of course—what

215

makes you think you can march in here, demand that I give her to you, and still get out alive?" His eyes malevolently elongated into the shape of flames as the dark lord inclined his head toward Jack.

Steeling himself not to back down, Jack responded defiantly, "I know your game."

The underlord narrowed his eyes. "My game?" The words rumbled from his throat, soft and low.

"You're stealing souls from other gods."

Zalnic spun on his foot and laughed, but Jack thought he'd caught a flicker of surprise in the glowing embers of the demon's eyes. "If that were true, surely I'd have heard from these other gods. Yet I haven't received any complaints."

"Because you take those who haven't sworn their souls to another. Those souls would rightfully end up in the underworld of their ancestors. You're circumventing this by taking them while they're still alive."

The lord of the underworld spun to face Jack, staring him down for a long moment. "Well, well. Aren't you the clever one?" The god's voice dropped an octave. "Too bad you'll never see the light of day again." The statement ended with a snarl.

Jack's heart thrummed and a sheen of sweat beaded along his hairline, but he stood his ground. "That would be a mistake. My death will bring the wrath of the other gods down on you—starting with those who own the girl you stole. Odin will not be pleased, and Hel, queen of the Norse underworld, will surely declare war on you."

From behind Jack, a door scraped open and then closed. He turned sideways, unwilling to have his back to either the approaching underling or to the dark lord.

216

A figure emerged from the shadows. As it bowed to the ruler, Jack realized it was an Enuuki. "Ah, Megedagik," Zalnic said. "A question." He motioned for the creature to follow him and they retreated from Jack.

The conversation took only a minute or two and then Zalnic waved the creature away. His burning eyes settled on Jack, boring into his soul. After what seemed half of eternity, he finally spoke. "Megedagik informs me a girl was taken recently. Perhaps we can come to an agreement. I release her soul, and you forget your allegations."

Jack didn't care for the sly smile Zalnic wore—a knowing smile. Striking a bargain shouldn't have been this easy. He'd studied Norse mythology—been prepared to argue. Still, this was exactly what he'd hoped to achieve. "Agreed." Jack felt more uneasy than triumphant.

"Let's seal it in blood." Suddenly the underlord had a dagger in his hand. He held out his hand, palm up, and sliced into it with a small groan of satisfaction. He pointed the dripping knife at Jack. "Next?"

The image of Kyle's artificial limb thumping on the table generated a surge of panic and Jack's heart pounded in warning. Using Zalnic's blade on his own skin was not an option. His thoughts raced, considering alternatives. Although they'd stripped him of his backpack, he could demand his own knife. Still, the underlord would expect their blood to mingle. Jack struggled not to shudder visibly at the thought of the demon's blood directly on his skin. His brain switched gears to the ramifications of refusing the blood affirmation.

The glowing orbs in Zalnic's eye sockets flared as he stared Jack down. His blood overflowed his black palm, the drops pattering to the stone floor. "Second thoughts, Shifter?" The raspy voice sounded equally amused and annoyed.

Jack hadn't let on that Emma had any personal significance to him, therefore Zalnic should have more to lose if they didn't make this agreement. "I don't need to spill blood to confirm my word. A handshake is sufficient." He offered his gloved hand.

A growl rumbled from Zalnic's throat and, for a moment, Jack thought he'd made a poor judgment call. Then, sneering, Zalnic engulfed Jack's hand in a vice-like grip. Icy cold permeated his glove and stung Jack's skin as if he'd gripped something metal barehanded on a sub-zero winter day. The petulant attitude emanating from the lord of souls made Jack wonder if the blood oath had been the reason for Zalnic's smugness while they bargained. No. The satisfaction gained from such a small act of cruelty must be trivial to the lord of the underworld. Jack's gut feeling of suspicion remained.

His cynicism was substantiated by Zalnic's next words.

"Bring in the prisoner!"

CHAPTER 11

The Rescue

A cold slice of fear cut through Jack as the door again scraped open.

Megedagik entered with a girl slung over his shoulder. He dumped her on the ground at Jack's feet. Zalnic approached and laid a hand on her shoulder. She jerked and then rolled to her back with a moan as Jack fought to calm his racing heart. Her eyes fluttered open.

It was Emma.

"Where... where am I?" she mumbled. "Who're you?"

Jack bent down, hiding his alarm. If Emma was here, what happened to Natalie? He swallowed hard. "My name is Jack. And I'm going to get you out of here."

This was not part of the plan. Once Zalnic agreed to release Emma's soul, Jack was going to admit to the underlord that he'd already stashed her in a safe place. Now he had no way of knowing Natalie's fate. Had she been caught helping Emma escape?

Emma rose to her elbows unsteadily and then sank back to the floor. With a hateful glare at Zalnic, Jack helped her sit, pulled her arm around his shoulder and drew her to her feet.

The underworld god smirked and shrugged his shoulders.

Jack pressed his lips together to keep from asking questions about Natalie. There was a slim chance she was safe, and until he knew differently, he wasn't going to slip up and put her in jeopardy. He turned with Emma shuffling next to him and headed for the door.

"Megedagik, escort them to the Void."

Jack froze at the words and looked back over his shoulder. "Our deal?"

Zalnic laughed. "Is sealed by our handshake. I'm doing you a favor. It's the fastest way back to the living world."

Megedagik strode past Jack and Emma to the door. As he passed, Emma shrank against Jack with a small whimper. The Enuuki opened the door and barked out orders Jack didn't catch, then stood waiting, his smoldering eyes marking their slow progress. By the time they made it outside, a vehicle had been parked at the front of the citadel.

In the murky half-light, Jack's first thought was of a go-cart. The contraption had two large tires on the back with a smaller tire in front. Completely open, even the small motor in front of the cockpit was exposed. The passenger compartment resembled a crate made from the same black wood Jack had noticed earlier.

The Enuuki gestured toward the vehicle. Jack didn't like it, yet he had a reason to believe Zalnic spoke the truth—Eric remembered being hurled into an abyss. Thing was, he had to get Megedagik off their back so he could find Natalie. He scrambled for a solution as he helped Emma into the back of the cart.

The vehicle left the compound from a side gate and Jack tried his best to pay attention to the surroundings so he could get back to the fortress. He noticed there was no sign of smoke in any direction. When the vehicle stopped, Zalnic's lair remained a distinct glow on the horizon. The Enuuki growled at them from the driver's seat, motioning for them to get out, and at the sound, Emma buried her face in Jack's chest. He held her for a moment, making low, soothing noises. "Come on, let's get out of here," he whispered.

Once they were on their feet, the Enuuki herded them toward a vast opening many times larger than the crevices Jack and Natalie had dodged on the way to the fortress. Jack turned to Megedagik. "Okay, we're good. You can go now."

The creature stood unmoving, its red eyes radiant in the dimness.

With Emma clinging to him, Jack sat down near the edge of the abyss to demonstrate their intention to leave. The hole was made up of unearthly blackness. Past the lip of the chasm, Jack could see nothing, not even walls. The space seemed the polar opposite of existence. He made a last attempt to get rid of their escort. "Just go, dude. You're scaring her."

The Enuuki opened its muzzle, forming a nightmarish grin. Then it lifted its clawed foot and shoved Jack over the edge. He yelled as he plummeted into the void and heard Emma's scream follow as she, too, catapulted into space.

Chirping crickets rang in Jack's ears. Flat on his back, he scanned the canopy of trees above him, his nose picking up the smell of campfires. Fallen leaves rustled nearby. He sat up and saw Emma struggling to do the same, fear and confusion knotting her brow. Behind her, the silhouette of a camper was visible through the trees.

They were back.

He wanted to wail in despair. Natalie. Oh God, no. He'd left her behind in the underworld.

Propped up on her hands, Emma studied him warily.

"I'm a friend of Natalie's," he said, unsure what she remembered. "You remember who Natalie is?"

She nodded and he caught the gleam of tears pooling in her eyes.

"It's okay," he murmured. Inside, he was screaming that it was not okay. He blinked rapidly to chase away the sting in his own eyes. His knee-jerk reaction was to leave Emma with some nearby campers—he remembered a site in particular with kid's bikes and colorful lights out front that should be safe—and he'd descend back into the underworld and find Natalie. Rising to his feet, he lifted his face to search the sky. His heart sank when he detected the gray light of dawn creeping over the eastern horizon.

He swore under his breath.

The window was closed. He'd have to wait for the next moonrise.

He helped Emma to her feet. "Come on." He spoke with quiet resignation. "I'll take you home."

The rearview mirror reflected the blinding light of the rising sun, though Jack barely noticed. He careened onto a dirt road and floored it. Natalie's car skidded

222

over gravel as he turned into Brody's driveway.

His adviser must have heard the car because Brody opened the door before Jack knocked. "Jack! You made it back." He knotted the belt to his robe, the excitement in his eyes dying as he got a good look at his student's face. "What happened?" He guided Jack inside with a hand on his shoulder.

"I need to get back. Now. I can't wait until tonight. Is there a way?" Jack babbled, finally allowing his panic to surface.

"Slow down, Jack." Brody pushed him into a chair and made him wait while he retrieved a glass of water and handed it to him. "Okay, now tell me what happened so I can help you."

"Natalie's still there. In the underworld." The surprised look on his teacher's face nearly pushed Jack over the edge. He put the untouched water on a side table and buried his head in his hands, hitching in a breath. The homey smell of coffee and toast intensified his despair. "I left her. I didn't have a choice." His encounter with Zalnic had played over and over in his head enough times to convince Jack that Natalie was surely a prisoner in the underworld. He relayed the night's events in a monotone voice. "It shouldn't have been that easy." He avoided meeting his adviser's gaze. "How could I be stupid enough to think he was just going to let me go?"

"But you brought back the other girl?"

"Yeah, I pretty much left her on her doorstep." Good thing Natalie had pointed out Emma's house. He stayed with Emma on the porch until the lights in the foyer came on and then he'd melted into the shadows. Even her mother's cry of joy couldn't crack his shell of remorse. He'd achieved nothing—merely traded one girl for another.

"Jack, you don't know for sure if Natalie was captured."

Jack pictured Zalnic's sly smile, the whispered conversation with Megedagik. "She was," he muttered. "Zalnic won."

"Not if you get her back."

Jack finally looked Brody in the eyes. He straightened in his chair and let his head bump against the back. "Sure. But I need to go back now. Is there a way?" He didn't dare to hope. He knew the answer.

"Not physically. Only in spirit."

"So I wouldn't be able to rescue her."

"No, but you may be able to help her rescue herself."

Jack brought his head forward. "Show her the way?" A spark of optimism ignited inside him and he nodded thoughtfully. His brain broke free of the numbness, exploring the idea. "Yeah, it could work. I could check the way ahead to make sure she wouldn't get caught, maybe cause a distraction or something." Then he frowned. "I'm not sure if I can find the void again, though."

"Then lead her somewhere safe and descend tonight in the flesh to bring her back."

Jack cocked his head sideways, raising his eyebrows. "Okay. Yeah. It's certainly worth a try. She has to know I haven't abandoned her."

"All right, so our next problem is that you're not prepared to spirit-walk."

"Right. No time to fast and meditate. But I thought David told me there are other ways. You know how, don't you?"

His adviser deflected Jack's question. "Also, you can't spirit-walk to a living entity. You'll need to seek the guidance of a soul—preferably an ancestor."

"Okay."

"Without meditation to call your ancestor, you'll need some kind of link—like a possession of the person—and there still is a chance you won't make contact."

"Whatever. I have to try."

Brody nodded. "We can try to induce the trance. But you realize, Jack, it's dangerous doing it that way? Men have left and never returned to their bodies."

Jack met the older shifter's eyes with his own unwavering stare. "It's a chance I'm willing to take."

CHAPTER 12

Spirit-Walk

Jack took a swallow of the bitter brew Brody gave him. The tea was barely reminiscent of seekers tea, which he usually enjoyed, but he drank it quickly without flinching and placed the empty cup on the table. He'd been relieved to find his house empty when he arrived to retrieve his grandfather's tincture pouch; still, the time it took to drive there, find the pouch and then drive back already seemed too great a delay.

"Will you call my dad at the shop and let him know what's going on?"

"Of course."

Jack perched on the edge of the chair, his knee bouncing restlessly. "How long before it kicks in?"

The older man shrugged. "Just lie down on the couch, relax. Impatience and anxiety will only be counterproductive."

Jack did as his adviser instructed, stuffing a pillow under his head and drawing in a deep breath. He let the air out slowly, trying to force his stiff muscles to go limp. Brody handed him the worn leather bag Jack's grandfather had used to carry various medicines. "You're calling on your grandfather?"

Jack nodded. "I've asked for his advice before. I think he'll be easiest for me to contact."

"All right. Close your eyes. Seek your grandfather and when you find him, show him Natalie."

"Show him?"

Brody touched Jack's forehead. "Here."

Jack closed his eyes and began the practiced exercise of mentally retreating inside himself in order to enter another realm. He pictured his grandfather—the tanned face, severe cheek bones and somber eyes. As a small child, Jack was at first afraid of his mother's father, until he learned that with a smile, he could make his grandfather's eyes sparkle. The man had taught Jack many lessons, and when he died, a piece of Jack's heart went with him.

All at once, a wave of vertigo spun the images in Jack's mind. He dug his fingers into the nappy fabric of the couch cushion and then felt a strong grip steady him. "Show me." No words, no sound, but his grandfather's message came through loud and clear. The image of his grandfather dissolved as Jack pictured Natalie driving, on their way to Harbor Springs. The mental rendering was as crystal clear as Wes's high definition television.

Caught up in the remembrance, Jack composed a montage of his favorite Natalie moments. Like the way she instantly came to his aid the night he got beat up at the coffee shop—screeching to a stop in the middle of the street and flying out of the car with the door hanging open behind her. The slight flush to her cheeks when she said she'd love to be his girlfriend. The feel of her soft and gentle fingertips as she applied make-up to his black eyes. The warmth of her hand in his...

"Jack? Oh my God, Jack, is that you?"

Wait. When did she say that? Jack didn't remember

this. He felt a poke on his leg. Brody? Jack frowned and opened his eyes.

He peered through a dusky haze into Natalie's shocked face and blinked repeatedly, disoriented.

Natalie backed away, her red, puffy eyes wide with terror.

Jack pushed up from the cold stone floor. "I made it." He stared at Natalie in disbelief. They were in a tiny room—a cell by the looks of it—dimly lit by a flickering light that emanated through a square opening in the door.

"You can't be Jack." Although Natalie had her back pressed against the far wall, the space was so small Jack would only have had to lean forward to touch her. "I heard them torture you." She sniffed, as tears welled in her eyes. "They told me you were dead. You and Emma," she said in a wavering voice, oblivious of the droplet that escaped her eye and ran down her cheek.

"It's not true." Jack wanted to reach out and dry her tears, comfort her, but first he had to convince her he wasn't a ghost—or a fraud. "They tricked you, Natalie—to break you down. I got Emma out. She's safe with her parents. I wanted to find you, but they kicked us out—literally," he added bitterly. "I couldn't come back. The moon had set."

Natalie pushed herself harder against the wall and eyed Jack suspiciously. She hugged her knees close. "But you just... suddenly appeared out of nowhere," she whispered.

"Because I'm only here in spirit—I'm spirit-walking. I'm actually on Brody's couch."

The only change in her expression was a few added worry lines that furrowed her brow. "Okay, I'll prove I'm me," Jack offered. "Ask me something only I should know."

Natalie narrowed her eyes, thinking for a moment. "Who is Jase?"

The corners of his mouth lifted. "My six-year-old brother. But that's too easy, be more specific."

"All right. What's Jase's favorite car?"

He replied immediately. "1968 Monte Carlo SS, black with white racing stripes."

The lines on her forehead smoothed out and Natalie raised an eyebrow. "My locker number?"

"Let's see, right of me so 328."

"What did you have for lunch last Saturday?"

He thought back. Saturday was the day they went to Harbor Springs. They stopped at a diner and he ordered…"Club sandwich. At a diner—with you."

"Okay… one more." She'd stopped hugging her legs and rested her gloved hands on her knees. "How did we get here?"

Jack hesitated. The question could have a couple of different answers, although he was pretty certain she was already convinced. He decided on a two-part response. "We shifted at the ancient burial mounds."

Natalie tentatively stretched her hand out and touched his foot. "If you're here in spirit, how come I can feel you?"

"Because we're both from the living world."

"I don't understand, but I don't really care." She unexpectedly sprang forward and threw her arms around Jack. He recovered quickly from the surprise and extracted his arms from her embrace so he could hug her back. "You were wrong, you know." The words were muffled; she'd buried her face in his shoulder.

"What do you mean, wrong?"

"The burial mounds. That's not really *how* we got here." She pulled away, just enough to look into his eyes.

She was in his arms, her face inches from his, so Jack gave her the answer she was looking for. He realized, as he leaned down and pressed his lips on hers, how many times he'd thought about this over the past few days. At some point what he wanted had changed, yet he stubbornly clung to his old aspirations. He could no longer deny his feelings, though—kissing Natalie felt so right.

"Yep. It is you." She spoke softly, a blush coloring her too-pale cheeks.

"Now that we've established that," he said, feeling his own face flush, "we gotta figure out how to get you out of here." He reluctantly released her to examine the small cell. "Do you know where you are in the compound? They didn't..."

She shook her head. "They marched me down here. They weren't nice about it, but they didn't knock me out or anything. We're in the bottom of the citadel."

Of course. Zalnic knew better than to put her in one of the pits. "Did they discover you with Emma?" Jack turned to the door and crouched down to examine the lock.

"Yeah. On the rope, after I'd finally convinced her to climb up. There was nothing I could do at that point—nowhere to run, nowhere to hide."

"Were you wearing the brimstone?"

She was quiet for a moment and Jack glanced over his shoulder at her. She stared at the ground. "I put it on Emma. She was in front of me on the rope. When they pulled it up—"

"They felt her."

Natalie nodded, her eyes still downcast.

Jack swore. "I should've given you mine. It's not like it was doing me any good." He scrubbed his face with a hand. "Man, I totally botched this whole operation."

"Stop it, Jack." Natalie put a hand on his shoulder. "I didn't think of it either. Besides, what I did didn't make much sense either. For one, she was in front of me, so once they saw me, they'd find her, and two, there'd be no surprise at seeing Emma in the pit. They would've never had to know I was down there with her."

Although everything Natalie said was true, none of it would've mattered had both girls been wearing brimstone. Belaboring their mistakes, however, was a waste of time so Jack didn't voice his protest. He reached to his neck. At least he could give her his amulet now.

Except his neck was bare.

"What the—" he sat back on his feet and groaned.

"What?" Natalie shuffled over on her knees, her eyes on the door.

"I was going to give you my necklace now, but it didn't travel with me." He felt his pockets and shook his head, frowning. "Nothing did." He sighed heavily. "Whatever. Let's start with trying to get this door open. Did they search you? Do you have anything on you?"

Natalie pulled her gloves off to thrust her hands into her jacket pockets. "They didn't search me at all, actually. They just threw me in here." She produced the packet of tissue, a flashlight and a pouch of bandages. Then she fished a pink Swiss Army knife from her jeans pocket. "Sorry, I put most of the stuff in my backpack."

"I'm just happy they underestimated you." Jack wore a grim smile as he picked up the knife. "Okay, here's the deal. My spirit-walk was directed at you, so I'm here only to you. To anyone—or anything—else here, I don't exist. I can use things from the living world," he nodded to the knife as he pulled it open, "but I will pass through anything else."

He turned to the door and slid the blade between the door frame and jamb. He wiggled the knife up and down, but the latch held fast. "Mmm, I need something else." His eyes flicked to her hair. "You're not wearing a hair clip, are you?"

Natalie started to shake her head and then her eyebrows shot up. "Wait." Pink spots bloomed on her cheeks as she slipped her hand inside her shirt. A few seconds later she held out a bobby pin which, Jack assumed, had been fastened to her bra. "Sometimes outfits don't have pockets," she explained before Jack could ask any questions. "I have a hair elastic too." She snapped the band she wore on her wrist like a bracelet.

Jack took the hair pin and spread the prongs until they were nearly flat. With his left hand, he poked the bobby pin into the key hole. His right hand held the knife blade against the latch. Concentrating mainly on the bobby pin's exploration of the keyhole, he intermittently pushed against the catch.

"So... how is it that you know how to pick a lock?"

Jack chuckled. "I was a curious kid. If it was locked, I assumed there was good stuff inside—I wanted in. Made it challenging for my parents at Christmastime."

A few jabs later, Jack was rewarded with a distinct click. He pressed the knife blade against the latch and the door swung inward.

Natalie held up her hand for a high-five and Jack tapped her fingers. "Unfortunately that was probably the easy part," he admitted. "I'm going to look around and find out where the guards are stationed, then I'll come back."

"Okay, hurry."

Jack slipped out the door into a corridor dimly lit by torches set in wall sconces. To the left was deep blackness. To the right, three separate flames flickered along the passage, so he headed in that direction first. A few other doors lined the corridor on either side. He heard an occasional scuffle as he passed and told himself the noise must be rats. He didn't want to imagine alternate possibilities and refused to contemplate the putrid smell coming from some of the cells.

Just beyond the last torch, the corridor turned right and became an open stairwell. Yellow light spilled from the space above and voices echoed downward as Jack mounted the steps. Although he knew the truth of his spiritual invisibility, his heart thumped at an increased rate as he poked his head above floor level. Two disfigured men sat a table tossing dice. Jack frowned. Getting Natalie through here would be tricky.

He returned to Natalie's cell, retrieved her flashlight and turned left this time into the dark end of the corridor, hoping there was another way out. Not too far down the hallway, though, he reached a dead end. On the way back to the cell, Jack pondered how to get Natalie through the guard room. As a visiting spirit, he couldn't fight, so he had to lure the guards out. Basically, create a distraction. While mulling over possible scenarios, his gaze fell to the flashlight in his hand and he was struck by an encouraging thought—he couldn't fight directly, but he could use the things Natalie had with her.

Back in her cell, they devised a plan.

"It's going to work," Jack said, reading the apprehension in her face. "Are you ready?"

Natalie put on a brave smile that didn't match her frightened eyes. "As I'll ever be."

Positioning himself in the corner at the base of the stairwell, Jack nodded to Natalie. She bent to the ground and skidded her pocket knife across the stone floor toward him. The rasping sound echoed loudly down the hallway.

As anticipated, a voice sounded from above. "What in the heck was that?"

Jack quickly stooped, slipped the knife into his pocket and then got out the cord he'd pulled from the bottom of Natalie's coat and entwined it around each hand. Natalie dodged back into her cell, leaving the door noticeably ajar.

Jack's elevated heartbeat bumped up another notch at the sound of a wooden chair scraping on stone—a guard was on the way. Footsteps grated across the floor and then clumped down the stairs. A dilapidated shoe appeared first, the sole ripped from the upper to expose toes that appeared to be rotting. Then, legs clad in pants too filthy to determine what they might be made from carried into view a rotund, hairy belly which protruded from beneath a greasy t-shirt. When the pockmarked face appeared, Jack was not surprised to see the man was missing an ear.

He let the guard pass and turn the corner, hoping he'd notice the open cell door. When the man paused, Jack stepped forward and tossed the cord over the guard's head, crossing the ends and yanking hard against the guy's throat. The sentry's hands flew up in a futile attempt to get what few fingers he still had under the string, but Jack held fast as the man thrashed and kicked.

"What's going on down there, eh?" guard number two shouted from the top of the stairs.

Fearing the other guard would come barreling down the stairs and save the floundering man in front of him, Jack tugged viciously. But the intermittent scrape and crunch from the stairwell told him the remaining sentry was advancing tentatively. As the guy in Jack's grasp finally crumpled to the floor, he let go of one end of the cord, stuffed it into his pocket and got out the knife.

Guard number two's tall, gaunt frame advanced slowly around the corner, slightly hindered by the length of wood which made up his lower left leg. A large spiked club, gripped in his bony hands, hovered over his shoulder like a baseball bat. With barely a glance at his partner's body, he continued down the hallway. When the man reached the door to Natalie's cell and paused outside to listen, Jack jabbed the knife into his back. The guard stumbled forward with a yell as Natalie swung the door open, allowing the man to fall to the ground.

Jack nodded to Natalie and she kicked the guy in the head, wincing as her foot made contact. She turned away and clutched her stomach with a retching sound. Jack touched her arm. "They're already dead," he reminded her.

His words also raised the thought that the downside of dealing with the dead was that you couldn't kill them, so they'd better hurry. Jack retrieved the knife from the man's back, motioning for Natalie to accompany him back into the corridor. He breathed a sigh of relief to see the first guard was still down. Natalie stared with revulsion at the man on the ground. "Thank God for gloves," she mumbled, bending to grasp the man's pudgy hands. She tugged. The body jerked, but hardly moved. Natalie grunted as she doubled her effort.

Jack paced, feeling helpless, but he couldn't touch the guards. His hands were tied. He could only act with—

Tied.

The cord!

"Here." Jack knotted the cord around one of the guard's wrists and then the other. He grabbed the length of string between them. "I'll pull, you push."

Natalie picked up the man's feet, turning her head slightly and lifting her chin to avoid smelling or examining them, then crouched down and shoved as Jack pulled. A moan issued from the cell and Natalie's eyes widened in her pale face. Jack guessed she received the same terror-fueled adrenaline rush that he did, because the heavy body shifted into motion. Scooting their load a few feet each time, they were able to heave the rotund body into the tiny cell. The scrawny man stirred and moaned again. "Quick," Jack whispered, retrieving the cord and setting the lock. Natalie dodged into the corridor, pulling the door closed behind her.

Jack led the way up the stairs, pausing to inspect the guard room before waving Natalie forward. Then he crossed to a closed door and listened for a moment. He turned to Natalie. "Wait here. I'll see where it goes." He passed through to find a spiral staircase leading upward. He took the steps two at a time. The arched entryway at the top of the stairs opened directly to the vestibule of the citadel. Zalnic had beefed up his security, posting sentries at each of the four doors leading to the throne room.

He returned to the guard room where Natalie waited, fidgeting with her hands. He saw her shoulders droop as she let out the breath she'd been holding. She shook her head. "Okay, that," she pointed to the door he'd just passed through, "is creepy."

Jack grinned. "All the horrors we've seen here, and me coming through a door is what creeps you out?"

Natalie allowed a wan smile. "It's just wrong."

He explained the scene above. "Looks like we need another distraction." His eyes combed the room.

Natalie picked up the dented metal cup containing the guards' dice then circuited the room. From a pile of paraphernalia on a table shoved in the corner, she lifted a good-sized knife. When Jack got a closer look at the formidable weapon, he drew in a sharp breath. The six inch blade was black as night and curved wickedly at the tip. He guessed the handle, also black, was likely obsidian—rock born of fire. Though he'd never seen such a thing in reality, his shifter's codex contained a detailed drawing which labeled the knife a shade dagger. Used to torture souls, the implement could harm the dead, causing wounds that never healed. The book said nothing about how the blade might affect the living. The weapon seemed dangerous to keep, yet too valuable to leave behind, so he settled for a warning. "That's no ordinary dagger. Be careful with it."

Natalie nodded. Jack pointed to the cup of dice which trembled slightly in her hand. "Try to toss the dice as far as you can to the opposite side of the room. I'll distract the guards, and when you see an opportunity—run. Head to the place we hid when we first got here, remember? It looked like an Anasazi settlement? I'll be right behind you."

She nodded again, face pallid.

"I could use your hair elastic." Jack noticed Natalie's quick breaths and felt the fear radiating from her. They needed to keep moving or she may become panic stricken and unable to act. She had it together enough to heed his warning and carefully transfer the dagger to the hand with the dice cup before extending her wrist toward him. As he rolled the elastic over her hand, Jack rejected his impulse to pull her into a last embrace, deeming the gesture too fatalistic. Instead, he grinned with a confidence he didn't feel. "Okay?"

Natalie opened the door and they climbed the stairway to the vestibule above. They exchanged a meaningful look, and then Jack slunk around the edge of the room, moving slowly. Closer to the guards, he recognized Pudgy and One-eye who'd captured him earlier.

The man guarding the small waiting room where they'd held Jack before his audience with Zalnic wore a funky vest that may have once had fringe at the bottom. He was an immense, bald, black man with a bushy beard. Jack hoped he never had to fight that guard. One-eye stood at the next door down and Jack stretched out the hair elastic with his fingers and fired it at the huge guy from One-eye's direction. The band struck him in the cheek.

The bald man spun toward One-eye. "What'd you do that for?" he rumbled.

"Do what?" As One-eye turned, Jack pulled out the jacket cord and flicked it into the man's hair. The guard swiped a hand across his head. "Blasted bugs!"

"What's gotten into you, Segenam? Afraid of little bugs?" Pudgy laughed.

The fourth guard, long-haired and barefoot, watched the others impassively.

Then Natalie threw a die. It bounced across the floor to the far side of the room, bringing the long-haired guard to attention.

Jack moved between One-eye and Pudgy and stabbed Pudgy in the calf.

"Ouch!" Pudgy cried, looking down at his leg.

The second die flew overhead and rebounded against the wall. Their ploy was working—the room erupted into chaos. Jack shifted position and stabbed the large bald guard.

Out of dice, Natalie threw the cup. A second later she made a break for the door. As soon as it opened, all eyes turned to the front of the room, but she was already through and the heavy door banged shut.

"The girl!" Segenam, aka One-eye, recovered from the shock first. "She's escaped!" He lunged toward the door and pushed through, Jack on his heels. Already Natalie was out of sight.

As an alarm clanged, a booming voice shouted. "Idiots! I told you to be prepared." Zalnic stormed from the citadel. His crimson eyes scoured the area and his nostrils flared. "It's the boy. The shifter. He's here."

Jack rounded the side of the building, heading for the Anasazi settlement. Zalnic roared again. "Get me that girl!"

A squeal sounded from behind the citadel and Jack accelerated his pace in that direction, fearing the worst. He skidded to a stop as two guards rounded the corner with Natalie held firmly between them. The one

240

on the left bled from a cut on his shoulder. Her frantic eyes met his. "Sorry," she mouthed.

Jack followed helplessly while the guards marched Natalie to the front of the building. Unable to break from their grasp, Natalie squirmed and kept her gaze down as she was held before Zalnic. The lord of souls reached out and grabbed her jaw, forcing her to look up. Although she tried to pull away, he held her fast.

Jack wanted to deck the underlord, beat him to the ground, but he had no power. Instead he watched with an aching heart. At the least, he must know what happened to her—what Zalnic would do with her now.

The black figure leaned his face close to Natalie's. "So tell me," he demanded in a soft, low voice that dripped with malice, "how did you escape?"

Tears leaked out of Natalie's eyes and Jack balled his hands into fists, fraught with frustration.

When she didn't answer, Zalnic pulled his hand from her face then brought it back, lightning quick, and slapped her hard. Her head snapped back. Had the guards not been holding her up, Jack was sure she would have hit the ground. She cried out and slumped between them.

Jack frowned and pressed his lips together. His fault. This was all…

his…

fault.

He never should have let her come in the first place. This was his deal—he'd wanted to seal his fate and tie it up with a bow. Instead he'd risked the one real thing he might have had a chance at.

"Now." Zalnic hooked a black finger under Natalie's chin and jerked her head up. "Let's try this again. How did you escape?"

"I…" Natalie drew in an uneven breath, "called the guards. Tricked them." She sniffed. "I locked them in my cell."

Jack's heart swelled at the defiance in her eyes.

"Mmph. Smart girl." Zalnic let go of her face. Her cheek was bright red where he'd hit her and indents from his fingers remained on her jaw.

The underlord paced in front of her, shifting shadows trailing behind him. "Or, perhaps, you had some help?"

Natalie shook her head, gaze averted.

"Look at me!" Zalnic's voice resounded off the stone walls.

Natalie lifted her head, not wanting to be hit again.

The ruler of the underworld grinned at her—an expression more terrifying than anything Jack and Natalie had encountered so far in this heinous place.

Horrified, she recoiled, her eyes darting to Jack for half a second.

"You're a liar," Zalnic said softly. "You had help." He spun in his tracks. His eyes traveled over seemingly empty space. "How dare you think you can come here and take what is mine, Jack Ironwood," he shouted. "I am a god. It's time you learned your lesson."

Jack's blood ran cold and his chest felt as though it was being crushed in a vise. Oh God, he'd made things worse by coming here now. He should have waited until moonrise.

Zalnic turned back to Natalie and considered her for a moment. "Take her to the Precipice of Delusion."

No! Jack wanted to scream.

He followed the guards as they led Natalie to an

open vehicle like the one used to take Jack and Emma to the void. "Don't worry, I'm going with you," Jack said as one guard forced her wrists together in front of her and the other bound them together. Then she was lifted and dumped unceremoniously into the box-like passenger compartment.

She stole glances at Jack full of fear and questions and he willed the creases in his forehead to relax. If she had any inkling of the panic and dismay swelling within him, she might arrive on the precipice feeling already doomed. And the only useful weapon she'd have out there was hope.

After a guard climbed into the back with her, Jack got in. The man rested a menacing stare on Natalie and she pressed against Jack's side. Then Jack noticed the gash on the guy's arm, still oozing blood, and realized this was the guard Natalie wounded with the shade dagger. He was in the best shape of any minion they'd come across thus far, with all of his fingers, both eyes, and most of his hair. He was either a new recruit, or very careful—possibly both. His arms were draped casually over the edge of the crate they rode in and his mouth was twisted into a wicked smirk. His posture alarmed Jack more than if the man had been screaming and cussing.

The bizarre craft roared to life and then regulated to a loud buzz like a dirt bike once they were underway. Jack leaned in close to Natalie's ear and slipped his fingers between hers. "If you can hear me okay, squeeze my fingers." She responded immediately so Jack continued. "You can survive this easily if you understand what's going to happen and take precautions. They're going to put you on a ledge inside a chasm filled with the souls of people who lived happy and just lives. They mean you no harm. They will, however, encourage you to join them." Her grip tightened on his hand. "The precipice isn't meant for living souls; it's meant for those reluctant to pass into this realm. You may hear voices, so put something in your ears—rip off pieces of your clothes if you have to. Even then, you may still feel the pull. You have to fill your head with something else. Think about life, Natalie, all the things you still want to do. Think about your dad… about Emma."

Her eyes were closed and Jack watched as a tear escaped from between her lashes. "I'll stay with you for a while. But then I'll have to return so I can come to get you."

Natalie could suffer a worse fate than taking the plunge into the Eternal Chasm—the equivalent of a Christian rising to heaven. Most souls went willingly, joyfully, to join the others who resided in an eternity of happiness. Occasionally, a soul with strong ties to the living world would rest on the precipice before giving in to the euphoria that rose from the chasm.

The experience was different for a living being, which is why only shifters referred to the ledge as the Precipice of Delusion. Abandoned alive in limbo, a person's will to live battled the ultimate temptation of eternal happiness. The ordeal was tortuous, regardless of the outcome. So the underworld god, resentful of the living that crossed into his realm, utilized the precipice as a last resort for intruders he could not bend to his will. Because of this, decades ago, the sect had decreed that shifters were not to interfere with Zalnic's affairs so long as the lord of souls did not meddle in the living world.

Zalnic had crossed the line when he took Emma, Jack decided to make things right and now Natalie was going to pay. And though her selflessness earned her the right to eternal happiness, she shouldn't have to forfeit decades of her life.

Jack vowed he'd do whatever it took to make it back before she succumbed to the enticement of the chasm.

The timbre of the motor changed to a lower pitch and Jack scanned the terrain. It was impossible to mistake the Void for the Eternal Chasm. This large cavity emitted a yellow-gold glow, as if the sun lay at the bottom of the crater. Jack slipped Natalie's small knife from his pocket and opened it behind her, out of sight from the guard. "I don't want to cut the rope on your wrists because they'll probably lower you down that way," he explained as he slid the knife under her arm and tucked it into her gloved palm. "Keep it hidden."

He felt Natalie take a shuddering breath as the vehicle slowed and rolled to a stop near the edge of the chasm. The guard in back with them tied a cloth around his head which had holes for his eyes only. He stood and yanked Natalie to her feet. She tore her arm from his grasp. "I can move by myself."

With a snicker, he dropped to the ground and crossed his arms expectantly, watching as Natalie rose and jumped over the black wood. She hit the dirt hard, landing in a crouch, but remained on her feet. Before she could straighten fully, the guard tossed a rope over her bound wrists, tied it firmly and then jerked her toward the chasm. The other guard followed, wearing a cloth over his face as well.

"Once they're gone, cut your bonds," Jack said, walking alongside Natalie. "If I had a way to get down there, I'd go with you. But I promise to stay for a while."

At the edge of the vast abyss, the guard with Natalie's rope briefly glanced down and then took a few paces to the right. He passed the coil of rope to the other sentry, retaining enough length to loop over his shoulders and around his blood-stained forearm. Eyes burning with malice, he turned to face Natalie. "Before you go, I've got a little score to settle." He drew the knife from his belt. Alarm blazed in Jack's chest as he recognized the shade dagger Natalie had stolen from the citadel. She shrank away from the man towering over her, eyes wide, face white as a ghost. But she was attached to the rope he pulled up short and could do nothing as he reached out and viciously slashed her forearm.

Her scream received an evil chuckle. "Okay, we're ready now. Off you go." He spun Natalie around. He slid his hands under her arms. Before she could protest, her feet dangled over the abyss and Jack watched help-lessly as she whimpered and went limp, fearing the man might drop her.

Jack swore under his breath. He crouched at the lip of the huge hole.

The man knelt and lowered her further. "Bye-bye," he hissed and let Natalie slip from his grasp. She cried out fearfully as she began to plummet and then screamed when the rope grew taut and jerked her arms cruelly.

The guard kneeled at the lip of the chasm, the rope held fast in both hands. He grinned. "Don't want you to die too fast, now, do we?" He stood and backed away before he began feeding the rope over the rim.

Heart pounding in his throat, Jack evaluated

Natalie's expression, wondering if her arms or shoulders had suffered any damage. Her wide eyes contained more terror than pain and he exhaled a twisted feeling of relief. Her balled fist looked as though she'd also managed to hang on to the knife. "You're halfway down," he called. "Keep your feet close to the wall." It was all he could do for her.

The guard didn't watch her progress, looking down only when the rope went slack to confirm she was on the ledge. "Enjoy your stay," he cackled. As he passed the other man, still holding the coil, he said, "Leave it." The guard dropped the bundle of rope which immediately began snaking across the ground and over the chasm rim.

"Natalie! Watch out. The rest of the rope is coming." Before Jack had even finished the warning, the length of rope hurtled downward. Natalie dropped to a crouch before the rope hit her and as the coils fell around her, she sat back on it. The guards hopped into the three-wheeler and took off.

Kneeling at the lip of the chasm, Jack stared at Natalie. She hadn't moved. Her head was bowed. Then Jack noticed her shoulders shaking and realized she was sobbing. The left arm of her jacket was soaked in blood. His heart ached with the need to comfort her. Every fiber of his being wanted to climb down and rescue her—except he had no physical being right now. Sure he could touch Natalie, but he couldn't throw her a rope.

All he had to offer was his voice. And what could he say? Tell her everything was going to be all right?

Without actually making a conscious decision, he started to sing. First thing that came to mind was a

Killer's song, *Believe Me Natalie*. "Believe me Natalie, listen Natalie, this is…" The lyrics weren't pertinent to the situation and he wasn't even sure of all the words. Still he fudged his way through it until, eventually, she looked up.

"That was pretty bad, Jack. But thanks." Despite the tears glistening on her cheeks in the warm yellow light, she wore a grim smile.

"Do you have your knife?"

She opened her hand to show the knife lying in her palm. Her eyebrows lifted.

"With your teeth," he answered. "Unless you can hold it between your feet."

Jack had to hand it to her; Natalie did not give up easily. She used her teeth to yank the gloves off, then clamped the knife between her rear molars so she could saw her bound hands across the blade. It took a while, and a change to the other side of her jaw, but she got through all the fibers and the rope fell away. To demonstrate her freedom, she held her arms outstretched and peered up at him.

"You're awesome," he said. "Might as well keep the rope. Who knows, it may come in handy." As she gathered it up he asked, "You remember what I told you, right?"

"I remember."

"I have to go so I can come back."

She nodded, sober-faced.

He locked eyes with her. "I will be back. Say it."

"You will be back."

"Keep repeating it out loud if you have to. I want you to be right there when I get back."

"I'm not going anywhere." She looked so small

248

and alone on the negligible shelf above the huge chasm. Jack had to tear himself away.

Somehow, he had to return to his body.

CHAPTER 13

Return to Hell

Jack found a clump of boulders in the endless expanse of wasteland, sat down, and closed his eyes. Since his grandfather had guided him here, he searched for the old man's essence. Reaching his grandfather's spirit turned out to be the easy part. Unfortunately, it seemed as if a virtual wall had been built while he was gone, barring him from returning to the land of the living.

"You put the wall up, Jack. In your heart, you don't want to leave," his grandfather finally told him.

"But I have to go. It's the only way I can rescue Natalie."

"Tell it to your subconscious."

Jack thought it over and admitted he was afraid to leave her again. "I feel guilty."

"Yes. And if you don't forgive yourself, you won't go home."

How could he forgive himself while Natalie sat on the Precipice of Delusion? As he began to admonish himself for dragging her into the situation, his memory argued back. Jack had offered her an out more than once—she'd insisted she come with him. She was here of her own free will.

Jack opened his eyes and at first didn't comprehend the speckled ceiling above him. He turned his

251

head and recognition fell into place. He was in Brody's living room.

Brody approached anxiously. "Thank goodness, Jack. I was beginning to worry. Did you get Natalie to safety?"

Jack sat up, avoiding his adviser's eyes. "No," he replied quietly. "She's on the Precipice of Delusion."

Brody said nothing, but when Jack raised his gaze, the older man's forehead was lined in concern.

"What time is it?" Jack asked.

"1:30."

Jack's gaze darted to the window. Daylight. So he had about twelve hours to come up with a plan. Drawing a deep breath, he related the events of his morning in the underworld. As he spoke, his hand went to his chest, confirming he was still wearing the brimstone amulet—this time, it would travel with him. He wondered if anything had changed—if the stone might work for him now. Either way, once he reached the Eternal Chasm, the necklace was for Natalie.

Brody grimaced. "He knows you'll come back for her and he'll do everything in his power to stop you."

"I know. Is there any way to throw him off my scent? I mean, I can find other sacred grounds to descend from, but I know he's tracking me."

Brody lifted an eyebrow, his eyes distant as he scoured his memory. Then he focused on Jack and snapped his fingers. "Water."

"What, like walking through water to throw dogs off your scent?"

"Kind of, except you don't need to get wet, just cross water. The bigger, the better."

Jack stared at his adviser and felt a spark of hope

followed by instant trepidation. They exchanged a look and Jack moved his eyes west, toward Lake Michigan.

Brody nodded.

Jack rose from the couch and picked up Natalie's car keys. "I'll meet you at the car." Brody dashed from the room. A minute later, the engine was running and Jack drummed his fingers on the shifter as his adviser approached with a small pack. "My climbing gear," he explained as he handed it through the window.

"Thanks." Jack looked Brody in the eyes. The older man bobbed his chin once.

After a quick stop at home for his laptop, Jack sped south on Highway 31 and pulled in at the first place he saw advertising Wi-Fi.

The connection slugged along at a glacial pace and Jack bounced his knee in agitation. Finally online, he Googled 'ferry Michigan.' The cursor hovered over the site for a Muskegon to Milwaukee ferry when Ludington caught his eye. Ludington to Manitowoc. Jack considered the choices—Ludington was only forty minutes away, Muskegon was at least twice the distance. Seemed like a no brainer, as long as the departure schedule fit his timing.

When a picture of the ferryboat plowing through waves and kicking up a wake came up on his screen, Jack groaned. Oh God, was he really going to do this? He hadn't been on a boat since his father's accident.

He chose the schedule and rates tab while his stomach churned in protest. The last boat left at three which didn't give him any time to deliberate—he should get on the road immediately. But he needed one more piece of information. Researching the existence of sacred grounds near Manitowoc was not a clear-cut search. Jack clicked and scanned, knee jiggling constantly as precious minutes ticked away. His digging paid off when he finally discovered Native American burial grounds located on Walleye Island in Wisconsin, about a three hour drive from the ferry. As long as he made the three o'clock departure for Manitowoc, he'd have plenty of time to drive to the island.

The clock on the car stereo read 2:13. Jack slammed his laptop shut and accelerated back onto Highway 31. He'd been on the road only ten minutes or so when he felt an odd vibration through his elbow which rested on the center console. "Crap," he muttered, lifting his arm. Car trouble had been his last worry in Natalie's new SUV. He pressed on the vinyl surface experimentally with his forearm. Nothing.

He let his arm relax. Obviously he was too on edge.

Another hum vibrated his elbow. A sudden realization dawned on Jack and he flipped the console open. A quick glance inside revealed a variety of items. Keeping his eyes on the road, he felt the objects inside until his fingers closed around her cell phone. One look at the display dropped a rock in Jack's guts. It was a text from her dad.

He plunked the phone into a cupholder. There would be plenty of time on the ferry ride to figure out what to do about this latest complication.

He arrived at the dock with minutes to spare—barely enough time to buy a ticket and get on board. He considered renting a car on the other side and sparing Natalie's car the extra miles, but decided he was better off saving time. As he drove up the boat ramp, he remembered Natalie's reluctance to let him drive on the way back from Harbor Springs—he shook his head at the irony.

With the window down to receive instructions from the parking attendant, the smell of hot grease and warm sugar assaulted Jack's nose, reminding him he hadn't eaten since the night before. When the car was safely parked, he followed the aroma to the concession area. Despite the anxiety gnawing at his insides, his stomach rumbled.

While waiting for his food, Jack pulled Natalie's phone from his pocket. The screen displayed the numeric keypad requiring her security code. A sarcastic laugh escaped as he stared at the phone. He knew her code. She'd told him when he texted her dad for her on the way back from Harbor Springs. Fearing the worst, Jack read the text from Mr. Segetich: *Late meeting tonight. Don't wait for me for dinner.*

He felt his shoulders drop as some of the tension ebbed away. Finally, something in his favor.

He carried his food to a table far from any windows and wolfed down the burger and fries while he contemplated a reply text. Natalie needed to be away from home at least until tomorrow and preferably not available to talk on the phone. Finally Jack sent: *No problem. Some girls were talking about going to the movies tonight anyway. I'll catch dinner with them. The movie is later so Renee invited me to stay the night at her house. I love you. See you in the morning* ☺

With that taken care of, he went back to the concession stand for a cinnamon-sugar pretzel. Since the large ferry was fairly stable, Jack scanned the area, thinking if he could find something to read—any sort of distraction—he might forget he was on a boat. Unfortunately the only printed material he found was a rack of brochures, but he collected a handful and went to find a seat.

Eventually the stress, a night without sleep and a full belly caught up with him and his eyes drooped. Learning more than he wanted to know about things to do and see in Manitowoc and Green Bay couldn't combat his extreme exhaustion. His chin dropped to his chest and he was asleep in minutes.

Next thing he knew, a hand shook his shoulder gently. "We've arrived at Manitowoc, sir. Welcome to Wisconsin."

Jack opened his eyes to see an attendant walking away. He straightened in the seat and scrubbed his face with his hands. He checked the clock. Ten minutes to seven. En route to the parking bay, he noticed an information desk he wished he'd seen at the beginning of the trip. Many of the brochures he'd already read were laid out on the counter, but what caught his eye now were the maps.

The information desk clerk highlighted two possible routes to Walleye Island. "You can catch a ferry in Miller Bluff or Eastport," she added. "I'm not sure how late they run. You may have to wait until morning."

Jack thanked her and took the map, though he was mentally kicking himself. The detail shouldn't have caught him off-guard. That it did was a testament to his inner turmoil and lack of sleep. Of course Walleye Island was an island—as in, land surrounded by water. Another boat ride was imminent.

And if the ferry wasn't running when he got there, he'd have to find a boat.

Fantastic.

The orange numbers on the car's clock read 9:37 as Jack rolled into Miller Bluff. He'd made a brief stop for gas as the surrounding area became less civilized. At the station, he also decided to grab a couple of water bottles and snack bars.

His nerves felt rubbed raw.

Apparently the small town businesses shut down early, and judging by the parking lots, the residents that weren't at home were in the bars. He found the Miller Bluff ferry depot as deserted as the downtown area. According to the posted schedule, the last one departed at three, just as Jack was leaving Michigan.

He got back on the highway to Eastport. He arrived in town less than ten minutes later, surprised at the signs of life—he'd expected this town would be a replica of Miller Bluff. But the low level of bustle gave him a spark of hope that the ferry might still be in service. He located the brightly lit terminal, encouraged by people milling about. Jack parked and jogged to the building. He bounded up the stairs and pulled on the door. It didn't budge.

"Ugh," he groaned out loud. According to the schedule posted near the door, the last ferry had left for Walleye Island at nine fifteen. He walked past the building and peered over the fence. The dock was empty. "Crap," he muttered. "So close."

Back in the car, Jack let his head fall against the headrest and closed his eyes, racking his brain for ideas. Determined to do something—anything—he drove beyond the town, staying as close to the shoreline as possible, open to any sort of inspiration. When he

257

happened across the marina, he pulled in, even though he knew many pleasure boats would already be dry-docked this late in the season. Regardless, he got out to poke around the few vessels still in the water, thinking he might run into someone.

The night was calm and the thinly populated docks seemed eerily quiet. The intermittent pools of light made the space between them seem darker. His footfalls and an occasional creak from the wooden pier echoed across the water. Jack stayed alert to movement in all directions, frequently checking behind him as well. He saw only one man, snoring among empty beer cans in the bottom of an aluminum boat, an open whiskey bottle hugged to his chest. Desperation nearly prompted Jack to try and rouse the man, but the sight of the aluminum boat gave him an idea.

Certain that he'd seen a brown and white state park sign just outside of town, Jack jumped into the car and back-tracked to find it. Then, following the arrow and subsequent signs, he proceeded along the coastline until he arrived at the park. In an area like this, a state park rowboat rental was a reasonable assumption. Since fishing was good well into the fall, he hoped the park still had boats at the ready.

He paused with the headlights illuminating a sign that directed visitors to various park amenities. Although the list didn't include boat rentals, 'pier' seemed the obvious place to start. Gravel crunched under the tires as he rolled into a parking area adjacent to a well-lit waterfront. Jack parked in the shadows cast by a row of pine trees, stuffed the water bottles and snack bars into Brody's pack, and then picked his way to the dock, staying off the sidewalk.

The black water glimmered in the lights, lapping gently at the shoreline. The mineral smell of the lake, combined with oil and gas fumes, instantly brought Jack back to time spent at the marina with his father. With those memories forefront, mixed feelings of terror and triumph coursed though him when he discovered a row of small aluminum boats bobbing next to the pier.

He had no other choice.

A ranger station situated close to the beach area showed lights in the window, but Jack knew there'd be no boat rentals this late at night. Nor could he stroll down the dock under the lights and simply take one of the rowboats without drawing unwanted attention. He sighed and stripped out of his jacket, socks, shoes, shirt and jeans. The crisp fall air stole across his exposed skin and Jack shivered as he tied the arms of his jacket together to form a bundle.

He strode down the shore, away from the ranger station, before wading into the water. Although goose bumps already speckled his arms and legs, the shock of the icy water took his breath away. Jack gritted his teeth and kept going. His skin crawled as the water rose above his waist. He fought past his urge to dash back to shore by imagining how Natalie felt on the Precipice of Delusion.

When he estimated he was about even with the boat farthest from shore, he turned and cut directly toward it. Panic shimmied up his spine as the water level rose nearly to his chest. Jack fought to breathe, as if the icy fingers of the lake held him in a vise-grip. He concentrated on his task to push away the rising tide of apprehension.

The floodlights posted on the beach barely penetrated the darkness this far out. Still, he prayed the ranger was busy looking at a computer or television instead of out the window. With his clothes in one hand and Brody's pack in the other, both held high enough to stay dry, he wasn't exactly inconspicuous. He breathed a relieved sigh when he reached the boat and lowered his things inside. His legs felt numb, but he forced them to do his bidding. As he'd suspected, the boats were locked to the pier. Rummaging through Brody's pack, Jack produced a knife and easily forced apart the lock—its purpose wasn't so much to prevent theft as to keep customers from helping themselves. When it was free, he pushed the rowboat away from the dock and the ranger station.

He waded slowly through the icy water, evaluating the boat he'd just heisted. A pull-start motor was mounted on the back, but the vessel was otherwise empty—no floatation devices and no oars. Although he planned to use the motor once he was out of ear shot, he had to get that far first. Besides, he'd be a fool to set out without oars or at least a paddle. Cursing, he turned toward shore and dragged the boat up on the rocky shoreline past the beach.

The air felt about ten degrees colder now that he was wet, and his shaking limbs slowed the process of getting into his dry clothes. Once dressed, he crept to the ranger station assuming that if the park officer dispensed the gear, it would be close at hand. Jack spotted the woman through a side window, sitting at a desk with her feet up, watching television. In front of the building, a cluster of oars leaned next to the door. The good news, they weren't locked up—the bad news, the jumble of oars was a giant game of pick-up sticks. Choose the right one, Jack, or they'll all come tumbling down.

He traced each oar with his eyes, forcing himself to stay calm and concentrate, though everything seemed to be taking too long. He clamped his mouth shut over his chattering teeth. One oar appeared not to be touching any others, so Jack plucked it from the group and set it aside. He debated on taking a second oar. One was enough for paddling a short distance, but suppose the motor wouldn't start? Or quit? Or ran out of gas?

Jack reached for another, easing it away from the rest. The stack shifted and he froze, hand still on the oar, holding his breath. When nothing happened for a long moment, he slowly let the air escape from his lungs, then gingerly continued to extract the oar. When it was free, he snatched the other off the ground and padded away from the building. As he reached the scrub trees, a loud scraping noise split the silence, followed by a noisy clatter as the group of oars crashed to the ground. Jack bolted without looking back.

When he got to the boat he dumped the oars inside, gave the craft a hard shove and quickly jumped aboard. His heart thrummed out of control as he fitted the oarlocks into their holes. Jack blamed his uneasiness on the ordeal with the oars, but in his heart he knew the real reason. As the boat moved away from shore, Jack dug deep into the water and pulled hard, propelling the vessel across the open water. From his vantage point, the ranger station was hidden in the trees and he, thankfully, couldn't make out any figures on the dock. Hopefully the ranger assumed a nosey animal knocked down the stack of oars.

Rowing properly with his back to the boat's prow, Jack was forced to watch the shoreline diminish while he fought the panic rising in the back of his throat. A sheen of sweat that had nothing to do with physical labor broke out on his forehead. When the only things discernible in the vicinity of the park's dock were the spot lights, he leaned forward and pulled the cord on the motor, but his tremor-weakened arm produced only a sputter. Grunting aloud, Jack used anger to push aside his irrational fear and yanked hard on the starter. The motor roared to life.

According to the map he'd picked up on the ferry, the burial grounds were located on the Fry Peninsula, which jutted out from the southeast corner of the island. The ride was mercifully short. Jack killed the motor as he neared the coast, even though no lights shone from the protected area. He picked out a short stretch of beach and rowed toward it, allowing himself a moment to breathe deeply when the boat touched land. Leaving the vessel beached and secured to a tree, he trekked inland, forging over sand dunes speckled by clumps of long grass.

Gray, slowly drifting clouds obscured the moon, but the openness of the area afforded decent visibility. Since he doubted he'd see anything to alert him when he reached sacred ground, Jack stopped periodically to listen or test the air, relying entirely on his intuitive skill. By the time the terrain began to flatten out, he was breathing heavily and had completely shaken his earlier chill.

Concentrating on his senses, he corrected his path to the east and was soon rewarded by a hum. A check of his phone confirmed midnight had already come and gone. Almost time.

Wriggling his fingers into his gloves, he slowed his pace, mentally pushing against unseen boundaries as he wove across the area that seemed to vibrate with afterlife. Finally choosing a spot that felt right, he paused and gazed upward at the leaden sky, hoping his ruse worked. He'd gone to a lot of trouble to shake Zalnic off his tail.

Without the moon's location as a guide, he concentrated on the membrane, periodically exerting pressure against the thin line between worlds. Then suddenly, without warning, the resistance disappeared and he fell to his hands and knees. The sour smell of sulfur stung his nostrils and his knees pressed into charcoal dust instead of sand.

He was back.

Jack dropped to his knees at the rim of the Eternal Chasm. Though it had been a challenge to get his bearings when he descended, he eventually located the yellow glimmer which marked the abyss. The distinct lack of resistance convinced him his trip to Wisconsin was not in vain. Also, it seemed as if the brimstone might have been in effect—perhaps the tide had turned in his favor.

Golden light bathed his face and he closed his eyes for a moment, afraid to look over the edge. If the precipice was empty…

There was nothing to be gained by pondering the worst, so he took a deep breath, opened his eyes, and leaned forward. Instant relief flooded through him. Natalie was there, lying on her side, curled toward the chasm wall.

263

"Natalie!" he shouted.

She didn't move.

"Hey, Natalie!" He pushed his voice even louder. "It's Jack. I'm back."

Again she didn't stir.

Jack frowned. Sure, he'd told her to plug her ears, but bits of cloth or tissue couldn't be that effective. The blood stain on Natalie's sleeve had spread to an alarming size, making Jack wonder if she might have fainted from blood loss. That thought was followed by the disturbing recollection that the wound had been made by a shade dagger.

He needed to rouse her or go down and get her—and do it quickly.

Rising, he awkwardly gathered a handful of pebbles in his gloved hands and hurried back to the chasm. Aiming carefully, he dropped a stone. It hit the ledge and bounced into the abyss. He tried again. This time he was pretty sure he hit Natalie's shoe, although she didn't flinch. He took a deep breath. "She probably just fell asleep," he mumbled, ignoring the quaver in his voice.

After another miss, the fourth pebble finally hit her cheek. Jack's heart soared when she jerked and lifted her head. She spied him immediately and reached to her ear. "Jack!" she yelled with a relieved smile.

Jack laughed out loud. Headphones? The thought that she'd been lying down there listening to music was surreal. "I'm getting you out," he shouted. Natalie maneuvered onto her knees and nodded. Red-rimmed eyes stared anxiously from her wan face. Jack held up his index finger and shrugged Brody's pack from his shoulder. His hand closed around a coil of rope and then he was suddenly struck by a tremendous force. The blow slammed him sideways and he ploughed into the hard ground with his left shoulder.

He instinctively rolled and attempted to get up, yelling in agony as he discovered his left arm was unable to support his weight. Steeling himself for the next attack, Jack was surprised he made it to his feet before being struck again—until he faced his foe.

A large wolf-like beast stood at a distance. Waiting. Apparently it wanted more than a kill—it wanted a fight. Jack slumped forward, right hand on his thigh for support. His left arm hung uselessly from his dislocated shoulder. He watched his opponent but avoided direct eye contact, buying time to assess his situation.

After jimmying the lock on the rowboat, he'd pocketed Brody's knife, so at least he was armed. He slowly moved his right hand to his back pocket and extracted the weapon. He held it loosely in his hand as his father taught him, finding the balance of blade and hilt. Then he straightened, keeping his knees bent slightly, ready to move in any direction.

The wolf hunkered down, its mouth curled to expose large pointed canines. When it lunged, Jack dove, letting out a groan as pain radiated up his left arm. The beast sailed over him, scrambling for purchase on the dry, cracked earth. It skidded to a stop and spun around to face Jack, snarling.

Recognizing him as a worthy adversary, the animal was finished waiting for Jack to be ready and it sprang forward immediately, snapping its salivating jaws. Jack jerked away, but the strike had been close enough that he felt the wolf's hot breath on his face and got a good look at its eyes.

Distinctively human eyes.

The wolf must be a skin-walker.

Although skin-walkers weren't part of the sect, shifters were aware of them because, in their animal form, the shape-changing humans possessed a spiritual element allowing them to cross worlds. Skin-walkers were seldom seen in the underworld, however, because of the risk that if they stayed too long they could become trapped—not only in their animal form, but in the dark realm.

Jack drew in a ragged breath. Lack of proper food and sleep, the lengthy journey and constant fear and stress had left him exhausted. The wolf charged toward his knife hand and Jack adjusted his grip, but at the last minute, the beast twisted mid-leap and hit his throbbing left shoulder. Fangs like daggers sank into his flesh. Jack yowled, wrenching away from the wolf.

He had to end this right now or both he and Natalie would end up dead.

"What a sorry excuse for a wolf," Jack sneered, rising to his knees, "playing with your prey like a pet kitty."

The wolf snarled, pacing.

"But that's because you're not a wolf," he taunted. "No, a wolf would fight much more fiercely."

The beast's muzzle opened, revealing a row of pointed teeth and allowing a low growl to escape. Jack watched as the wolf licked blood from its chops—his blood.

"You're only a man. Less than a man, really. I bet you sold your soul. You're just an underworld lackey. And that's all you'll ever be." Jack could read the anger in those human eyes. "You're nothing more than a slave, a dog on a leash. I bet—"

He'd pushed hard enough. Furious, the wolf leaped.

Dropping to his knees, Jack leaned backward as the beast flew at him. He jabbed his knife up as the wolf came down, impaling the creature on the blade. Jack heard an agonized howl before the massive animal landed on top of him, slamming his head into the hard ground. His vision became grainy, almost pixilated, and then went black.

Jack blinked, nearly gagging at the fetid smell of the body on top of him. He worked to roll the stinking corpse to the side as he wriggled out from under it. He lay on his back for a minute, gulping in fresh air. The human form next to him confirmed that he had indeed killed a skin-walker. When he was first attacked, Jack thought he was wrong and the brimstone amulet wasn't working for him after all. But skin-walkers trapped in the underworld were living beings; they would be immune to the effects of a talisman. And also susceptible to death.

Jack knew he had nothing to fear from the body next to him. He rolled to the side and balanced on his knees and right hand, pausing as his head swam. Apparently, he hit the ground harder than he thought.

That he was covered in blood wasn't a surprise, but his clothes were sticky and the pool where he'd lain had spread considerably before soaking into the parched earth. He must have blacked out. A surge of fear got him on his feet.

He stumbled to the edge of the chasm, a sigh of relief escaping his lips when he saw Natalie on the ledge below. "Got a little waylaid," he shouted as he grabbed the bundle of rope, ignoring the tackiness of his saturated gloves.

But Natalie didn't look up.

Jack realized she was standing awfully close to the edge of the precipice. "Natalie!" he yelled.

She didn't take her eyes from the golden abyss, but she called out. "I think it's okay now, Jack. It'll be okay if I go to them."

Oh God, how long had she waited for him to come with the rope? Obviously, too long. "No!" Jack bellowed. "Natalie, listen to me." He rushed to a large boulder and wrapped the rope around it, cursing his slow and clumsy one-handed progress. "What about college? You want to be a teacher, don't you?" He finally achieved a secure knot and rushed back, dropping the rest of the coil over the side and down to the ledge. "What about love? Marriage?"

She didn't look up. Just kind of swayed, transfixed by the swirling yellow brightness of the chasm.

If he couldn't get her to climb up, he had to go down and get her. Jack peeled off his blood-soaked jacket and gloves, paying little heed to the searing agony of his dislocated shoulder. He threw Brody's climbing pack over his shoulder, grasped the rope with his good hand and rolled to his belly. Holding tight, he slipped his legs over the rim and maneuvered his right foot until the rope twined around his calf. Then he began to slide downward. "Natalie, listen to me. Are you listening to me? Do you like kids? Don't you want to have kids of your own?" He wished he knew more about her—things that really mattered.

She squatted at the brink of the precipice as if she hadn't heard him. Jack let himself fall faster, the rope burning his palm. "What about Emma?" he pleaded desperately.

Natalie cocked her head. "Emma's lost." Her voice held no emotion.

Then she stood upright, and without hesitation, stepped into the chasm.

"No!" Jack cried. His feet hit the rock shelf and he sprang toward her, nearly following her over the edge. Tears stung his eyes as he watched her body cartwheel into the whirlpool of yellow radiance. He'd been so close—so close.

When Natalie's body disappeared into the brilliance, he let out a wail of grief and frustration.

Jack stared up at the eternally overcast sky. How long had he lain here? He didn't know.

Nor did he care.

Zalnic won.

Jack saw no point in leaving the precipice. He was a failure.

The thought of joining his ancestors in the chasm settled over him like a comforting blanket. They would welcome him with open arms despite his mistakes and inadequacies.

Even his grandfather.

Jack moaned. Open arms or not, he wasn't sure he could face his grandfather. Not after the man had helped him visit Natalie in spirit—his first botched rescue attempt. Jack threw his good arm over his eyes. Not only had he let down the living, he'd dishonored the dead.

269

Returning to the living world wasn't an attractive option either. Although he'd rescued Emma, the sect couldn't possibly deem his quest successful. Shera's father would break the betrothal. Shifter Premier was out of the question. Ironically, he'd be free to shape his own future.

Great. He'd escaped his fabricated fate after all.

In the worst way imaginable.

Rolling to his belly, Jack scooted to the edge of the stone shelf and rested his chin at the lip of the chasm. He knew it was the coward's way out, yet taking the plunge was so inviting. The Precipice of Delusion was exactly where he deserved to be—in limbo.

Why had he allowed Natalie to come with him? What had made him think he could keep her safe?

As he stared into the golden abyss, over and over he saw Natalie's figure as it plummeted into the swirl of brilliance.

She was gone. He had no way to retrieve her. Not even the most accomplished sect member could undo this tragedy.

No one could undo...

Wait.

Jack tore his eyes from the chasm and wriggled away from the edge. He sat up.

There was someone. A human couldn't free Natalie from the Eternal Chasm, but a god could. One god in particular.

Zalnic.

Jack shook his head to try and clear out the distraction emanating from the abyss. There must be a way to persuade the lord of the dead to release Natalie's soul.

His thoughts racing, Jack attempted to stand, wincing when his left arm refused to cooperate. He rose to his feet slowly, contemplating the rope dangling on the cliff face. He couldn't scale the wall one-handed.

His gaze fell to Brody's pack. His adviser had simply retrieved it and handed it over—aside from rope, Jack had no idea what else was inside. Kneeling, he dumped the bag. With a silent thank you sent out to his teacher, Jack donned a pair of climbing gloves while he inventoried the equipment that would get him to the top of the chasm wall. Brody was an avid climber. He'd taken Jack with him a few times, teaching lessons in faith, trust and focus. The ascension process was complex—Jack wasn't positive he could configure the harness, straps and ascenders properly.

As it did in his lessons, the methodical assembly of a climbing apparatus pushed all other thoughts from his mind. The ascension method Brody had taught Jack used one leg in a strap to raise the climber up the rope. Oval-shaped ascenders provided a handle for each hand and included a toothed cam that bit securely into the rope when weighted. A climber usually used one hand and then the other to slide the ascenders as he moved up the rope. Jack had to use his right hand to adjust both, slowing his progress.

As he repeated the procedure over and over, slowly scaling the thirty to forty foot sheer wall, Jack mulled over his options. By the time he hauled himself over the rim, he knew one thing for sure—he was about to make a deal with the devil.

Again.

CHAPTER 14

Buying Time

Jack wiped the sweat from his brow with the sleeve of his shirt. Now that his body was at rest, the sheen of perspiration from the climb chilled him to the bone. He couldn't seem to stop shaking. Exertion, adrenaline, fear, cold, pain—all ganged up to take a piece of him.

His shoulder screamed in agony and Jack knew he had to address the issue, no matter how distasteful the thought. He crawled to his jacket. The blood was dry, thanks to both the fleece fabric and the arid environment. His phone looked like hell; he'd have no idea if it still worked until he was topside. He left his wasted gloves where they lay.

Removing the brimstone amulet from his neck, he then bent to retrieve Brody's knife from the skinwalker's corpse. Whether Jack was worthy of the amulet's protection or not didn't matter. He was leaving the necklace behind for Natalie. A nearby patch of wilted grass and a good-sized rock sufficed to hide it along with the knife and phone. Then, with his right arm, Jack draped the jacket over his shoulders and pulled it together over his chest. His trembling decreased somewhat.

Facing the orange blaze on the horizon, he set off toward Zalnic's lair. He had an idea of how he might fix

273

his dislocated shoulder, although the thought of agitating the sensitive injury made his stomach roil. Instead he concentrated on searching the terrain for items that would serve his purpose. His eyes roved and evaluated each rock formation he came across until he spotted a fairly flat-topped boulder. Then he sought out a good-sized rock he thought would weigh a few pounds. Jack scooped up an oblong stone, set it on the large boulder's flat surface and climbed up next to it. He lay on his good arm, near the edge. A moan slipped from between his lips as he lifted the oval rock in his weakened left hand and levered it upright vertically with his elbow resting on his hip. He breathed in and out deeply a few times and then began lowering his arm as slowly and evenly as possible, letting his elbow follow when his fist passed the edge of the boulder he was on and continued toward the ground.

He cried out when his arm was fully extended over the side. A bead of sweat trickled across his forehead. His sore shoulder protested in anguish, but Jack let his arm hang, willing the muscles to stretch and allow his bones to slip back into place. A moment later, one final jolt of pain radiated through the arm and then sweet relief flooded the area and spread throughout his body.

Jack dropped the rock and stayed in position a minute longer. Then he sat up, gingerly drew his jacket over the left arm and snaked his right hand into the other sleeve. He was better—still scared out of his mind, blood pumping at an accelerated rate—but better.

As he drew close to the compound, he trudged forward with his hands in the air, telling the sentry who apprehended him that he wished to bargain with Zalnic. He was marched directly to the underground prison. Where Natalie had been given the courtesy of an empty cell, Jack shared his with a foul smelling heap of bones that made his stomach heave.

Zalnic let him stew for a while. Apart from the fetid odor of his decaying roommate and the ache in his left shoulder from having his hands bound behind his back, Jack was grateful for a little rest and time to collect his thoughts. He was banking on Zalnic's greed to get the better of him. The underlord's scheme to steal souls from other gods spoke volumes. Since he already had Natalie, Zalnic would want to see if he could get Jack too.

Jack had actually started to doze off when he heard shuffling and the rattle of keys outside the door. Megedagik prodded him up the stairs and deposited him in the same room where he'd waited for an audience the first time. The guard with the cap of charred flesh instead of hair stared at him dully so Jack studied the flames flickering in the small hearth.

As his gaze absently drifted over the stone fireplace and the crude bench next to it, Jack's heart missed a beat. Natalie's amulet—the one Emma had been wearing—lay atop the bench. Jack shifted in his seat and then stood slowly. He glanced at the guard. "I'm cold," he mumbled, and took a few steps to the warm hearth. The heat did feel good and he paused a moment before turning to warm his back. They might usher him into the throne room at any minute.

Jack backed to the bench until his calves touched the wood and then he sat down, keeping his bound hands out of the guard's sight. He made a show of putting his feet out, one at a time, to warm by the fire. Behind his back, his fingers raked the wood surface for the amulet. He had to scoot back and repeat the process with his feet before he finally snagged the rawhide.

The door to the throne room opened and he quickly balled the necklace into his hand, shoving it into the sleeve of his jacket, and then clamping the sleeve shut with his fingers.

A sense of déjà-vu settled over Jack as he entered the throne room.

"Jack Ironwood." Zalnic's voice rasped dryly, as if the sound scraped along the parched earth of his kingdom. "It's been fun, hasn't it? I must say you've been a worthy adversary." The lord of souls wore a wicked smile. "Had you been older—and wiser—perhaps you would've fared better," he sneered. Then he laughed, his eyes flaring crimson.

When Jack didn't reply, Zalnic leaned forward, the shadows rearranging themselves into his form. "I heard you want to bargain. What makes you think I'm interested? Let's check the score, shall we? The girl I released to you was living, her soul pending. Now, I have an actual soul. Of a dead girl." He paused to watch for Jack's reaction. "I'm ahead."

Jack clenched his teeth. That Zalnic knew of Natalie's plunge was no surprise. The lord of the dead was aware of every soul that passed into the underworld, whether into his service or the Eternal Chasm. "You fully intended to have the soul of the girl you stole." Jack emphasized the last word. "In the long run, I'd say you just broke even."

Zalnic's glowing eyes shrank to red pennies as he contemplated Jack's statement. Crossing his legs, he reclined on his throne, stroking the highly polished skulls on the armrests. "What are you proposing?"

276

"Free the girl's soul from eternity. At the end of my life, my soul goes to you. I'll serve you for a year before joining the Eternal Chasm."

The lord of souls chortled.

Jack was unfazed. He knew how to negotiate—you don't start where you want to end up. He'd opened the exchange with plenty of bartering room.

"Do you really think I intend to let you live out your lifetime?" Zalnic scoffed. "How about if I just kill you now and instantly be one soul ahead of the game?"

"Without my return to the living world, I can't uphold my end of our earlier agreement. In my absence, the gods of other realms will be advised of your treachery."

Silence stretched out as Zalnic tapped a skull with a talon-tipped finger. "Then I'll let you live out your life if you pledge your soul into my service for eternity."

"Five years servitude."

"One hundred."

"Ten." Jack knew he had Zalnic interested now—he'd dropped from eternity to a mere one hundred years. The debate wasn't about the servitude, but getting the best bargain.

Greedy.

Zalnic sat up straight and narrowed his eyes. "Numbers aren't getting us anywhere. Let's try it this way. However many years you wish to live, I get that many years of servitude. The amount of time is up to you." He looked immensely pleased with himself. He wanted to know how badly Jack wanted Natalie's soul.

The newly proposed parameters were clever. For each year he wanted to extend his life, he'd spend the same amount of time serving the ruler of the underworld. Live long; serve long. He couldn't even imagine—didn't want to imagine—the despicable things he'd be forced to do under Zalnic's rule.

Jack pictured One-eye, Charred-head, and the various guards with missing fingers. He'd seen a number of disfigurements he assumed were punishments for displeasing the underlord.

But how could he choose when to die?

"I'm waiting, Mr. Ironwood."

Jack couldn't afford to think in long-term ramifications. He needed to get Natalie back before Zalnic tired of the negotiations. He'd just leave himself some time to figure out the rest. "Fifteen years," he blurted. "And our earlier agreement remains intact."

"Done." Zalnic's smile revealed a flash of yellow teeth causing a tingle to crawl up Jack's spine. The underlord motioned with his hand. "Megedagik, escort Mr. Ironwood back to his cell while the contract is drawn up." His gaze bore into Jack's eyes. "You'll sign in blood. No alternatives."

The contract was short and concise. Jack opted to rub the clotted blood off one of the punctures from the skin-walker's bite. He then insisted he hold the vial himself to the oozing wound. Megedagik passed him what appeared to be an old fashioned calligraphy pen, and Jack dipped into his vital fluid. He hesitated with his hand poised over the parchment, his gaze fixed on his own blood.

Closing his eyes, he exhaled in acquiescence. There was no other way. Then he scratched his name on the document, arguing with himself that he wasn't selling his soul.

He was buying time.

Soulshifter

He was warned that his safety could not be guaranteed once he left the compound, but Jack had expected no less. At the contract signing, as he jostled his jacket off his shoulder to open a wound, he'd slipped the brimstone amulet into a pocket. Once he found cover, he removed the necklace and pulled it over his head. He had a hunch it would work for him now.

When he reached the Eternal Chasm, it was as if time had reversed back to when he'd been attacked by the wolf. Natalie looked up at him expectantly and he threw the climbing harness down to her. When he hauled her topside, he immediately put the other brimstone amulet around her neck and then pulled her into an embrace.

"I knew you'd be back," Natalie murmured into his shoulder, gripping him tightly with her uninjured arm.

Jack closed his eyes, his cheek against her soft hair, relishing her warmth, the beat of her heart and the rise and fall of every breath. "Always," he whispered.

She sighed. "Let's go home, Jack."

He decided not to seek out the Void for their return trip for two reasons: he wasn't sure he could find it, and if they did, he assumed that Natalie would emerge at the campground and he would return to Walleye Island. More so, Jack wanted to escape the underworld at the first opportunity, so he employed his shifter senses and found a thin spot between worlds. They crossed into a small cemetery surrounded by a rust-speckled wrought iron fence with an open gate hanging crookedly from one hinge. Judging by the full-blown color of the trees, Jack surmised that they were farther north than home.

279

"How's your arm?" he asked as they made their way through the gate and down an overgrown path.

"It hurts like heck," Natalie replied dryly.

Jack took his cell phone from his pocket and checked to see if he had service. "It's roaming. But I hear cars in that direction." He pointed to their left. "If we find some kind of civilization, hopefully I'll be able to call for help."

The path ended at a narrow blacktop road so they headed toward the rumble of passing vehicles. The sun was just peeking over the horizon and when it reached them, they paused for a moment to savor its light and warmth, glad to be out from under the gloomy, overcast skies of the underworld.

"We need somewhere to warm up and get some food."

Natalie glanced at her sliced and bloody jacket sleeve and then examined Jack, whose torso was soaked with wolf blood. "I'm not sure we should be seen in public. We look like a couple of axe murderers."

"Crap." Jack sighed. "You're right." They approached the main road hesitantly. "Maybe we should ditch our jackets." Natalie nodded and he helped her out of her coat and then took off his own. He rolled them to hide most of the blood. "It seems like a bad idea to leave them out here."

About a quarter mile up the road they found a truck stop. Jack carefully put his arm around Natalie to cover her bloody arm and they made a beeline for the restrooms. Natalie cranked the handle on the women's room and pushed the door open. "It's a single, Jack. Just come in with me," she whispered. They cleaned up the best they could. Jack didn't look so bad—his clothes were randomly blood-stained, but Natalie's entire right sleeve was soaked. "I need a different shirt. Or something to wear over this."

"Wait here," Jack said.

A minute later he was back, offering a worn flannel shirt. "Custodial closet," he answered Natalie's quizzical look. "Right next door." He helped her with the shirt and then pulled a dingy sweatshirt over his head. "Hopefully the attendant won't recognize this stuff. It looked like it'd been there a while."

Natalie wrinkled her nose. "It smells like it, too."

They stole into the diner side of the establishment and Jack grabbed the local paper before they slid into a booth. He turned it so Natalie could read the front page header which revealed they were in Newberry, in Michigan's Upper Peninsula. A waitress took their order and then Jack called Brody and relayed a brief summation of their situation.

Natalie curled her hands around her mug of hot chocolate, took a sip and let the hot ceramic warm her fingers. When he was finished with his call, Jack stirred cream into his coffee. "Someone from the sect will come and pick us up."

She didn't respond, and when he looked up, Jack found her troubled expression trained on him. "So… what really happened down there, Jack? I feel like I have some less than lucid memories."

He stared into his cup, swirling the spoon around idly. "What do you remember?" He hadn't decided if he would tell her she jumped if she didn't remember. It would be better if she never knew about his bargain.

"I clearly remember when you came back—in the spirit-walk—and I got caught. They lowered me onto that ledge. You told me you'd come back." She sipped and thought for a minute. The surface of the brown liquid shimmered, betraying the slight tremor of her hand. "I cut my tank top so I could pull it off and tie it around my arm to stop the bleeding. I also put small pieces of the shirt into my ears. But the voices were getting to me. I kept repeating what you told me, that you'd be back. I chanted it to myself. Then I thought how great it would be if I had my iPod. I'd brought it to listen to in the car and assumed I left it behind, but on a whim I checked the MP3 player pocket in my coat. It was in there."

Jack smiled and shook his head. "Yeah, I couldn't believe you had it with you. I didn't expect to come back and find you jamming to some tunes down there."

"It totally saved me. Not only did it block out the voices, but a lot of the music I listen to I like because of the way it makes me feel, you know?"

Jack nodded.

"Those feelings helped drown out the emotions coming from the chasm. The urge to join the souls was overwhelming, just like you warned. I curled up and tried to concentrate on the lyrics, hoping I might fall asleep like I do at home when I listen to my iPod."

"Were you sleeping when I came back?"

Natalie gazed out at the street and narrowed her eyes. "That's what I'm not sure of." She shifted her eyes back to Jack. "I remember you looking over the edge— you'd come back for me." She frowned. "Next thing I knew I was sitting up and there was a rope hanging down the cliff. I don't remember you throwing the rope down. I feel like I missed something. Did I black out?"

He could say yes. She didn't remember. He'd be

doing her a favor, right?

"What is it, Jack?" She studied his face anxiously. "Something terrible happened. Something I don't remember, right?"

Jack stared into her sapphire eyes and realized he didn't have a choice. He wanted a relationship with Natalie. Something real. That couldn't happen if this lie was always between them. And if she was interested in the same thing, she had to know. It would be unfair to promise forever if forever wasn't his to give.

"You jumped," he said quietly.

"Jumped? No... I... what do you mean?"

Jack told her. About the wolf, how he lost consciousness. "It didn't seem like a long time, but you were waiting for me to get you off that ledge, your defenses were down. I saw you teetering on the brink and I tossed the rope. I slid down as fast as I could." Jack turned his right hand over to show the rope burn on his palm. "I wasn't fast enough. You jumped."

"But you were able to pull me out? Get me back on the ledge?"

Jack shook his head. "No, I—"

The waitress arrived with their food. "Breakfast special." She set a plate in front of Jack. "Veggie omelet." Natalie's plate. They both murmured thanks but the unanswered questions still hung suspended between them. The waitress raised her eyebrows. "Everything okay?"

"Yeah, it's great," Jack assured her. "Thanks."

She bustled off, leaving them alone, staring at one another. Neither picked up their silverware. "I had no way of getting you out myself." He held his gaze steady. "Only a god has that kind of power."

"What god?" Natalie whispered, though her drooping shoulders said she already knew the answer.

"Zalnic. I made a bargain."

"A bargain?" Natalie choked out a hollow laugh. "You made a deal with the devil?"

Jack nodded. "Basically," he mumbled.

"What did you offer the ruler of the underworld?"

"My services for your soul."

Her eyes were wide. "Your services? What does that mean?"

Jack explained the contract.

"Oh, Jack," Natalie said softly. "You shouldn't have done that."

"The idea was to save Emma. Not trade her life for yours."

"Yet you gave up yours for me."

"No. I didn't give up my life," Jack said. "I just bought some time."

Jack hammered out the last few chord progressions of the song and grinned at Natalie, who was bouncing up and down in front of her seat with a hand raised in the air. Emma was on Natalie's right, also bobbing to the beat while maintaining enough space between them that she didn't jostle Natalie's immobilized right arm. All the students—as far as Jack could see—were on their feet, waving their hands to the pulse of the music.

He finished his last strum, lifting his arm dramatically as the stage lights went out. The curtain dropped. A second later, the area was flooded with normal fluorescent light. Jack ducked out of his guitar strap and ran a hand through his curls. Tommy passed by, winding the microphone cord around his arm and ignoring Jack completely. Jack couldn't help smiling. He'd earned the highest praise he'd probably ever get from Tommy: no comment.

Wes approached wearing a smirk. "Keep it up and he may eventually speak to you civilly someday."

"God, I hope not." Jack laughed. "I wouldn't know how to act then." Hearing a chuckle from the corner of the stage, he looked up and met the gaze of John, who was collapsing his keyboard. The piano player delivered a crooked grin and a nod, which Jack returned.

When their guitars were cased, Wes and Jack helped Fletch break down his drum set. "Nice job today, Ironwood," Fletch said as he stacked his tom-toms.

Jack smiled and nodded his thanks. He'd never imagined what an immense feeling of gratification he'd get from being in the band—not only the validation from fellow musicians but also the infectious excitement of the crowd. Add to that the earnest enthusiasm on Natalie's face as she watched him perform, and Jack wondered how he could have been so narrow-minded to think his happiness was tied only to the sect and Shera.

He stacked cymbals on a drum and folded the stand. "Want help carrying this stuff out?"

Fletch shook his head. "It's cool man. My brother's bringing his SUV." Jack picked up his guitar case and amp, meeting Wes offstage. They pushed through the metal backstage doors, emerging into the hallway. Their band had been the last act in the talent expo so school was dismissed when the show ended. Only a few clusters of kids lingered in the halls. Peering around the group closest to the door, Jack caught a glimpse of Natalie and a thrill warmed his chest. Though the sensation was becoming familiar, he hoped it would never fade completely.

"What the..." Wes's voice was almost a whisper. Jack glanced over, taking in his friend's stupid grin and wide-eyed gawk at the group of girls. Following his line of sight, Jack realized the blonde with her back to them was Kelly. As far as he knew, Natalie and Emma didn't really know Kelly, which meant she must be waiting for Wes.

Jack elbowed Wes and they exchanged a grin.

Natalie spied them first and waved. Jack parked his amp and guitar case next to the wall and then circled behind her. He slipped an arm around her waist, leaned over her shoulder and gave her a quick kiss on the cheek. She turned, still flushed from the show—or maybe the kiss—and grinned. "You were great!" She leaned in and gave him a one-armed hug.

"Yeah, good thing they saved you guys for last," Emma said. "No one would've wanted to sit down after that!" A good-sized stack of books weighted her arms down.

"Thanks. So how was your first week back at school?" Jack held out his arm and Emma shifted the top two books to him.

"Well, aside from the ba-zillion times I had to tell people I couldn't really remember anything, the week was fairly mundane—in the best way possible."

"Right. Never undervalue ordinary life."

Emma turned to Natalie. "Since your knight in shining armor has arrived, I should go."

286

"Do you want a ride?" Jack offered. "I've got my dad's truck."

"No thanks. My mom is outside the door." She shifted her gaze to Natalie. "Literally."

"I guess that's understandable." Natalie shrugged sympathetically.

"I know, it's okay with me too." Emma pulled the zipper on her coat up to her chin. "For now."

While Natalie said goodbye to Emma, Jack heard Kelly saying, "... looked kinda envious when I told them we went out."

"Envious... of me?" Wes replied.

Kelly laughed. "Sure. Why not?"

Jack turned to see Wes wearing a wide smile. He locked eyes with Jack for a moment, lifting his eyebrows. Then he shrugged his guitar case strap up on his shoulder and took Kelly's hand. "See you guys later." He said it casually, but Jack detected a hint of swagger to his voice.

Jack hid his amused grin by bending down for his guitar.

"Here, I can take my books." Natalie reached for them with her good hand.

"Whoa," Jack exclaimed. "What do you think you're doing?"

"Come on Jack, my left arm isn't useless. You've got enough stuff to carry."

"That's not the point. You should have a free hand in case anything happens. You can't let your..." He trailed off when he noticed she was fighting to keep the corners of her mouth from curling upward. "What?"

Her eyes sparkled. "I was zoned out in trig today when I realized I was rubbing on my bandage. It itched."

It took a moment for Jack to process what she was telling him and then his eyebrows shot up. "It itched? Are you sure?"

"Puh-lease, I know what an itch feels like." Natalie laughed.

"That's awesome!"

"I know, right? My dad's going to be beyond happy."

While someone was dispatched to fetch Jack and Natalie from the Upper Peninsula, other sect members retrieved Natalie's car from where Jack had left it in Wisconsin. Solving that problem had been a piece of cake compared to providing an explanation for Natalie's wounded arm. They'd finally settled on the story that Natalie went hiking with friends Saturday. She fell in the woods and cut herself on a bacteria-laden hunting knife.

Fortunately, Jack's mom was at the hospital to corroborate the account, going out of her way to attend Mr. Segetich's questions. Even better, she'd encouraged the doctors to treat Natalie's wound as if she had a flesh eating bacteria. They'd cut away all of the damaged skin and muscle, including a five millimeter margin. Then they waited to see if the wound would heal. Her arm was not only sore, but weak from the muscle damage so the doctors had advised her to keep it immobilized.

Jack set the books on the amp and drew Natalie into a loose embrace, keeping his left arm low. He felt like a weight had been lifted off his chest. "You're healing," he whispered.

"Yeah, it's gonna be okay," she murmured into his shoulder.

He released her with a broad grin. "I'll let my

mom know, too." He slung his guitar onto his back and picked up the books and amp. They strolled toward the exit.

"I'll never be able to thank her enough." Natalie's voice was soft. "And not just for my arm, for you, too."

Jack chuckled. "Believe me. I've thanked her for that more than once." Mr. Segetich had been impressed and charmed by Jack's mom and thought very highly of her. So Natalie made sure to let it slip that Jack was 'the awesome nurse's son.' Her father had been very cordial to Jack ever since.

A blast of chilly air buffeted them as they pushed through the exterior doors, cutting off their conversation until they made it to the truck. Jack opened the passenger door and helped boost Natalie into the seat. Then he tossed the books, amp and guitar into the back seat and climbed into the driver's side.

Natalie scooted across the large seat to snug up next to him. "This is the one time I'm glad it's my right arm that's out of commission."

Jack smiled as he started the engine. He put his arm around Natalie. "Better let it warm up a minute."

"Perfect. Then you can warm me up for a minute."

He leaned down and kissed her, lightly at first, and then with more intensity, pleased to see the rosy color of her cheeks when he pulled away. He started to lift his arm from her shoulders, but Natalie reached behind his neck and pulled him into another kiss. This time when they broke apart, she burrowed her face in his jacket and tightened her arm around his neck. "He can't have you, Jack," she whispered. "I want you forever—not just fifteen years." She pulled back to gaze into his face. "And why fifteen? How'd you come up with that?"

Jack shrugged. "I just wanted to buy some time, and I needed an answer before he got bored negotiating." He used his thumb to smooth the creases from Natalie's forehead. "Hey, he's the ruler of the underworld, Natalie. He's greedy. He'll screw up. He'll break the contract himself."

She looked down for a moment, then lifted her gaze to meet his. "What if he doesn't?"

"Well… then I've got fifteen years to figure out how to find the contract and destroy it."

She narrowed her eyes, evaluating his expression to make sure he was serious. Deciding he was, she sat up straight. "Then I'm not going to wait around for him to mess up." She extracted herself from his arms and reached for the seat belt. "Buckle up. We've got work to do."

ACKNOWLEDGEMENTS

Because I aspire to share my writing adventures with my readers, I ran a titling contest for this novel. *Soulshifter* was the suggestion of Rebecca Robinson, the winner of the contest. Thank you, Rebecca! Not only did others like your title suggestion, my publisher and I are extremely pleased with it as well. Thank you to everyone who submitted suggestions and/or voted in the second round—it was your participation that made the contest fun and successful.

Every day my husband gets up early and goes to work for 'The Man' while I work part-time and write. I appreciate this more than words can say. Making his sacrifice worthwhile motivates me to work relentlessly to succeed. My daughter, Nikki Pietron, makes all of my work better because she's not afraid to tell me what's good and what's not—for that I am eternally grateful. I also owe thanks to Judy Skemp who is always willing to read my stories and ensure that they make sense.

I don't play the guitar, so when Jack emerged as as a guitar-playing rock-and-roller, I knew I needed an expert to educate me in "musician lingo." Fortunately, I live next door to an accomplished guitar player. Special thanks to Jim White for passing along examples of challenges a guitar player may face and the words he might use to describe them.

This book was made possible by Scribe Publishing Company and the final, polished copy is the result of hard work by Jennifer Baum, Mel Corrigan and Inanna Arthen. Their time, dedication, critique and thoughtful comments are invaluable. *Soulshifter's* amazing

291

cover is credited to Miguel Camacho who successfully brought to life images that previously existed only in my imagination.

I would be remiss not to mention NaNoWriMo (National Novel Writing Month), as the first draft of this novel was written during my first WriMo experience. I'm grateful to the people behind the website (www.nanowrimo.org) and for their idea to challenge writers to complete a 50,000-word novel in thirty days. I greatly appreciate the inspiration, encouragement and support from this community of like-minded writers. In their own words: "Valuing enthusiasm, determination, and a deadline, NaNoWriMo is for anyone who has ever thought fleetingly about writing a novel." I highly recommend it!

Finally, I must thank all of my family, friends and readers whose support means the world to me. Whether at events, on social media or even one on one, their encouragement and enthusiasm urges me onward.

ABOUT THE AUTHOR

After years in the corporate world, Barbara found herself with a second chance to decide what she wanted to be when she grew up. Her lifetime love of books and the written word returned one answer: writer. Drawing from her experience with technical writing, she began by writing non-fiction magazine pieces and achieved both regional and national publication.

In addition to *Soulshifter*, Barbara has also published *Thunderstone*, Book One of the Legacy in Legend series. A prequel to *Thunderstone, Heart of Ice,* is also available in e-book format. Barbara is currently working on the rest of the Legacy in Legend series.

If she's not reading or writing, she likes to walk, garden, and sew. She works in a library and lives in Royal Oak, Michigan with her husband, daughter, and their cat—who often acts like a dog. You can join Barbara's writing adventures at www.barbarapietron.com for bonus content, giveaways, presales and insider scoop. Also find Barbara on Facebook at facebook.com/barbara.pietron.19